'Aye, I was expect said, painting the as much scorn as she could. 'Expecting you as one does a plague or a pestilence. And I welcome you just as much.'

She shifted her stance, getting ready to throw the dagger in her hand.

'You need to leave. I've warned you.'

'We haven't begun, Lioslath. Why would I leave?'

He was so arrogant. Vibrant. Too full of life. She made another signal and Dog, with a noise deep in his throat, came to her heels.

The sound always raised the hairs on her neck, and she had no doubt it did the same to Bram. But he did not take his eyes from hers, did not see Dog as a threat, and so he forced her hand.

'You need to leave because I was expecting you, Bram, Laird of Colquhoun.'

Lioslath stepped into the light and lifted the dagger, making sure it glinted so he'd know what she intended.

Nicole Locke discovered her first romance novels in her grandmother's closet, where they were secretly hidden. Convinced that books hidden must be better than those that weren't, Nicole greedily read them. It was only natural for her to start writing them (but now not so secretly). She lives in London with her two children and her husband—her happily-ever-after.

Books by Nicole Locke

Mills & Boon Historical Romance

Lovers and Legends

The Knight's Broken Promise
Her Enemy Highlander
The Highland Laird's Bride

Visit the Author Profile page at millsandboon.co.uk.

THE HIGHLAND
LAIRD'S BRIDE

Nicole Locke

THE HIGHLAND
LAIRD'S BRIDE

To my friends, for your chiding encouragement
and constant bewilderment that
I've survived this long. Here's my secret:
I wouldn't have made it without you.

Renee, it is infinitely precious to me that
we can still be five years old together.

Anita, I know you thought I'd never grow up and,
as always, you were right.

Corrie, full of grace, love and life. Your vivaciousness
and unheard-of-before cocktails are my sunshine.

Sue, I'd be lost without your meticulous brain and
lists, but even more so without your laugh.

Karen, I know you didn't want your name in the
acknowledgements but, alas, you can't edit this
sentence as you have all the others. I want you to
know how much I cherish our friendship.

Chapter One

❦

Scotland—1296

'You were expecting me.'

Lioslath of Clan Fergusson stopped pacing the darkness of her bedroom and adjusted the knife in her hand. From years of training, she knew simply on the utterance of his four words where Bram, Laird Colquhoun, stood in the room, and the precise location of his beating heart.

She knew it, even though her back was to him and she'd been caught pacing. Defenceless. Or so he thought.

The laird was right; she had been expecting him. Expecting him as one views a storm on the horizon. Ever since he and his clansmen, like black clouds, crested a nearby hill. Since he alerted her young brothers, who raced to the keep, giving them precious moments to lock the gates. All the while the storm of Laird Colquhoun and his clansmen gathered strength and lined up outside the keep with arrows and swords like lightning about to strike.

But they hadn't struck. And it had been almost a month. Which meant weeks of her climbing the haphazardly rebuilt platform to look over the gates; weeks of hearing the Colquhoun men below her even before she climbed the rickety steps.

It had been almost a month, and still they didn't strike. Although she barred the gates, though the villagers shunned him, Laird Colquhoun hadn't struck like the harshest of Scottish storms. Rather, he and his clansmen enclosed the keep. Surrounded, she felt choked by his stormy presence, suffocated by the battering wait.

But this morning, she knew the wait was over when she spied the carefully placed food at the outside entrance of the secret passage. Her captor had discovered her tunnel. She knew, despite the fact she locked the gates, the storm would get inside.

When he hadn't come during the day, Lioslath expected Bram of Clan Colquhoun this night. She was no fool.

But she hadn't been expecting his voice. Deep, melodious, a tenor that sent an immediate awareness skittering up the backs of her legs and wrapping warmth around her centre.

So she didn't immediately turn to see him, even though a man was in her bedroom. Forbidden and unwanted. She didn't pretend maidenly outrage as she had carefully planned, to provide a necessary distraction and give her an advantage before her attack.

It was his voice. It was…unexpected.

It didn't fit here, in the dark, in the intimacy of her bedroom. It didn't fit with what she'd seen of him so far.

Arrogant, proud, superior, Bram rode through her broken village to her weather-worn gates thinking himself a welcome benefactor with his carts of overstocked gifts. Or worse, as laird of the keep bestowing treasures to his people.

Since Laird Colquhoun began the siege, he'd been an abrasive force, from his vibrant red hair to the length of his strides as he walked amongst his men. His voice booming orders; his demands to open the gates. His constant laughter. Everything about him she instinctively rejected.

But not now.

Now his voice reverberated with some power, some seductive tone she'd never heard before. She felt his voice. And it shouldn't have felt like this. Not to her. She calmed her wavering heart.

Never to her.

Allowing the cool night air into her lungs, she turned and immediately wished she stood elsewhere.

The full moon cast light through the window and holes in the roof, but his back was to the light and Bram remained in darkness.

She knew the darkness would give his voice an advantage. She adjusted the knife, careful to keep it close and ready. Her plan might have changed, but not her intent. Bram of Clan Colquhoun was expected, but he was not wanted. He had arrived too late for that.

'Get out,' she said, without menace. Dog hid in a corner. She needed not to alert him to her tumultuous feelings; she needed to remain calm and keep to their routine. For years they'd hunted together. Dog knew what the knife in her hand meant: for him to lie in wait for her signal—and surprise their prey. 'Get out of my room and away from the keep. Weren't the closed gates and the hurtled dung enough deterrent? Leave, Laird Colquhoun. You never should have come.'

Bram could only stare.

Weeks of being barred entrance to the keep of Clan Fergusson, of wasting time while determining the layout of the keep and the village. Of glimpsing the woman who, without schedule, would appear at the top of the gates. Visible, but never near enough to truly see her.

But now, as shafts of moonlight illuminated her form, he did see her. It was as if the night created another star. One brighter than those poised in the sky above this tiny room.

He glanced around. A single bed, a small table at the opposite wall. Something large, like a trunk, in the dark corner nearest her. A simple room and too meagre for her beauty, but at least they were alone.

'You were expecting me,' Bram repeated, now realising the meaning of finding this woman fully dressed and pacing. 'You received my gift this morning. You observed us today. You knew I was coming.'

'Your gift?'

'The deer and vegetables by the entrance,' he said. 'I didn't know if you would take them.'

She frowned, a darkness marring her eyes.

He knew she'd been stealing their food for the past week. Until yesterday, he hadn't known how. When he discovered the tunnel, he knew he had to let her know his intentions. So this morning, he placed the food at the entrance. He only meant it as part of his negotiations.

But now he knew, instantly, he failed.

'You didn't want to take them,' he answered for her. He was a master at diplomacy, but his gift hadn't softened her towards him. She locked the gates against him and his clansmen. The food was only a reminder.

'Why aren't you leaving?' she said instead.

Because what he came to do wasn't done. He had to be here. Tonight. While he'd been waiting for the gates to open, danger came to his clan. His duty as laird necessitated he end this stalemate, but it wasn't duty he thought of now.

Lioslath's short black hair curled and spiked defiantly. It highlighted her sharp cheekbones and softly angled chin. Her skin was pale in the moonlight, and it emphasised the size and brightness of her eyes. And the colour…

They were blue, intense and startling against the blackness of her hair and thick eyelashes. It was as if under her finely arched brows shone the brightest of summer skies.

In the moonlight, he couldn't fully see the outline of her body, but he didn't need to now. Every time she stood on the platform, the wind plastered her paltry clothing to curves that made beggars of men. Including himself.

His reaction to her wasn't in the plan he and his brothers devised: for him to make amends to the Fergussons, to wait out the winter and to hide from a certain English king.

A complicated plan made simple by the fact that all of it could be done on Fergusson land and that Lioslath needed to know only one of those reasons for his being here. The one he explained in the letter he wrote last April. To remedy the wrongs that had been done to her clan and family by lending aid and comfort to the Fergussons' orphaned children.

After all, he'd tried to ally the Colquhoun clan with theirs, when he had married his sister Gaira to Fergussons' laird and Lioslath's father. When Gaira had refused such a marriage and fled to their sister at Doonhill, Lioslath's father had been killed.

Unfortunately, the Battle of Dunbar had delayed Bram's arrival by summer. It would soon be winter, and his intent to help this clan would prove more difficult. Yet he was here now.

Here, now, and in her room. It had been a simple act to arrive here by a cleverly hidden passage. He'd been surprised the tunnel led to under her bedroom. When he found her here, he'd been pleased. After the political and personal turmoil of the past year, his brothers' fateful arrival and portentous messages, he needed something to be simple.

But there was nothing simple about Lioslath. A woman who was created as if the moon and sun deemed her beauty worthy of them both. Had he known the quality, the sheer magnificence of her beauty, he would have breached the weak defences a fortnight ago. Any man would have.

He cursed himself at his use of reasonable diplomacy. The food he tried offering failed because he'd been laying siege to a decrepit keep instead of laying siege to the beautiful female inside.

Suddenly, everything became clear to him on how easy it would be to get her cooperation. And he needed her cooperation if his plan to remain here for the winter were to work.

'You want me to leave? After all, we need to… negotiate. This is your first meeting with Laird Colquhoun,' he said. Self-assured, he knew who he was, what his power meant to any lass. 'You couldn't desire this to be so brief.'

She was beautiful and probably used to men and flirting. He'd been a fool to stay outside the gates. A fool thinking not to frighten the children and families with force. All he had to do was to coax, to flirt, to please.

'Brief? I *desire*—' she put emphasis on the word '—for it not to happen at all.'

He liked the word 'desire' coming from her mouth. He liked the shape of her full lower lip, the deep dip on her upper one. Her lips were shaped like a bow, as if an angel had pressed its fingers there to keep a secret.

'But it has.' He shrugged, pretending a nonchalance his body didn't feel. 'I'm here to get past our introduction. You are Lioslath, after all,' he murmured. 'The eldest daughter?' He'd introduced himself when he came to the gates, but she hadn't. Maybe some sense of propriety was needed, even here, in her bedroom.

In her bedroom, where she stood waiting for him. His anticipation tightened. Maybe she knew this game as well as he.

Her frown increased. 'You came to this room not knowing who I am?'

Satisfaction coursed through him. She did know the game. She was coyly, if not suggestively, asking him to guess who she was. Flirting would be easier than he thought.

'I know exactly who you are.' He stepped towards her as she held still. The room was small; it wouldn't take much to be right against her. 'The lass I will soon kiss.'

Her lips parted as her brows drew in. She shook her head once as if answering a question inside.

Did she think he wouldn't kiss her? Then she didn't know him very well. Another regret for his delay. She would soon learn that he kept his word.

'I am not fond of jests,' she said. 'Nor those who try my patience.'

She stepped outside the shafts of light and he

felt the loss of vision. He might be within the gates now, but she continued to bar him with her sparring words. A game she clearly played well.

But it was late, and although he was known for his game playing, he knew when to steal forward, especially when he had the advantage. She was a woman, after all. He always knew how to get his way with women. She would be no different.

'Come now, enough of this game,' he said. 'It is night and we are alone. Isn't there something else you'd rather play?'

Play? Games?

Lioslath didn't understand this man.

At first she blamed the lateness of the night, the way his voice seemed to reach into her. Blamed her continual hunger and thirst for her addled mind. She knew she was addled, because when he mentioned game, her mouth watered with the wanting of succulent meat. But that wasn't the type of game he meant.

'I never play games.' She found the very word offensive.

He waved and she followed the gesture. His hands were finely tapered, with a strength and eloquence that was as unexpected as his voice.

'Come, I've seen this ploy before,' he said. 'In the past, it has made the reward sweet. But we have waited long enough, love. Trust that my willingness to participate in this game you play could not be any truer.'

Was this man flirting with her? Since childhood, and until only recently, she'd been ignored. She slept in stable lofts and no man flirted with her. Ever. They wouldn't dare.

No, it couldn't be flirting. It was merely his abrasive ease with words, with manners, with everything. A man who thought himself charming as he used words like 'lass' and 'love'.

He didn't charm her, yet he didn't seem to be leaving. She had a choice to make. The knife or Dog? It was late, a knife would make a mess she'd have to clean and she needed her sleep.

'You need to leave now,' she ordered.

With a wave of her hand, Dog rose. Bram's eyes widened, not with fear, but with surprise.

'That's a dog? I thought it was a trunk.' His grin changed. 'Hardly welcoming having a—is that a wolf?—in your room, since you were expecting me.'

He took his eyes off Dog, which was foolish, or arrogant.

It didn't matter. His time with her was over. It had gone on too long. She blamed her hunger, his voice, the fine movement of his hands. She blamed him for *everything*. It was time to remind him of it.

'Aye, I was expecting you,' she said, with as

much scorn as she could paint the words. 'Expecting as one does a plague, or a pestilence. And I welcome you just as much.' She shifted her stance, getting ready to throw the dagger. 'You need to leave. I've warned you.'

'We haven't begun, Lioslath. Why would I leave?'

He was arrogant. Vibrant. Too full of life. She made another signal and Dog, with a noise deep in his throat, came to her heels.

The sound always raised the hairs on her neck and she had no doubt it did the same to Bram. But he did not take his eyes from hers, did not see Dog as a threat, and so he forced her hand.

'You need to leave because I was expecting you, Bram, Laird of Colquhoun.' Lioslath stepped into the light, lifted the dagger, made sure it glinted so he'd know what she intended. 'But I do not think you were expecting me.'

Chapter Two

Waking in the morning and needing to relieve herself, Lioslath rose from bed, only to collapse as dizziness overcame her. She'd sat up too quickly. The lack of food, the continual hunger, had made her faint the past few days. Was her dizziness worse? If so, she knew who to blame.

Anger giving her strength, she slowly sat up. Anger that had only one direction: towards Bram…who had laughed. *Laughed.*

She still didn't understand what had happened the night before.

Dog at her heels, and a knife in her hand, she'd readied to strike. At her most dangerous, Bram laughed as if she told the funniest of tales.

Startled at the sound, she almost dropped the knife. So she hadn't, couldn't have, reacted as he shook his head, told her he enjoyed her games and would see her the next day.

She simply stood there incapable of comprehending his actions.

Worse still, Dog, who never let prey escape, who should have attacked, abruptly sat, canted his head and stared as Bram eased himself through the trapdoor.

She didn't know what was more incredible. Her own inability to attack or Dog's sudden meekness.

No, she did know. The most incredulous moment was when Bram told her he'd see her today. He expected her to open the gates.

She might not have attacked, but she wasn't opening the gates today. His grating laughter had ensured that. If she could shut the gates more firmly, or again, and preferably right in his face, she would. At the idea, satisfaction coursed warmly within her.

Desperate now to use the privy, she walked out of the room. Dog only lifted his head as he stared in her direction.

She scowled at him. Bram had laughed, she had almost dropped the knife and Dog had sat.

Since weaning him from a pup, he had been her friend and protector. More wild than tame, no one dared approach Dog. She'd always thought they had an understanding. She slept in the stables when it rained and outside when it didn't. He'd never lost the wild side to him and she hadn't either. But at the moment he canted his head, he had been no more than a weak, useless, domesticated dog.

She leaned against the wall as dizziness overcame her. A well-fed dog at least, just like the rest of her clan. She ensured that. Or rather, Bram ensured that.

He had reminded her that it was he who hunted and provided the food. He who discovered the secret tunnel, and her anger at that gave her the strength to stand straight.

The tunnel was hers, maintained through sheer will. She told no one of it. When she was a child, there had been several of them, but time had passed and the residents either didn't remember them or believed they had collapsed. But she had maintained one, had cleared and buttressed it for years. It was narrow and precarious, and a way of escaping from her punishments, from her family and what had become of them.

Simply knowing the tunnel was there kept her calm. And now, with the siege, it allowed her to steal much-needed food. But she hadn't been stealing. Bram had been leaving gifts.

She should have known—she *had* known—but it was a bounty she hadn't been able to ignore.

In the darkest part of the night before last, she had left the tunnel to steal, only to find venison hanging in the tree closest to the tunnel. And underneath? A sack of cabbages and onions.

Immediately, she had recognised it for the bait it was, but she had no caution as she cut it down. Caution didn't matter when necessity did. Her clan was starving and, even while she resented it, she took the trap.

So all day she looked over her shoulder, all night she kept herself dressed and pacing in her room. She thought of barricading the tunnel, but a mere day's effort wouldn't keep out a determined intruder and she didn't want to bring attention to the tunnel.

But she had vowed that would be the last time she stole food. Since it was their last stolen meal, she needed to feed the few people still in the keep; she needed to feed her brothers and sister. What she didn't do was feed herself.

It didn't matter. She didn't need her energy for much, since she was trapped inside with no way to roam. Trapped, and she knew who to blame for that as well.

As she left the privy, Dog was waiting for her at the end of the narrow corridor. From there it was a short turn with a few stairs that led to the main Hall.

She wished she could avoid the central room even though the Hall's permanently rancid smell was weaker now, which was the siege's only benefit.

They had cleaned the keep when the gates were first barred. Old mouldy rushes, thrown bones and rotting food were swept clear to be thrown at the Colquhoun clansmen surrounding her home.

But even without the old rushes and food, the Hall stank from the rotting wood and stones that hadn't been scrubbed in years. When she was a child, the Hall had gleamed, the smells had been of home, of a time when her mother and father had been alive and happy. Now it held only mould, stains and regret.

She resented that she was forced to stay in the keep, forced to walk through the Hall that mocked her childhood memories. Patting Dog's head, she hurried outside to the low building that was the kitchens.

Cook, making a soup from the venison and vegetables, gave a cautious, respectful smile.

Ignored most of her life, Lioslath forced herself to nod a greeting in return. For over a month, her clan had treated her with loyalty, with…*respect*. Their tentative friendliness continued to startle her.

It was difficult to change a lifetime of avoidance. With the siege, she was no longer left to roam free. She was forced to acknowledge her clan and her family. No. In truth, it was before the siege that she'd been forced to acknowledge her family...but she didn't want to think about that now.

As soon as Dog grabbed the generous bone from the preparation table, they exited out the back of the kitchens. Again, a change. Usually, this area was rife with rotting carcasses. But since the Colquhouns came, this area, too, had been swept.

She didn't take any pleasure in it, though. After meeting Bram last night, nothing today would bring her pleasure except his departure. He was all that she hated: conceited, arrogant, jovial.

Regretting not plunging her blade into Bram's heart when she'd had the chance, Lioslath walked to the platform that allowed her to see over the gates.

The structure was a hastily erected disaster they ripped from her father's stair extension. Stairs he ordered made, even though there were no walls, floor or ceiling to support them. Another impetuous folly of her father's, just like his marriage to the Colquhoun's sister.

She felt the weight of her loss rise and settle in her chest. Her father was dead. It wasn't the English knight who had killed him who bore the full brunt of her wrath. No, the man she hated above all had better be breaking his camp or she'd throw the first bucket of debris today.

'You rise late again.'

Lioslath stopped to face Aindreas, the hunter's son. As usual, Aindreas's appearance was marred by his thickly tangled brown hair.

'Does it matter?' she retorted. But it mattered to her; she had never woken late in her life.

'You're rising later and sleeping in the keep. You're becoming a lady of leisure. Already the men and I cleared the debris into buckets. They are ready to throw on command. I also checked and reinforced the snares in the back, and re-limed the branches to catch the birds.'

She snorted in derision, but she envied him his duties. They had given him a purpose. She felt lost in here. 'You had to wake up early to do the snares because you've never been good at them.'

'I've improved since we were five, and since you sleep late I'll be a sight better than you the next time we hunt.'

Hunting. It was what she lived for. In her childhood, Aindreas's father, Niall, had been the chief hunter for the clan. When Lioslath's father had remarried, her stepmother had prohibited her from staying and then sleeping in the keep. She'd followed Niall like a shadow until he showed her his skills. Aindreas was only a year older and they had become like siblings.

'You have been making snares for years. You couldn't possibly become better than me in only a few weeks,' she said. 'You'd have a better chance using a handful of your own tangled hair.'

Aindreas cocked a brow. 'The lasses have nae trouble with my hair.'

She saw the curve to his lips that displayed the familiar dimple. The one that made all the Fergusson lasses sigh with want.

'That's because they didn't have to listen to your mother lament about you never combing it.'

Those years in childhood at the hunter's cottage had been the most precious to her. It had been a chance to be around a family, since she didn't have one of her own.

Except...she did have a family now. Maybe not her father or mother, but her half-brothers and half-sister. They were here.

'The whelps have already risen,' Aindreas said, seeming to know her thoughts. If her brothers and sister had risen, she had more pressing concerns.

'Have they been fed?' she asked, looking around her.

'Do you truly care?'

'Aye, if someone else looks after them, I

doona have to.' She gave him a pointed glare. 'Your continual calling them puppies won't make me tend and care for them.'

He shook his head. 'They think matters are different now.'

She didn't want to think of her father's death or what that meant to her younger half-sister, Fyfa, and two half-brothers, Eoin and Gillean. She was still adjusting to being trapped inside the keep with them when, for her entire life, they'd been kept separated. 'Even if matters are different, what would I do with them? They're... idle.'

'They're not idle. They play.'

'What would I know of play? Other than it accomplishes nothing.'

'Just because you weren't given the chance—' Aindreas's eyes softened. 'You wouldn't have to do anything with them. Simply be their sister.'

She didn't know how to play or be a sister because she'd never had a childhood. So how could she understand theirs?

'You can't avoid them forever, Lioslath.'

'I'm not avoiding them.' It was impossible to. They were always underfoot, playing, laughing. Her clan's tentative smiles and wary looks continued to startle her. Her siblings' open smiles and constant chatter terrified her. 'Will you take them today?'

'You know I will.'

'Just keep them away from the platform.' She didn't care how he took her words.

'Caring if they get hurt? You *are* becoming soft.'

'Nae,' she said, wondering if that was why she said it. 'I doona need the annoyance of tending injuries on top of everything else I have to do today.'

'What is it you're doing today?'

Turning away, she said over her shoulder, 'Saying goodbye to the Colquhouns.'

She heard the camp outside before she reached the steps. Grabbing a bucket, she listened as icy frustration and hot anger coursed in opposing rivulets inside her body. Bram wasn't breaking camp. Already knowing which unstable steps to avoid, she bounded up the stairs. Before she reached the top, she heard his laughter and gave a feral grin. Bram made such an easy target.

Chapter Three

B ram found Lioslath in the kitchens. It was night and darkness blanketed every crevice of the long spaces surrounding them. Soot covering her hands and face, Lioslath slept curled up near a dying fire with that wolf next to her. Like this, she looked soft, inviting—

The dog suddenly growled and Lioslath woke with a start. Her hand reached out, but there was nothing there. If she were a man, he'd have thought she was reaching for a weapon.

The dog's ears twitched as if to flatten them and Bram pulled himself back. The dog was only a reminder of their differences, of why he was here.

'You didn't open the gates,' he said, more gently than he meant. Her softness was now gone, but his body hadn't caught up with his thoughts. How she barred him, denied him again, when she should be grateful he showed up at all.

He had not expected Lioslath to open the gates without a pretence of a fight. After all, it would make no sense if she were to open the gates after denying them access for so long. When she threw the bucket of debris and the others did the same, he thought it all for show.

Which was why he controlled his anger when some of it hit his foot. But the entire day came and went, and he didn't see her again.

'Yet, you came anyway,' she retorted.

Wobbling, she stood. Like this, the fire's light illuminated what he hadn't seen before: a black mole, small and just above her upper lip. It was placed as if a mischievous faery kissed such perfection. He knew if *he* were such a faery, there would be others…

'What can I do to make you unwelcome?' she said.

Obstinate. Their encounter last night had been brief, but he thought he'd controlled the situation. After all, Lioslath was a beautiful woman and his flattering words had always been enough in the past, but it didn't seem enough for her. Maybe flirting wouldn't work with her. Difficult, when her beauty affected him.

No. More than that. It was her fierceness at the platform, her throwing the debris, her contemplative observing of them. All of it affected him. But if his flattery wouldn't work, there were other methods of persuasion.

She took his gifts by the tunnel and he saw the state of the clan and their lands. She needed his supplies and manpower, even if she pretended she didn't.

The current level of desperation should be enough for him to be accepted over the winter.

'Those gates are barred, but I can get inside,' he said. 'This is nae a real siege and it is time to end it.'

'I never told you to come. I held a dagger to you and told you to leave.'

Her amusing threat of last night. At the time he thought it a jest. Now he was beginning to think she meant it. It was still laughable, but for other reasons.

'I may be unwelcome,' he said, 'but my supplies are not.'

'You stay because of the gifts?' she retorted. 'You could have left them and gone. I doona even know why you're here.'

'I sent you a missive. When your father died, I would come with help.'

'Only because you feel guilty for the crimes you committed here!'

'I committed nae crimes here. I forged an alliance.'

She pulled herself up, then wavered before

she widened her stance to gain her balance. He looked at her feet. There was nothing that tripped her.

'You bribed this clan, married my father to your sister, who at the first opportunity didn't honour her vows and ran off!'

'Careful, Fergusson. There was nae bribe to this clan. I offered a marriage and alliance between your father and my sister Gaira. I offered a total of forty sheep—twenty immediately, and twenty more after one year. It was a profitable and a stable alliance, and one which your father accepted.'

'Which your sister didn't honour! With nae possible reason, she ran away.'

He didn't know how to answer this. Either way, it would not be good. Something about this woman's father, Busby, frightened Gaira, but his sister had also been hurt when he forced her marriage. 'It matters not why she ran,' he said.

'Of course it matters why she ran. If she hadn't, my father wouldn't have pursued her and wouldn't have been murdered by an English knight.'

This conversation must be avoided. He hadn't lied in the missive he sent to her, but he'd skirted the truth regarding how her father died and by whose hand. He knew exactly who murdered her father and he wasn't an ordinary knight. He was also no longer precisely English. No, Robert of Dent, the famed Black Robert and King Edward's favoured knight, wasn't dead at all, but married to Gaira, and living in secret on Colquhoun land.

'My sister ran from him,' Bram said. 'I didn't order him to follow her.'

'Nae, you merely threatened to take the sheep and bring the force of Clan Colquhoun down on his head if he didn't find her.'

He hadn't known how else to keep Gaira, his only surviving sister, safe. When Bram made the alliance with Busby, he had concerns only for his own clan, for his own selfish desire to marry. When he made the alliance, the English massacres at Berwick and Doonhill hadn't yet occurred. The war against England hadn't been lost at Dunbar. How was he, how was anyone, to guess that the Scotland of only months ago would be so changed?

If he'd known, he would have kept his family close to him. He would have spent the months preparing and fortifying his keep. He would have closed the gates and locked them all safely inside.

Instead, he forced a temporary marriage between Gaira and Laird Fergusson. Under normal politics it would have been astute. It brought strength for his clan by having someone in the south and Gaira would be nearer to their youngest sister, Irvette.

Irvette, the youngest and sweetest of them all, who married a man she loved. Irvette, who was murdered by the English at Doonhill.

Since April, his family had seen too much danger, suffered too much loss. And worst of all, he could have avoided most of it.

Now he needed to right these wrongs with this clan, but he could not be gentle any longer. Her stubbornness aside, he was laird and knew what was at stake. He wouldn't fail his clan and family again, and he fully intended for his new plan to work.

'What happened to those sheep, Lioslath? I didn't take them and I see scarce livestock on your land.'

'Why does it matter to you?'

He felt a roiling frustration and fought to keep his patience. He would not give up his power. 'I wrote to you. I told you that Gaira returned to Colquhoun land. I explained I'd come here to make amends.'

'But you're late.'

'Dunbar occurred. I am late because our country went to war!'

'Aye, but that doesn't explain why you were late. Everyone knows you didn't participate in Dunbar.'

No, he hadn't participated in that fateful battle against the English last April. Scotsmen had been slaughtered; the ones who survived hid in Ettrick Forest. His brother Malcolm was one of the survivors, but he carried a terrible wound.

Bram could tell no one why he hadn't participated in Dunbar. He made his choice not against his country, but for his country. King John Balliol himself ordered Bram not to participate, to stay on Colquhoun land and receive two messages. The messages, he had been told, would protect Scotland.

Bram stayed, had advised his family and clan to stay, but he never received two messages. Balliol was defeated at Dunbar and was now being held at the Tower of London. It was the English King Edward who ruled over Scotland now.

If Balliol expected Bram to protect Scotland, he was falling far short.

Then, his brothers, Malcolm and Caird, arrived whilst Bram waited for Lioslath to open the gates. The messages that were supposed to have come to the Colquhoun clan became clear. They were not actual messages, but a dagger and the legendary Jewel of Kings.

Though the jewel was safely in Malcolm's hands, he now fled to Clan Buchanan land to secure the dagger. He took a spare horse to make the journey faster for him. Bram was all too aware it might not be fast enough. As long as the jewel remained in the open, his brother, his clan, were in terrible danger.

For now Bram must stay on Fergusson land for the winter and await news about the jewel. Come the spring, he would know whether he was to ride north to the safety of his land, or south and commit treason with Balliol in the Tower of London. Either way, King Edward would find him then.

'It matters not whether I was at Dunbar. It delayed my arrival,' he continued. 'But I'm here now.'

'And I want you to leave.' She waved her hand towards the door and he knew he didn't imagine her unbalance.

'What is wrong with you?'

A hesitation. 'Nothing that your absence wouldn't cure.'

She lied. There were dark circles under her bright eyes, the natural angle of her cheekbones sharply exposed because of the hollows of her cheeks.

'I've given you food,' he said.

'I took your food.'

He narrowed his eyes. 'But you haven't eaten it.'

'What is it to you what happens to it?'

'Have the others eaten?'

'Again, I ask, what is it to you what happens to it?'

Too much. He never would have been waiting outside the gates if he thought anyone inside was suffering. 'Answer me.'

She crossed her arms around her midriff, which outlined the smallness of her frame and… her ribs?

He cursed. 'You little fool, you haven't eaten.'

'Fool? Better a fool than what you've become. You didn't participate at Dunbar. You're a traitor. So, too, what of your acts for this clan? You probably knew your sister would run away and endanger my father!'

Traitor. He was no traitor, but he'd have to get used to being called one.

'I could not prevent your father's death,' he said instead.

'I'll never believe you! Without him, without his protection, just look at what has happened here!'

'What do you mean what has happened here?'

He knew it. Something worse than poor management had caused the damage here. For the first few days, he questioned the villagers, but they ignored him and his clansmen. So he observed them instead. Their homes were in tatters; the crops were burned. It was too early for the crops to be burned. He thought…he hoped…

they harvested early. That the winter supplies of food were locked safely inside the keep. But Lioslath stole food from him and she looked half-starved. She had no food inside the keep. There could be no food anywhere.

This year, he committed more wrongs than he could ever mend. Irvette had died and he'd broken his trust with his sister Gaira. He was committing treason, but not because he hadn't fought at Dunbar, as Lioslath or any of his fellow countryman believed. Still, he paid the shaming price of it. Now, with the jewel in their hands, his family held another secret and this was far more dangerous than he, than any clan, than a king, could prepare for.

Whilst Malcolm carried the jewel with him, the thought that Bram wasn't there to protect him weighed heavily on him. And that didn't end the list of his wrongs.

Although he hadn't killed Lioslath's father, Busby would be alive if they hadn't made their alliance. He might not be able to bring her father back, but he could help this clan prepare for winter. He bore too many wrongs. For once, he would make amends and he would do that here with this clan.

'Answer me,' he bit out. He wouldn't be able to hold back his anger much longer, and if he did, he'd lose control entirely. He never lost control in negotiations.

Something seemed to snap in her as well. 'Answer you? The all-mighty laird wants me... *depends* on me...to answer him. You doona deserve my answers.' Swaying, she unfurled her arms and clenched her fists.

'You're not dependable, you doona honour your vows. You want to make amends? You're too late to make amends!'

She raised her fist. Her intent clear. She didn't have a dagger, but she would hurt him. She took two steps before her eyes suddenly closed, her legs crumpled beneath her and he rushed to catch her fall.

Chapter Four

~~~~~~~~

Jostled, and held too tightly, Lioslath woke. With long strides Bram carried her through the Hall.

He was too close. She noticed the shades of red in his hair, the blonde tips of his eyelashes. She could smell the scent of leather, of outdoors…of him. It was almost as jarring as him carrying her.

'Put me down.'

'Nae, you little fool. How long have you been like this? How long did you think you would last?'

Bram cradled her against him as if she was no more than a babe. She shouldn't have felt him through the layers of clothing, but she did. She felt the hard planes of his chest, and the grace and strength of his legs. His arms had no more give than the rest of him, and yet he held her gently.

She couldn't remember if she had ever been

carried or held like this. He was Laird Colquhoun and his holding her should have felt uninvited and unwelcome. At the very least it should have felt foreign. Instead, he felt…warm.

Fighting the warmth, she turned her head and saw the light through the Hall's doors. A spike of fear woke her up. 'Put me down,' she ordered again.

The keep would wake soon. She didn't need her two brothers seeing her. At six and five, they would ask too many questions. Her sister, Fyfa, at eight, would think it romantic. Lioslath knew that would be worse.

Brows drawn, Bram didn't look at her, but she felt the flexing of his fingers against her arm and leg. 'Not until we reach your bedroom.'

She was too weak to fight him, but she wasn't too weak to hold herself rigidly. She felt the tightening of his hold and saw his frown, though he ignored her tiny defiance. When he laid her on the bed, she sat up, and his frown deepened.

'Stay there.'

She wouldn't take his orders. 'This is ridiculous.'

'You fainted.'

Forget the room or her siblings, her fainting was the most embarrassing bit of all of this. Worse, because an enemy had seen it and carried her. 'I didn't faint—'

He quirked an eyebrow.

'Or if I did, it's over with. It's daylight. The keep will wake soon.' Her eyes darted around.

'Your dog stayed in the kitchens. Shouldn't he be protecting you?'

'As if you were a threat?' How did he know she wanted Dog and why wasn't Dog protecting her? The edges of her vision wavered and she put a hand to her head. 'You need to leave or you'll be discovered.'

'We're in your room. I'll take the tunnel.'

By now the platform by the gates would be manned. 'Someone will see you.'

He tilted his head, studying her. 'Worried for me?'

Looming over her, he was everything arrogant and domineering. His red hair waved loose to his shoulders, but it didn't hide the broadness of his jaw or his eyes, which were grey, like the colour of the sky before a storm broke. His sun-browned skin highlighted the soft dusty colour of his lips. His jaw was broad and square. His nose looked as though it had been broken and straightened many times, but it didn't disfigure his face. In fact, she found this part of him... interesting. It gave him a certain fierceness she wasn't expecting of the weak-kneed Colquhouns.

Like this, Bram looked like the warrior he was reputed to be.

She felt a fluttering in her stomach and her skin flushed. But was it from hunger or fear? It couldn't be fear. Her father had been a giant of a man and had ruled the keep with intimidation and punishments. When he loomed over her, never once had she felt this sort of helpless breathlessness before. It must be from hunger.

Bram shook his head. 'Not worried for me. You're worried for your tunnel. Why is there a tunnel and room beneath your bedroom?'

He didn't need to know about the tunnel, or the empty storage room beneath. He didn't need to know this wasn't her bedroom. All he needed to know was—

The door burst open. Bram, ready to fight, leapt in front of the bed.

Two muddy boys were chased into the room by an older girl. Lioslath's gasps of surprise and anger were drowned by the girl's shrieking. Gleeful, the boys taunted the girl until they were all fully around the bed. Just as the boys swerved to run out again, they spied Bram.

'The giant outside the gates!' the littler boy cried, dashing out of the room.

Bram lunged for the door to trap the other two inside, then turned to face his captives.

Curiously, the children hadn't run to Lioslath for protection. Instead, they stood on the other side of the bed, their hands locked together.

Unlike the boys, the girl's appearance was immaculate. Her hair was freshly brushed and a rudimentary ornament held back tiny plaits around her face. Her dress was thin, overly mended and far too short for her, but it was clean. As was the girl herself, except for one long drip of mud from her left cheek that stretched down and along her gown.

The boy standing next to her looked as though he'd emerged from a mud puddle; the girl looked as though she'd never seen a mud puddle.

There were now witnesses to his being inside the keep. He didn't know who they were, but he suspected.

Lioslath stood when he closed the door. She looked as though she'd never seen the children before, but there was no mistaking their similarities. The children had brown hair with golden highlights, but their eyes were Lioslath's.

She waved to the children. 'Leave now!'

'I think it's too late for that.' Bram heard footsteps. This would not go well.

'Are you smiling?' she choked out.

Bram stepped aside before a man stormed into the room with the littler boy at his heels. When the man saw Bram, he brandished his axe.

'Aindreas!' Lioslath cried.

'Get away from her!' Aindreas bit out.

Lioslath's embarrassment over fainting was

now swamped by frustration and fury and a helplessness she'd never felt before that made it all worse. Too late she realised that when Bram stepped away from the door, he'd stepped towards her. It only reinforced the damage done.

She felt like kicking Bram, shouting at Aindreas and shoving the children out the door, but she could do none of it. She was trapped.

'Are you harmed?' Aindreas kept his eyes on Bram.

'Nae harmed—merely plagued.'

'What is he doing here, Lioslath?' Aindreas asked. 'How did he get here?'

Neither question could she answer and already she saw the children's comprehension that Bram was inside the keep, though the gates were closed. 'It's not as it seems,' she said.

'Not as it seems!' Aindreas almost roared. 'He's in your—'

'The children!' she interrupted.

Aindreas clenched his jaw as his eyes, warning of retribution, returned to Bram. 'Did you harm any?'

'Nae harm and I came alone,' Bram said calmly, yet there was no mistaking the silent challenge in his words. Lioslath and Aindreas had observed Bram training his men. He was daunting from afar, now, up close, he was formidable.

'Why are you here?' Aindreas said.

'That is between Lioslath and me,' Bram said.

'Not while I have breath in my body, Colquhoun. You are leaving. Now.'

'Why would I do that?' Bram said.

Aindreas raised the axe again, his stance widening. He was skilled in axe throwing, but Bram stood too near to Lioslath and her siblings were here. He couldn't throw it and he couldn't attack. They all knew it, but Aindreas looked as though he was beyond caring.

'He will go now,' she said. 'He knows by staying the consequences will be dire.'

'You're unwell,' Bram said.

Did he think her a fool to believe that he stayed because of that? 'I have care now,' she pointed out.

Something about Bram's demeanour said he didn't like that. 'Nae good enough. We need to negotiate.'

'You'll negotiate,' Aindreas said, 'only at the end of my axe.'

Lioslath knew it was up to her to end this. The room was brightening with the rising sun. She could hear people waking and she needed no witnesses to her fainting embarrassment.

'Aindreas, you need to leave and take the children.' She turned. 'And you three need to keep quiet.'

'Nae!' Aindreas waved his axe. 'He's trapped. We can use him to barter. We have an advantage.'

'Do you truly?' Bram said, amusement lacing his words.

Lioslath's insides roiled. Did he find nothing serious?

No, he did. She'd been watching him all these weeks, and Bram was Laird Colquhoun and a warrior in every sense. The years, the authority and the training were ingrained in the way he held himself. Even without a weapon, he was too worthy a foe. And his all-too-knowing smile that belied a friendly easiness told her he wouldn't leave here quietly.

Her siblings, for once, remained still, but they were not silent. Increasing her alarm, they held hands and whispered something between them.

'Aindreas, go, please. Keep them quiet and nae harm will come to me. I'll converse with Laird Colquhoun and we can end this.'

'Alone? You expect me to leave a man in your room alone?'

'I was alone with her before we were interrupted,' Bram said.

Lioslath's breath left her lungs. 'Mere moments and unwanted! Aindreas, only we know he is here. If we delay much longer, this cannot be kept secret!'

Aindreas eased his axe hold. 'To negotiate?'

She nodded. 'I trust this to you.'

Aindreas lowered his axe and nodded. 'I'll take them to the courtyard outside the Hall's door. Nae more.'

It was the most she could ask.

'Wait,' Bram said, turning to the children. 'Who are you?' he asked.

'This isn't necessary,' Lioslath interrupted.

'I won't go,' Bram said. He meant it.

Her siblings visibly twitched, but Eoin and Fyfa faced this intimidating man with their chins stubbornly set. She'd seen them like this when facing her, but never with someone they should fear.

'Did you... Did you hurt her?' Fyfa asked, a fierceness to her eyes.

'Nae,' Bram said, 'but it'll hurt your sister if I stay.'

Aindreas made some sound, while Lioslath tried not to reveal her surprise at her siblings' bravery.

'How will it hurt her if you stay?' Eoin asked.

Fyfa tugged on her brother's arm. 'I'll tell you later. Now they want us to pretend he wasn't here.'

'How are we to do that?' Eoin said. 'He's huge!'

'Later,' she hissed at her brother before turning her eyes to Bram again. This time there was a gleam to them. 'What do we get in return?'

Her siblings had been chattering to themselves and this was what they planned? It was confusing. Their protectiveness was confusing. As was Bram's increasing amusement.

'Do you know what you want?' he asked.

Eoin and Fyfa nodded, but Gillean, who remained by Aindreas's side, looked lost.

Bram pointed to him. 'When he knows, come to me to discuss your terms.'

'Are you finished?' Aindreas demanded.

Bram shrugged. 'For now. When you return, bring food. She needs it.'

Aindreas's lips thinned as he looked at Lioslath. She nodded. For now, she was safe. She'd deal with the Colquhoun's arrogance after the children left.

Keeping his eyes on Bram, Aindreas ushered the children out of the room.

The door latch clicked with an ominous sound and Lioslath felt more alone with Bram now than she had before. At the very least she was more... aware of him. Which made little sense, but she couldn't shake the feeling that he was suddenly, vibrantly here.

Had he always been this tall or broad of shoulder? He was a well-trained man and it showed in this morning's light. Showed...a little too much to her. And she didn't want to guess on why. Faintness or hunger. That was all this fluttering awareness had to be. She'd never felt it before and she hoped she wouldn't faint again.

To prevent it, she sat, but she raised her chin when she saw his brow arch. He wanted to negotiate and she'd do it. 'What do you want?' she said.

'What are the children's names?'

This information was useless to him, to her, and she wanted to argue. By his demeanour, she also knew it was futile. 'Fyfa, Eoin, he's six, and Gillean's the youngest at five.'

'Fyfa's age?'

'Eight, she's eight.' She had just had her birthday, which was something her father celebrated in the years before his death. Lioslath hadn't known what to do to mark the day, so she hadn't done…anything.

'Are there more?'

She shook her head. Her siblings were orphans like her. They had to learn the harshness of life, too. Except—

'Why doesn't Aindreas know of the tunnel?'

Of course he'd notice that. 'A conversation about the tunnel is what you want?'

He shrugged. 'I am curious.'

She knew better. 'Your reputation precedes you, Colquhoun. You are asking questions to obtain leverage for your famous negotiation skills. What do you do? Find facts to use against your opponent? I think you've harmed us enough.'

Bram clasped his hands behind his back and rolled on his heels. It was a casual pose, but she sensed his displeasure underneath.

She liked it. 'Nae talking of kissing me now like you did last night? It took me a while to know what you did. Another manipulation from Laird Colquhoun. You won't find those weaknesses with me.'

A small smile. 'I may find others.'

'You won't be here long enough.'

'Ah, but you make me want to find others.' He released his stance. 'You are…not as I expected.'

A play on their words last night or something else? He probably expected her to have courtesy, manners and a calm demeanour befitting a lady of the manor. She had none of those skills. When she hunted, if she wasn't direct, she missed her target.

Oh, she wanted to argue more, but Bram had spent too much time in her room. Aindreas could become impatient. 'I'll open the gates,' she said, 'if you stay quiet on the tunnel.'

His head tilted as if he sensed a trap, but he didn't hide the smile of victory. 'Not expected, but you have, indeed, made me a curious man. A hidden tunnel, but also hidden from the keep's residents? A private tunnel for you only. Now, what use is such a tunnel to a woman?'

Irritated at his smile and the way it made something flutter inside her, she answered, 'Its use is to get you out of here so I can open the gates.'

He narrowed his eyes on her. 'This morning.'

She nodded.

'This seems sudden. I can't imagine keeping a tunnel secret would be so important to you. What trick do you play?'

Tricks. Play. She knew nothing of such things. Unlike this Colquhoun with his pampered existence, her life had always been hard work.

She would always remember when her father first set off to secure the wealthy Gaira of Clan Colquhoun as his wife. With laughter ringing out, her siblings clung to him. They had been joyous, as if he'd soon bring home their every childhood wish.

And her? Her father, with his head held high, gazed at her, his arms full of children, the rest of his clan waving proudly. At that moment, her father looked at her as if he loved her again. Tears stinging her eyes, she hadn't wanted to break their gaze. She hadn't seen her father look at her with such emotion since before her mother died so many winters before.

In that moment it felt as if she had her father

again. Not the man he had become since his second marriage and since their fortunes changed for the worse. After that he became bitter and the knot of hate that began with her mother's death grew until every word he ever uttered, every action he ever committed, was a reflection of that hate buried in his heart. His runaway bride only made it worse.

When he pursued Gaira, her father was killed. Then the English came and the Fergussons lost what little wealth and pride they had left.

Fate or God already played the cruellest of tricks on Clan Fergusson. Now this Colquhoun came to humiliate them further.

'I make nae tricks,' she practically choked on the word.

'This is too easy,' Bram said.

'Doona you like easy?' she said.

With no bride and only resentment, her father had boasted of the Colquhouns' decadent home and the excess of comforts strewn about. How their tables were laden with food and the freshest rushes were underfoot. He even spoke of laughter, jests…entertainment.

And the more her father spoke, the worse that knot of bitterness grew until barbs slashed at his insides. When he left to pursue his bride, he was filled only with vengeance.

And he never looked at Lioslath again.

'You like easy,' she repeated. 'It's what every Colquhoun likes. So I'm opening the gates because that's what you expect—everything comfortable.'

Gaira, the Colquhoun bride who was supposed to have saved them all, never arrived at Fergusson keep. Lioslath knew why: she was soft like the rest of their clan. No doubt she'd fled prettily to the safety of her luxurious home.

His frown increased. 'Comfortable?' he said the word as if he'd never said it before. Maybe he hadn't. Maybe he was so used to food and entertainment he took it for granted. That thought made her angrier.

'You insult me and grant me a boon,' he said softly. Almost too softly. 'Why are you doing this?'

She had work to do and she needed him gone. Barring him had not worked, so she would open the gates. Once he saw that there were no comforts, that there was only work here, and lots of it, he'd be gone, just like his sister. For once, she was proud of the wreck of a keep she lived in.

She shrugged as she'd seen him do. 'Because it's easy,' she said.

Chapter Five

Bram dropped into the room below Lioslath's and hurried through the tunnel. He was walking around the keep's corner when Finlay, his first in command, strode up to him.

'Where have you been?'

Bram kept his eyes on the man he'd grown up with. 'Walking.'

Finlay frowned. Bram never simply walked like his brother Caird did. He enjoyed activities such as hunting and fishing, but that would mean witnesses.

'We heard activity inside the keep. I think the gates are opening,' Finlay said.

That was fast, he thought. Had Lioslath ordered it done or did she have council? Too many unknowns. 'The men?'

'Preparing.'

They'd talked of the different strategies they should employ if the gates were opened, but something in Finlay's voice made Bram's heart thud. 'Preparing for what?' he asked, but he had his answer as he walked towards the gates. His men were preparing for battle.

Their weaponry was already in their hands. Their camp's spiked fence was now raised and angled menacingly outward.

His men knew of Gaira's marriage and alliance to this clan. When his best-trained men and carpenters followed him, they were as surprised as he by the lack of welcome. Since they now laid siege, for all they knew he could be preparing to take the Fergusson clan for his own. In these turbulent times, he was surprised no other clan had tried.

'They have barred us for weeks and there was nae call out of greeting,' Finlay said. 'They cannot be friendly.'

He could see the villagers gathering in the few winding streets behind him. Most had their hands full of some form of weaponry.

He should have told Lioslath to wait. If the first sight Lioslath saw was his men prepared to fight, she would think he betrayed their understanding.

Understanding. They didn't have an understanding and he didn't need one either. He only needed her to cooperate and he expected his men to as well.

'Have the men stand down,' he ordered. 'Immediately.'

'The gates are opening. The villagers—'

'Are only reacting to what we have done. It's not the time for weapons, it's the time for the other plan we discussed.'

'There's been nae indication of why they are opening the gates now.'

'When those gates are fully open, I'll not have these people see fully armed men. I want them to see a feast and the full extent of our generous offerings we began yesterday. The boar's ready?'

'Aye, but as to the other?'

'I know it is short notice, but it must be done.'

Knowing Finlay would implement his orders, Bram strode through his men. There was little confusion when he told them to stand down. One benefit to idleness, his men were well-prepared. He did, however, order the spiked fence to remain up. He might have been careless when not asking for time, but he wouldn't be so when it came to the safety of his men.

When he got to the gates, they were fully opened. As he suspected, the men inside held bows. No, not only men.

Lioslath stood in front with a bow and arrow in her hands. Two more arrows were strapped to her belt. She'd also changed her clothing. No longer was she in a gown, but in a tunic and hose.

He'd never seen a woman with weaponry and certainly none with her beauty. His instinct was to dismiss it, but it surprised him how natural she looked. She'd held a blade to him the first night as well. He didn't know what to make of it.

Regardless of her abilities, the men, including Aindreas, were also armed. Weeks of treading softly with this clan and it had all been for naught.

He looked behind him. Many of his men put their weapons down, but they did not give up their strategic positions inside the camp or their narrowed focus on the keep and the village. No hope for a bloodless solution unless he defused this situation and fast.

Bram's men were armed and facing the gates. He talked of tricks and of play, yet it was him all this time.

'Stand ready,' Lioslath cried.

She hid her quivering voice, knowing Aindreas would hear it and the others standing behind her would notice her unease.

Now, of all times, she must remain calm. Dog at her heels helped. His familiar warmth comforted her. Unfortunately, he was the only thing familiar to her now.

Certainly, standing in front of her father's clansmen with weaponry wasn't familiar. Men who expected her to give orders, who had been looking to her for leadership since her father's death. Like everything, it continued to surprise her.

The Colquhoun men were shifting and Lioslath eased her stance to take advantage of the arrows at her waist. Their sole advantage was the narrow opening in the gates. If they were forced to engage Bram's men outside, they would not survive. Even as she thought that, she felt the familiar heat of a hunt flow through her.

When she'd requested Aindreas to prepare the men to open the gates, her friend hadn't been surprised that that was the result of her conversation with Bram. He had, however, been angry about Bram being in her bedroom.

Aindreas hadn't known of the empty storage room under her bedroom, nor of the derelict tunnel. When he'd argued further, she'd promised to tell him everything later. He hadn't liked that, but there had been no more time.

Now Aindreas stood behind her and she felt his tumultuous thoughts. She was in turmoil, too.

Suddenly, the Colquhoun men lowered their weapons. Walking amongst his men, Bram emerged. His hair and fine clothing were filthy from the tunnel. He carried no weapon and hadn't prepared for battle. As he swept through the men, a few swiftly left their positions, but with the narrowness of the gates, she could not see where they went.

When Bram faced her, she took a step forward. As if he didn't have arrows pointed at him, he strode through the gates like a conqueror.

So she notched the arrow to her bow. It was pointed at the ground, but her position was clear. Bram slowed and appeared surprised. Did he think her tamed? *He* knew that he'd forced her to open the gates, but her clansmen did not.

When he reached her, she called out for all to hear, 'Welcome, Laird Colquhoun.' She knew her frosty tone did not match her words.

Bram gave a small bow, a quirk to his lips that only she could see. As he looked around at the arrows aimed at his heart, he answered, 'I feel most welcome, Lioslath of Clan Fergusson. Thank you for opening the gates and allowing my men respite within your dear keep.'

Her fingers flexed to draw the bow tighter. How cunning this Colquhoun was with his courtly ways and booming voice. This wasn't the man who'd stolen into her room armed only with smiles and coaxing ways. Nonetheless, his formality was equally unwelcome. She might have been forced to open her gates to him, but she didn't have to be gracious.

'I'm afraid you'll find nae respite here,' she

said. 'Or did you know we have been recently ill-treated?'

He smiled then. That easy, carefree smile she hated and in reflex her arm drew back on the string.

Never lowering his eyes nor his voice, Bram said, 'Then perhaps you'll accept our humble offerings.'

With another courtly gesture, he turned towards the gates. Within moments, Colquhoun clansmen ceremoniously carried upon their shoulders planks of wood laden with food.

A whine in his throat, Dog restlessly lifted his front paw at the overwhelming smells and sights. Roasted boar, turnips, onions, parsnips, glazed over with…butter. All from the supplies Bram brought.

Her own men held on to their weapons, but their arrows now pointed down. None of them looked to her, their eyes were wide on the feast being carried into the keep; it would all need to be set down on—

She stopped short. Her Hall. The planks of wood would never fit. Then there was the filth and damp. She couldn't be in there today of all days. She'd conceded too much of her position to the Colquhoun today. She wouldn't give in any more.

She was just about to order them to stop when

more Colquhoun men brought in trestles to support the heavily laden planks of wood. As if at her request, they set them down in the centre of the courtyard. They couldn't have travelled from the Colquhoun land with them.

So his men hadn't been idle these past weeks. She'd watched as they made the spiked fence and crafted additional arrows, watched as they trained and trained again. But secretly, surely, they'd been preparing for this banquet as well.

Returning her arrow to her belt, she looked to Bram, who was carrying a thick wooden bench as easily as if he carried an armful of kindling. He said something to his clansman and they laughed as they gathered the other benches.

The morning was mild and it hadn't rained for days. She opened the gates, food appeared and now even the weather cooperated with this man.

Dog certainly was cooperating. Someone had thrown a hunk of venison against the furthest wall and he was busily dragging it outside the gates. She didn't know when she'd see him again.

When the food was all set, what would be expected of her? She was used to being alone, not surrounded by people with expectations. She hated these questions and doubts. Her weaknesses conceded even more power to Laird Colquhoun.

'He'll be done soon.' Aindreas stepped closer to her. 'Will you accept it?'

The food? Bram said nothing about it. But now that her clan saw it, she couldn't refuse. 'It'd be a waste, since the clan is hungry.'

'I doona like the way he looks at you,' Aindreas said.

She knew what he meant. Even though Bram organised the feast before her, it felt as if he was assessing her every move and emotion. Knowing him, he'd use it to his advantage. 'Nothing happened.'

'Aye, and I doona believe you,' he said. 'Still, whatever did happen, I didn't expect an apology from him.'

'Is that what this is?' She couldn't imagine Bram apologising. This had to be more of his famed diplomacy and negotiation. Perhaps he expected her to let down her guard with his generosity. Ha! Generosity! More like strategy.

'He's doing this here, but also down in the village.'

She gasped. There was more food?

'You need to let the villagers know whether you accept his apology.'

The villagers had looked to her for leadership since her father's death. She tried to lead them, but failed, and when the English had ravaged, ordered, stripped away every—

She clamped down on her anger and helplessness. The English were gone now, just as the Colquhouns would be soon enough.

Aindreas's expression darkened and she knew Bram approached from behind her. She wouldn't have the strength to stop a fight.

'Go, tell them to accept the food and see what Donaldo has baked,' she said.

There would be precious little bread, but there would be some. They couldn't have the Colquhouns controlling the entire feast. The Fergussons might be poor, but they had their pride.

With a look over her shoulder, Aindreas headed out of the gates.

'Tell them what?' Bram said.

She turned. He was closer than she thought and she barely stopped herself from stepping back. This close she was all too aware of his height, the way he held himself, the way he was just…there. She shook herself. 'That your apology is accepted.'

'I am grateful,' he said, but there was an undercurrent, some hidden meaning she didn't want to think about. He was always hiding something and resentment roiled within her.

She wasn't used to being around people, wasn't used to hiding her feelings or emotions, but if it kept her clan protected from the Colquhoun, she'd learn fast.

'It's easier that way, isn't it?' she said.

A muscle ticked in his jaw. 'Aye, easy.'

So he didn't like her reply. She didn't like anything about this. She didn't like that this close, and in the sunlight, his features weren't glaring, but vibrant. Alive. This close she heard, but also felt, the low timbre of his voice.

The Colquhoun laird was handsome. No, more than that. Aindreas was handsome. Bram was *more*. It was the way he held his powerful body and those unearthly eyes that pierced right through her skin. Like now. She felt that fluttering again and knew it had nothing to do with hunger and weakness.

It was him.

'Do you need to talk to your council?' Bram pointed over her shoulder. 'You couldn't have had time to do so before now.'

Lioslath glanced behind her. Everyone from the keep was standing in little groups. Bram was gazing at the group of elders.

'I'll take care of your siblings,' he said. 'While you go and talk.'

'My siblings?'

'Aye, your brothers, who are already grabbing food, and your sister, admonishing them as she usually does.'

Despite the tension in the courtyard, and her men pointing arrows at his heart, he noticed the children. She felt a pang and knew it had nothing to do with hunger. In the mere moments he'd spent with her brothers and sister, he knew them better than she. Even after all these months, she still didn't know how to approach or talk to them.

Chuckling as Gillean barely missed Fyfa's reach, Bram answered, 'I'll make sure they get enough before they scamper outside the gates.'

Was that what they wanted to do, to scamper? Maybe so. They had run into her room and they'd never done that before. But she couldn't blame them.

The keep and the courtyard weren't large. Hardly enough space for adults, let alone children used to running where they pleased. In fact, the children were almost frantic now, as they worked their way along the tables and towards the gates.

'There is nae council,' she said absently, contemplating Eoin's feet shuffling in barely restrained elation.

'Since when?' he asked.

Bram's sharp question pulled Lioslath's thoughts from her siblings. At Bram's assessing gaze, she cursed herself for admitting any weakness to him.

Clan Fergusson didn't have a council. A council meant order, trades and barters. It meant a keep that was well-run and fair. They'd had a council in her youth, but her stepmother, Irman, wouldn't allow any opposing opinions. The elders had been ignored or shamed until none came forward any more to offer advice.

It didn't matter. No council would have been able to steer her father away from his follies. And she didn't need a council to steer her away from getting rid of the Colquhouns.

'In matters regarding this clan, you'll deal with me.'

For a moment, Bram stilled and she felt as if he laid a trap she couldn't see. Foolishly, she might have opened the gates to him, but it didn't mean she agreed to anything more.

'Shall we eat?'

She didn't want to sit. She wasn't the clan's mistress. He probably expected traditions and courtly manners. But she never sat with her clan and she didn't know what to do. 'Nae.'

'A walk, perhaps?' Bram said.

A walk would get them outside, where she could breathe. Once he said what he was here for, perhaps he'd leave her alone and she could have peace in the forest.

'Aye, a walk.'

Chapter Six

He'd done it. Satisfaction brimmed through Bram. The wait was over and the plan could be implemented. In the meantime, the obvious reparations to the keep and land could begin. Either something had happened here that Lioslath wasn't telling him or the Fergussons lacked decent farming and carpentry skills. The houses were riddled with overlapping patches, the roofs covered in thinning thatch. The keep was in worse shape.

There were many improvements to make before winter. They would need cooperation between the clans to get them done and getting the clans to cooperate would take time.

He knew this visit would not be a welcome one, but this clan's anger had an edge to it. Since they arrived, they'd kept extra guard to prevent bloodshed. Lioslath barring the gates for weeks had imbedded the animosity between the clans.

Even now with the feast beginning, it was there. Beneath the sounds of scraping and tearing of food, and the adjusting of elbows and shuffling of legs, there was the air of anticipated battle.

He needed to come to some agreement with the clan's mistress. But would she be agreeable if she was hungry and fainting? Even more so, could he remain reasonable when she was so breathtakingly beautiful to him?

In the sunlight, her hair was raven black and just as incandescent. If it had been long, he knew its darkness would have consumed even the brightest of summer skies.

But its chopped length surprisingly pleased him. It didn't hide any of the womanly figure underneath. So he saw the graceful arch of her neck, the creamy texture along her nape. He could so clearly see the intimate spot where he might hover with his lips, where he might graze with his teeth, where he might kiss.

He'd teased her about a kiss. But what had started as calculated flirting, now, in sunlight, became something more like a truth.

It was a complicated attraction and one he didn't want, and which she didn't reciprocate. She wasn't accepting his food and she didn't raise her eyes to his. In fact, she kept looking outside the gates.

'We can take food with us,' he offered.

'With us?'

'I want to know the extent of the necessary repairs to be done before winter.'

'Are you expecting me to show you around the…my clan?'

'Certainly.'

'Doona you have responsibilities here?'

He shrugged. 'Doona you need to eat before we go?'

'Aindreas brought me food while I dressed.'

'The venison. Do you not want to take some of what is offered today?' Bram asked. They may be talking of only food, but at least she talked. Sometimes, the most heated discussions started with banalities.

'Ah, aye, the food today was conveniently made.'

'There was more yesterday,' he said, letting her know he'd expected her to open the gates yesterday.

He caught the slight curve to her lips before she looked away. He'd let her enjoy her victory, since he didn't intend to give her others. 'You must be eager to leave the confines of the keep?'

'Very,' she answered with the expected anger in her eyes. But there was also vulnerability. A complicated emotion he didn't want to see.

It wouldn't do to feel more for this clan or this woman. Curbing his tongue, keeping his patience, he stepped back so she could walk in front of him.

He had managed tough negotiations before; this was no different. When tempers were high, coming to any agreement was often protracted. But in the end, he always prevailed and he'd do so again. But how?

There were secrets here and he knew precious little about this woman. A woman who held daggers and arrows. Whose hair was black as night and whose eyes were bright as a summer sky. 'Are you averse to our making improvements and of using our supplies?'

'It would be foolish of me otherwise, wouldn't it?'

'But you do not like it.'

'Nae,' she said bluntly.

He'd get no further in that argument. 'The fences surrounding the keep and the gates need minor changes,' he said, changing the subject. 'What of the keep?'

'The stones hold, but much of the timber needs replacing.' She hurried her pace towards the gates. 'I doona want to talk of the keep today and I doona want to talk of improvements. What repairs are needed we'll make in the spring.'

They couldn't make repairs on their own. The platform by the gates was crooked. The entire village was riddled with haphazard structures as if the maintenances were hurriedly or half-heartedly done.

'Why are the keep and village like this?'

'You knew of our clan's poverty when you made the agreement with my father.'

He knew something of their poverty, aye, but now that he had a closer look, it appeared as if the damage was purposefully done. He couldn't imagine any carpenters with so little skill.

'You're not telling me everything.'

'Nothing has ever been easy or comfortable here. That is all you need to know,' she retorted.

There had to be more to the damage here than her words belied. There were few horses, no sheep, and their fields were bare. There were too many repairs and winter stores to make up as well, if he was right about her lack of stored food. He knew what it was like to be hungry and he wouldn't wish it even on this obstinate woman.

Their survival was precarious here, as was their future prosperity and stability. With King John Balliol now held prisoner at the Tower, the English King Edward began to set up many sheriffs and governors. This clan's protection, and its alliances, would be more important than ever.

His brother Caird had warned him that there was a lot of work to do here, but even now he could feel his blood coursing excitedly at the prospect. Bram enjoyed hunting and he enjoyed play. But he also loved a challenge and the work needed here filled him with a sense of anticipation.

No. He had to stick with the plan, which meant, come springtime, he would be gone.

They walked around his camp, but Lioslath's eyes remained resolutely on the village ahead. If she continued to ignore him, he wouldn't be accepted by this clan despite the supplies he brought.

She said she would accept his help, but she clearly didn't want to. She was full of contradictions. He wanted to implement his plan, but she forced him to remain idle. He offered the feast in friendship and supplies in goodwill; she didn't want to eat or discuss repairs. There were too many contrasts and contradictions. Too many factors competing.

Competition. The thought sparked an idea.

They'd never mend relations with tempers so high. They had to make peace if he and his men were to stay the winter and he thought he knew how to do it. 'Winter is coming and some improvements can't wait until spring. Our clans must work together to begin these repairs.'

'Isn't that why you feed us?' she said.

'It isn't enough. What is needed after these

many weeks is distraction. A faire. Some competitions.'

'You want us to do what?' Lioslath gasped.

'We must have a competition between clans,' Bram said.

Games. He wanted to play games in order to defuse a fight. 'How are games supposed to stop fighting?'

Lioslath could feel the air clearing since they'd walked out the gates. Near the village was the forest she treasured. Even though she was supposed to be showing him the fields and the village, already she was walking to the trees, to peace.

And he mentioned *games*?

She was done with this conversation. She didn't want to stay around listening to him until he twisted his words so she agreed with him. He wanted to talk of the village and of the fields, but to her the forest beckoned. She couldn't wait to get to the trees, to feel the soft dirt under her feet. To hear…silence.

'Are you being wilfully obtuse or do you truly not realise?'

'What will it take for you to leave?' she said, not wanting him in the trees with her.

'Go?' He frowned as if trying to guess what truth she told. 'As the clan's mistress, doona you want to appease ill tempers?'

She wasn't the clan's mistress. The only temper she ever cared about was her own. 'Nae.'

His frown increased, his eyes troubled. Then everything eased and he stepped back.

'You're a lady, I apologise. You've never been in a situation like this before. However, I ken what will start riots and this competition will help.'

A lady? Clan's mistress? He might as well have been speaking French. Even his manner had gone all courtly. She wasn't gentle born. She had never cared about cookery or ensuring freshly swept staircases, or gentling tempers. She had given Aindreas her bow and arrows, but she felt the comfort of her small blade hidden in the folds of her tunic. The small blade she currently wanted to throw at Bram.

'You cannot be sincere about these games,' she said. Although what else did she expect from a Colquhoun who laughed all the time? 'This is a trick, a…jest.'

'Nae a jest. Nae a trick. Simply games. A competition,' he enunciated. 'We need a swimming contest across the lake, wrestling, bowls, horseshoes and archery.'

'With teams, scoring, prizes?'

'Aye.'

He sounded relieved, as if she agreed with him! After everything she'd been through this year—death, vulnerability and soon starvation—he wanted to play games. 'Frivolous amusements. They serve nae purpose.'

Bram rolled back on his heels. Lioslath understood nothing, or she wilfully battled against him. Neither would do. This woman wasn't who he thought she would be. Her father died in April. Surely, by now, she had knowledge of clan affairs? After all, women cared about the temperaments of the people around them, even if they did not deal with the politics of leadership.

And now, in both of the clans, the men's temperaments were too high. They needed cooperation and a way to release the tension.

'They serve the purpose of men who want to fight each other. They give direction to their aggression so it is not spent on each other. We need to set it all up and fast or these men will be at each other's throats by midnight.'

'Those games will not feed my clan, or make their homes stronger, or provide—'

'Those issues would have been addressed weeks ago if you had opened the gates.'

Lioslath winced and he knew he'd hit his target. Being blunt wasn't normally in his nature when courteous words worked just as well. But courteous words were wasted with her.

'We need cooperation and there's nothing else more expedient to address raised tempers than a competition. What they need now is a test of wills.'

'This isn't a test of wills. I've hunted plenty to know when a prey is being manipulated from the safety of their lair. Come here, little vole, you'll get some food for your belly and then I'll get food for mine!'

'I set this up so our clans doona start fighting!'

'You make it all my fault. Aye, vole, it's all your fault you're in my soup because you were so hungry you ate the scraps in my trap!'

He would have his way in this. 'Are you saying I manipulated you when I put the food outside the tunnel?'

'Aye, what else was it?'

'A peace offering. A gift to show nae ill will!'

'And the fact that I took it? Didn't that obligate me then to open the gates?'

He'd done it to soften her towards them. 'You opened the gates to save your honour.'

'Because you were in my bedroom,' she pointed out. 'Ah, I've been blind. You've done it over and over. Here, starving people, here is some food. Here, Clan Fergusson, here's the promise of sheep and a strong alliance.'

Her words cut too close to the truth. 'Careful, Fergusson. Who is twisting words now? The deal we made was a matter of diplomacy between your father and me, made by consenting parties—'

'We're not consenting. You merely starve our bellies until we feel as if the starvation is somehow our fault! These games you suggest aren't a compromise, they're coercion!'

'I am Colquhoun. I am laird. I do not coerce!'

She smiled. 'Of course you wouldn't, how silly of me. We are only here for your pleasure.'

Shaking his head, he looked around. Their words were not going unnoticed. They were outside the gates now, past the camp and too near the village. There were no benches and tables here, but freshly cooked food lay on carts. Many villagers were taking the food and carrying it to the communal tables. Too many villagers who walked slowly and could hear their every heated word.

Bram ran his hand through his hair. Frustrating Fergusson! Did she not know women were meant to be gentle? To smile? To be meek? That was what was needed today, a biddable female. She was unexpected. And he was constantly guessing with her. It wasn't only her beauty he couldn't ignore, it was the mystery of her. How she hesitated around her siblings and clan.

How she ignored his status as laird and his coaxing smiles. How she angered at his reasoning. Frustrating female!

He was again brought to a point he didn't want to be with her. So quick to lose his patience. She put him in a position of defence again and he would not have it. 'Are you saying you doona want this competition?'

Lioslath pointed to the village. 'Aren't we walking so I can show you what you so generously want to improve?'

He'd get no further with her. Stubbornness. She might have eaten, but he hadn't. He eyed their offered food, but the colour of the pottage wasn't appetising, so he grabbed two of their rolls and some boar.

Following Lioslath, he took a bite of the bread and quickly spat it out lest he risk breaking a tooth.

'Bread not fresh enough for you?'

'Nae, 'tis fine.' No bread should have stones and pottage shouldn't be grey. But he wouldn't admit that. She believed he liked easy and thought him pampered. Confirming this idea wouldn't get her agreement to the rest of his intentions for today.

The feast was only the beginning of mending relations with this clan. It would take the games event to truly achieve cooperation. Then his plan to remain for the winter would be secure.

As if she knew he lied about the bread, Lioslath smirked and hurried her steps towards the village.

* * *

Restless, agitated and still too far away from her forest, Lioslath wanted the afternoon to end. It wasn't only Bram and his demands, it was their clans observing each other, observing her and Bram. Though she was outside, she felt trapped. Trapped by the role here that she didn't know how to do and trapped by her longing to be better.

Barely keeping her temper, she pointed to the roofs, and to the wood rot. Talked of the ploughing still to do in the fields and the trenching through the village. All needing to be done before the dirt froze.

Bram asked questions, and she knew he missed nothing. She felt the familiar prick to her pride. Fergusson keep and land were falling apart.

It hadn't always been so. When she was a child, her parents had worked tirelessly and the keep had been beautiful; the clan had been prosperous.

Then the wolves had come and raided the village right before a sudden frost descended. The wheat harvesting hadn't yet been completed and most of the bales of oats and barley hadn't been stored properly. They suffered too much as the harsh winter continued. Suffered more with her mother's cough and sudden death.

They'd never suffered a winter like that again, but they never recovered from it either. Her father most of all.

As the years went by her father took riskier chances. Desperation to recover what they lost engulfed his every action. The marriage to the Colquhoun clan was simply another attempt. When the letters of agreement occurred, when her father left to secure his bride, he regained some pride. His sense of purpose, of optimism, returning.

But Clan Fergusson was cursed. For when her father returned from that fateful trip to Colquhoun land, he had no bride. Determined, desperate, he left again and never returned. Then Bram sent his letter offering help, but he never came. When the English garrison stormed the keep in July, they'd been too vulnerable to withstand the demands. The English caused far worse damage than an ice storm. They arrived just as the barley was harvested and they stayed to harvest the oats and wheat before burning the rest.

The clan was gleaning for remains when the Colquhouns arrived. Lioslath had had enough.

She was tired of being told she didn't understand. She was sick of feeling as though she didn't understand. She did understand. Laird Colquhoun wrote a letter saying he'd come with aid, but then days, weeks, months had gone by.

So it was up to her to help her clan. She hunted; she provided food. She confronted the English until they left and she intended to confront Bram until he left as well.

She thought closing the gates would be enough. She thought giving supplies to the English would be enough. She failed on both accounts. She wasn't ruthless like her father, or gentle like her mother. Bram's very presence was a bitter reminder of how inadequate she was.

When they turned a corner and she saw her siblings playing with Donaldo's children, she couldn't go any further. She couldn't walk through her land with the weight of Bram's pity on her shoulders like this. It would only be worse if he saw she couldn't talk properly to her siblings as well.

'I'm leaving!' she said, turning away from the villagers and their clans. Turning away from the decimated fields and the derelict keep, and a Colquhoun laird who noticed everything.

His eyes widened in warning, but she marched around him. She didn't need to see him to know he followed her. It was simply that awareness. Like when he spoke, the low timbre of his voice. It was something that curled inside her. She hated her acute awareness of him almost as much as she hated his accusations and pity.

All day she walked beside him, answered his

questions and talked to her clan. All day she watched him. As a huntress, she admired how a man his size strode so stealthily, so deadly and silently.

She shivered. Why was she noticing him? Of everyone she had ever known, why did she feel this...desire for him?

She couldn't avoid it now. It wasn't hunger and it wasn't weakness. Her body was acutely aware of him. After all those weeks of watching him, she knew that her eyes were no longer filled with hate, but something like admiration. For Laird Colquhoun!

She was almost out of breath by the time they reached the forest on the south side. The forest was deeper and darker here. It was her favourite part of her land and one she could not see from the Fergusson keep.

A few steps inward and she smelled the musty earth and the sharp bite of autumn's leaves. The smell was freedom and home. Bram might have thought he trapped her in her home with his siege. In truth, he kept her away from her home, which she always found in her forest.

Bram remained silent, but his will was a force she could feel and its force was ruining her sanctuary. Bram practically hovered as he walked beside her and he almost blocked the sky through the trees. He looked wrong in her forest.

The brightness of his hair didn't blend, the broadness of his shoulders and bulk of his build like a boulder that suddenly appeared amongst the tall and graceful tree trunks.

He was wrong to be here as well. This forest was hers. Clan Colquhoun had no place here. But he was there, like a storm that kept battering against her.

Her hand fluttering to the hidden blade at her waist, she rounded on him. 'I showed you what you wanted to see. Why did you follow me?'

'We were in front of your clan and mine. My not leaving the village with you would have looked like a slight. So I strolled out with you as if we wished to talk privately.'

Stroll, she had practically ran here, but he kept his pace with her and wasn't out of breath. To everyone, they probably did look as though they walked away from the village. Again, she made a foolish choice. She was unused to wondering what others thought or what appearances should be.

She had been hidden away most of her life, and for the rest of it, she hid herself away. She was hiding now, but the Colquhoun wouldn't leave her alone. She clenched the blade she'd hidden in her clothes.

'So we talked privately and now you can go!'

'Nae, we must truly talk. We must come to an agreement.'

The competition again. His tone changed until it was as blunt as hers. It wouldn't make her change her mind on its futility, especially when he used the word 'must'. The very word curbed her freedom. She had heard it from her stepmother and in the end from her father.

She knew he would continue to argue about the games until she couldn't refuse. However, what Bram couldn't control was how the competition would go.

Bram might bring his food and his supplies. He might order this competition. But *she* would choose who the winner would be.

Bram didn't move. He didn't even realise he needed to move, until she threw the knife just past his left ear.

She knew he hadn't seen the blade, but there was no mistaking the fury and the shock in his eyes when he heard the *thunk* of it embedding in the tree behind him.

Brutal silence as storm-grey eyes stared at her.

Lioslath smiled. 'That's my agreement to your competition. Satisfied, Colquhoun?'

Chapter Seven

Trying to remember it would all be over soon, Lioslath suffered through the hanging of tabards and flags. She grimaced as her clansmen built hay men and targets, as they argued on markers and where to pin them to trees. It was all so wasteful.

Dog reappeared and walked next to her, his keen eyes taking everything in. Unlike her, he seemed happy about the proceedings. Probably because he was finally fed and had roamed the forest last night.

She wished she was as content as him. But she continued to feel yesterday's turmoil of telling her clan about the competition and waiting for Bram to surprise her in the night.

Needing to remain calm, she knelt, keeping her head just above Dog's, and waited until he leaned into her so she could put her arms around him. She never squeezed, though she wanted to. She never forgot he was a wild animal, so she kept their hugs brief and infrequent. But she needed it and was glad he gave it. He was her familiar when everything around her was unfamiliar.

Standing again, she noticed her brothers busily making hay men. At least Eoin made them, while Gillean undid them. There wasn't enough hay for large ones. She knew it had to have been a Colquhoun who suggested using the hay. The Fergusson clan knew they needed it. Every stalk would have to be picked up and stored before winter.

The cold would be upon them soon. This was a day wasted when her clan needed to work, not to play.

Her clan. Only since her father's death had she started to think of them this way. Amongst all her Fergussons, the Colquhouns stood out. Not only because they were strangers. It was because of the sharp contrast between the clans.

The Colquhouns were properly dressed, their shoes worn to comfortableness, their clean weapons at their sides. Her own clansmen were too thin from the siege and English greed, and what bows and arrows they had left were greatly mismatched.

Even if this was a friendly competition, it was

not fair. Already Bram's clansmen had the advantage and she seethed with the comparisons.

'Aren't these celebrations fine, sister?' Fyfa skipped to her.

Fyfa glowed with an eagerness and shyness to her eyes and voice. Even while she was skipping, her mannerisms were ladylike and full of grace.

'These aren't celebrations.' Lioslath watched Dog slowly walk away. He was as unused to her siblings as she was.

'There are flags and hay men. I'm told there will be music afterwards and Donaldo is already making her sweetened oatcakes.' She sighed exaggeratedly. 'I've heard tales of faires like this.'

'It's not a faire.' To be a faire, there would need to be trade and commerce. They had nothing but air to give away here, and with all the people, even that seemed precious little. Now Donaldo made her honeyed oatcakes, which had to be using the last of their hidden supplies. They'd fall to further ruin before the day was over.

'Where are your brothers?' Lioslath asked instead.

'*Our* brothers are arguing and muddying themselves as usual.'

'Have you talked to them?'

Lioslath knew Gillean couldn't possibly have said anything about what he wanted from Laird

Colquhoun in return for keeping quiet. Whilst she knew little of them, she was sure the children couldn't have forgotten the bribe. But if Bram had given the children their gifts, Fyfa would surely be beaming with the news. Bram probably had ribbons hidden in his camp for just such a manipulating purpose. Just as he hid that well-calculated feast.

'As little as possible now that we're free.'

Lioslath felt a pang. The confinement had been hard on her. At Fyfa's age, it would have been unbearable. Still, she hadn't expected her siblings to feel the same way. She thought them too different from her. But Bram said they wanted to scamper... Bram, again, and his too-observing eyes. 'We're not free while the Colquhouns plague us.'

'Plague, when there's a feast and festivities? Although I will have to bring Eoin and Gillean under my wing again. I've told them the dangers of stilt walking, but I do believe they weren't taking me seriously.'

Oh, Fyfa and her flourishing speeches. She acted very much like the lady of the manor. No doubt when she was grown, she'd make a fine lady.

It was one of her father's dearest wishes. One of the reasons Busby married the Colquhoun's sister had been to obtain a mother for Fyfa. One who would raise her gently to be a lady.

But Gaira fled and their father was killed. Looking at Fyfa only reminded her of the loss of her own mother and the horrible years of pain and banishment in between.

'You need to find work,' she retorted. 'You and the boys are too idle.'

She worked when she was their age. What did they think made anything better? Hard work. That was what she'd done all her life. All she got was meagre results, but she got them. Play earned nothing. These festivities were as useless.

Fyfa's expression fell flat and the light died in her eye. 'Work again.'

'Aye, work again.' Even as Lioslath said the words, there was something in her heart that ached as Fyfa's smile faltered.

'Someone has been stealing my oatcakes.' Donaldo took great strides towards them.

Fyfa's expression immediately changed to outrage. Clenching fists to her sides, she declared, 'Those boys! I haven't had any!' Without looking back, Fyfa stomped away.

'Did those boys truly steal oatcakes?' Lioslath asked.

'Do you think they'd dare?' Donaldo said.

No, they wouldn't have dared cross broad-shouldered, broad-hipped Donaldo. No one would.

Donaldo had been Lioslath's mother's closest friend, and while she couldn't call Donaldo a friend, she didn't feel as awkward with her as she did with the rest of her clan. When Lioslath's father died, it was Donaldo who had first given her loyalty to Lioslath, who stood beside her when the English came. She was always fierce, but now Donaldo's usual scowl was deeper.

Lioslath felt a fissure of worry. 'What has happened?'

'Preparations for the celebrations are going well.'

'That isn't it.' Lioslath couldn't care less about the celebrations and Donaldo would know that. 'What didn't you want Fyfa to hear?'

'All day he's been watching you.'

Lioslath knew what she meant. She knew Bram was watching her, just as she kept watching him. Had their watching become a habit because of the siege? No, it felt different this time. She wasn't only observing him from a distance. This close, she felt as though she participated in his preparations.

Everything about him was vibrant, his smile ever ready. He talked with his clansmen, attempted to talk to hers. There was an energy about him she'd never felt before. A purpose.

She frowned. He had a purpose she admired. But she wouldn't admire the Colquhoun. His purpose here was to play foolish games.

She shrugged. 'Should it matter?'

'Aye, it matters when he gazes at you like a man does a woman,' Donaldo said.

'He's probably only checking to see if I'm going to stop the competition.'

'Are you?' Donaldo knew her well.

'It's wasteful when so much has been prepared.'

'Ah, then you intend on showing off.'

Lioslath more than intended. Although weakened, she was still the best marksman of her clan.

'He won't like it,' Donaldo warned. 'There will be consequences.'

'He's not the English.'

'You took too many risks then as well. Facing them the way you did. Not consulting with any of us before you ran out of those stables. Offering them everything, when some of the men would have fought.'

'If they had done so, they would have died. I gave them everything and nae one was hurt.'

'You could have been. So easily, like now. You shouldn't test this man too far.'

Lioslath didn't miss Donaldo's sharp tone.

'Are you siding with him now? You, who

have kept the villagers silent and against the Colquhouns?'

'There are nae sides now that you've opened the gates.' Donaldo looked around. 'There can be only cooperation.'

Donaldo expected cooperation because she didn't know that Lioslath had been forced into letting Bram inside the keep.

'The only cooperation will be to do this competition, accept the supplies and say goodbye to the Colquhoun clan for good.' It seemed so simple. So easy. Why hadn't she cooperated when they arrived? Maybe if she had, the Colquhouns would be gone now. 'Has it all been for naught? Did I make more trouble, more waste, by not simply doing this in the beginning?'

'You didn't know what he was about when he came and he deserved to know his presence was unwelcome.' Donaldo shrugged. 'It's been difficult letting those supplies go to waste when we need them, but Fergussons are known to be stubborn and it felt good to shove their arrogance in their faces.'

It had felt good, but Lioslath was usually practical. She hated to accept his help because he hadn't been there when the English ravaged her land. It hadn't felt right to suddenly be his ally. Then again, since her father's death, nothing felt right.

Maybe after the competition, it would be better; maybe once the Colquhouns left, she would be able to finally breathe again.

'Does she intend to win the competition?' Aindreas asked, approaching.

Frowning, Lioslath stepped aside to allow them a more private conversation. Anyone could have heard him.

'Aye, she does,' Donaldo said, disapproval in her voice.

Aindreas looked relieved. Lioslath didn't want Donaldo to guess why. 'How does everyone fare?' she said to Donaldo, needing to change the subject.

'Better now, child,' Donaldo said. 'Although most continue to share your views. For this time, everyone is in accord to stay quiet about what happened. Although it has been difficult to hide the extent of the damage the English did when they came through here.'

'They continue to question?'

She didn't understand why Bram was asking questions; why he wanted to know the reason for so many repairs. After all, he never thought highly of the Fergusson clan and was aware of their poverty. Why wouldn't he leave it at that?

'Constantly,' Donaldo said. 'For now I bite my tongue. But if the Colquhouns are not asking about the fields, they ask about the scorch marks against the houses.'

The English had come through like locusts, what they did not devour they tried to destroy. When the Colquhouns crested the hill, Lioslath had little time to decide what they would do, so they kept to a simple plan: bar the gates and tell the laird nothing.

'Harder times are ahead for the clan,' Aindreas said. 'That doesn't mean we're a charity for the likes of the Colquhouns.'

On that Lioslath agreed. 'Then we keep our silence.'

Donaldo nodded, but looked over her shoulder. 'I'll happily keep our silence, but he doesn't watch you like a charity. Remember, do not test him too far. There will be consequences.'

'He needs to leave,' Aindreas said. 'Her insulting him in the games will make that message clear.'

'Aye, but she opened the gates,' Donaldo said.

'She was forced to!' Aindreas said heatedly.

At Donaldo's pointed gaze, Lioslath inwardly cursed Aindreas's outburst, but she knew she couldn't avoid telling of how Bram found her in the kitchens and her fainting.

'Gracious, child,' Donaldo said, after Lioslath was done. Then her gaze grew perceptive.

'Is that all that happened in the kitchens? He watches you as if he knows something.'

'I fainted,' Lioslath said. 'I've told him nothing!'

'He does know more.' Aindreas cursed. 'It wasn't the only time he was in your bedroom, was it?'

'He was there the night before,' she said.

'*Twice* he's been to your room?' Donaldo's voice raised before she vehemently whispered, 'If the children tell, there may be calls for you to marry him. There's nothing we can do to protect you on this, you ken?'

Lioslath nodded, keeping her eyes on her closest allies, who had now become her accusers. As if she had any control over Bram. As if she had control of anything that had happened this past year. She wanted none of this.

'Nothing happened,' she said. 'Dog was with me and I had a knife.'

'You should have thrown it!' Aindreas said.

She had thought the same. What had stopped her? Maybe they were right to accuse her.

'I was imagining you observed him as I did,' Aindreas said. 'With hatred. Imagining what you'd do to him if he ever did breach the gates. But you didn't, did you? Lioslath, he's the reason your father is *dead*!'

Rage flared through her. 'You think I've forgotten?'

Flushing, Aindreas eased back.

She didn't worry for her reputation, but she did worry that marrying the Colquhoun would be unforgivable. His actions added to the destruction of this clan, and he could destroy her, too. He'd probably expect her to be the lady of the keep. She'd never hunt again...never have the solace of her forest.

'When this competition is over, the Colquhouns will be gone.' Without looking at either, she whirled around and walked away.

Chapter Eight

Bram watched Lioslath walk heatedly away from Aindreas and Donaldo as they left in the opposite direction. But then Lioslath abruptly stopped. She was surrounded by the celebrations, by laughter, but her eyes scanned her clansmen with an emotion he couldn't interpret. What he did know was enjoyment or anticipation wasn't one of them.

He felt like a hunter who didn't know if the animal trapped before him was prey. Days in her presence and he didn't understand her. It was critical that he stay here during the winter. To do so, he would need to be accepted. The feast was to begin that acceptance. Lioslath made it clear when she threw the dagger that she hadn't accepted him. Since Lioslath had the loyalty of the clan, he needed to gain her approval.

But how to do that?

Yesterday, he had seen her interactions with

her clansmen and discovered that she never did anything predictable. He thought it was because of the freshness of the siege, the tenseness of the clan. Yet today, she was the same, and her eyes scanned the trees as if with…longing.

'Thinking of escaping all this?' he asked.

Gasping, Lioslath turned. 'How long have you been standing there?'

'Long enough,' he said 'You doona want to be here.'

'I already told you how ridiculous this competition was.'

'Nae, that's not it, it's—' Bram waved his hand, indicating the activity around them. 'It's everything else.'

'I doona like being around you,' she said, before turning and walking away from him and the faire.

Catching up to her, he saw her eyes scan the sparse trees surrounding them, noticed how the tension around her eyes eased as she entered the tree line. Yesterday, she went to the trees as well.

Was this where she found peace? Maybe he could understand this part of her. Satisfaction and something else warmed his chest at the realisation. The forest was where he found his peace. He needed the trees, the hunting, the *sol-*

itude. The lack of quiet was the price he paid for being laird.

His father had trained him well. Taught him lessons he'd never forget. They made him a good laird to his clan, made him an unparalleled negotiator. But the lessons of listening and observing people took something of himself. He returned to the trees to hear his own voice again.

And Lioslath kept returning here to the forest, which was always dangerous. He remembered her accuracy with the dagger. Was her precision not simply luck? 'The trees are where you want to be,' he said, certain.

She turned on him again, anger and frustration in her voice. 'I want to be left alone. Shouldn't you be preparing for the competitions?'

Too much anger. He gave an inward shake. He must have been wrong about her finding peace amongst the trees, must have been wanting to see a common thread between them that wasn't there.

'Why are you here?' she further accused.

To find some commonality with her! For a moment he thought he had. But it had been a fleeting thought, a *wishful* thought. And inexplicably, he felt a loss. She was not what he expected, but even so why would any woman find peace amongst trees?

He'd have to find some other way to connect with her. Something swift. With his family's lives at stake, he had to find some acceptance from her...and fast.

Lioslath wasn't like any woman he had ever met. But she was a woman and they could be persuaded, seduced. It hadn't worked so far with Lioslath, but could he try to coax her? It was a tricky thought, since he desired her. But if he persuaded, just enough...

No, he wouldn't fool himself that he wanted Lioslath because of the clan. This was for himself and the way she made him feel.

Did she feel it, too? There were times when she looked at him as if it were true, but then she'd scowl or avert her eyes.

Maybe if she did feel it, it was unwanted. After everything she accused him of, the desire couldn't be any more convenient for her than it was for him.

And he did desire her. He took too much pleasure merely at the sight of her. Lioslath's hair was almost blue in this light, her eyes rivalling the sky behind her. That mole above her lip alluring...tempting. Could he only taste her, only kiss her, and not have more? He wanted more now.

How could Lioslath be alone and unmarried? He never felt such longing for a woman before and he didn't even know if she was available.

Did it matter? He didn't know. Maybe if he did risk a kiss, it would be enough to end his torturous wondering.

'You talk much with Aindreas. Is he your betrothed?'

Lioslath's limbs trembled and she crossed her arms to hide her shock. Somehow, Bram had guessed she needed the forest.

And in his voice, when he had spoken of it, it was as if he wanted her to long for the trees.

But she must have been wrong, as she always was about people, because now he asked about Aindreas. As if her one true friendship in life was any of his concern. 'It matters?' she asked.

The heat and curiosity in his eyes cooled at her tone. 'It matters that you have gained influence with your clan and are yet unmarried. Mayhap they do not wish you to marry a Fergusson? Perhaps they wish for you to marry another from a different clan? A more…profitable match?'

Marriage. The thought was laughable. She, the huntress, who slept with horses, who wore her hair like a boy's and the clothes of a man when in the forest. Who would marry her? She remained silent.

'That's it, then. Aindreas wants what he cannot have because your clan wants another.'

Let him believe what he wanted. She knew

nothing of her clan's wants. 'I do not ken this conversation.'

'Do you not? It's about wants.'

He was flirting with her again. She was sure of it, although there wasn't a teasing note to his voice as there had been before. Nor was he looking at her through his eyelashes in that way she was becoming familiar with. His gaze was too assessing for that.

'I should go.'

He took another step. 'Why should you? There is only revelry now and anticipation for what is to come.'

'For the marksmanship.'

'Of a sorts,' he said, his eyes holding a teasing glint.

What could he be teasing about with marksmanship? Teasing meant being frivolous and there was nothing frivolous about hitting targets.

'Do you not know of wants?' he asked.

She knew very well what she wanted. 'What I want is for you to be gone.'

'You give up that easily?'

Something flared within her. Not a feeling of embarrassment, but the familiar flare of challenge.

'You do need to marry,' he continued as if she'd answered him.

So that was what he meant with her clan's

wants. Marriage. Donaldo and Aindreas talked of it often since her father's death. She knew they meant it to help her clan. There was no laird or protection here now. They suffered once at the hands of the English; after the winter, other clans would likely challenge them as well.

She wanted to help her clan, just as she wanted to help her brothers and sister, but she wanted to do it in the way she always had. By hunting and by taking care of the crops and the animals. Marrying would mean taking care of the house, of the stores, and setting tables. Ensuring laundry smelled of heather the way her mother had done.

She was nothing like her mother.

And she didn't want to talk marriage and marriage beds with this man. The fact they were alone was too keen a reminder of how she noticed the fluid movements of his hands and heard the low timbre of his voice. The day was bright, beautiful. Crisp with the cold coming and she was surrounded by her beloved trees. Yet, right now, it was Bram who held the vibrancy of her trees.

'But maybe Aindreas is not the man you want?' Bram asked. 'It must be the accuracy of your dagger throwing that distracts him.'

His continual talk of Aindreas grated. 'Do you always ask questions and never wait for answers?' she asked.

'It helps when having a conversation and the other party doesn't answer.'

'What I want is to end this conversation. I think you're insulting me.'

'Nae, what I'm doing is merely asking a question. And you do have an uncanny ability to throw a knife, lass.'

Unsure how to answer, she shrugged. She could have killed him with the dagger. Today, he acted as if he didn't care she had thrown it.

'Would it help if I told you what I want?' Bram said.

She could simply turn and leave, she knew that. There was nothing holding her here. But Bram was standing steadily in front of her. Though she was surrounded by the smell and feel of her beloved trees again, she felt arrested by his presence.

So she held still and foolishly answered him. 'I thought it was obvious what you wanted.'

His brows rose as he gave a wolfish grin. 'I am obvious?'

'You arrive in your fancy dress ready to bestow your generous gifts—aye, I'd say that was obvious of a man whose arrogance rivals a king's!'

'Not so obvious, then,' he said, his voice filled with amusement. 'But maybe that is my fault.'

He took the remaining steps to her until she looked up to catch his expression.

'Is there nothing you want?' His eyes were searching hers, but it seemed as if he found what he was looking for, because he continued. 'Ah, you're wondering if I'm negotiating with you again.'

This had to be Bram manipulating her again. But for what? He believed he'd gained what he wanted already. The gates were opened, he fed her clan and now a competition was about to begin at his request.

'You're always negotiating,' she said readily. But she knew she was wrong. Bram didn't have the same ease as before. There was an intensity about him. On this cloudless day, his hair rivalled the sun and this time it didn't contrast with her Scotland. Not when the sunlight lit through it until he became part of the warming rays. As though he was part of her precious Scotland.

Another matter she didn't understand and it put her at a disadvantage...again.

'Perhaps,' he said. 'But there's something more here and it surprises me as well as you.'

'There can be nothing more here.' But again she lied to herself. She felt that breathlessness in her breast, that heat pool both heavy and light throughout her. The desire flaring through her, made worse by his voice, his words, by his proximity.

'I agree.' His hand caressed the back of hers hanging by her side and she gave a start.

His hand was only a skimming caress, but she felt it deeply and felt his touch more as he trailed his fingers up her arm. 'There can be nothing more here, but there is. Too complicated. Too unexpected. Still, I want to kiss you, lass. Have been wanting to kiss you since I saw you stare defiantly down at me from the platform.'

His hand reached above her elbow and was descending again. The caress seemed almost casual, but she knew better. Everything he did was deliberate.

'I wanted to shoot you with an arrow.'

She tried to recall her anger, tried to remember that he was touching her deliberately, for some purpose, but her body held still and accepted, wanted, his touch.

'Aye, you were standing there with a bow, weren't you now. Nothing could surprise me more than that weapon in your hands.'

Surprising? What else would she do with it? Maybe it was her turn to explain. 'If I had one now, I'd use it.' The way she accepted his touch mocked her words.

'Aye, but there will be games soon. I look forward to those.'

'Am I a game?'

A wolfish smile. 'The very best kind.'

The smile seared her, as it changed his grey eyes. They held something hidden in their depths. Something he was showing her, but which she shouldn't fully want to understand. Not with him.

'I doona ken this *flirting*. Just before we were arguing. I threw a dagger at you.'

'Before, we were merely taking positions and discussing terms. I'll not lie and say the dagger surprised me. But it is a new day and now our bartering is over. It is just…us.'

She didn't know how to separate their argument from who she was. Like now she didn't know how to separate her anger from the way her body felt around his. She blamed her motionlessness on the clashing emotions inside her. She blamed it on his touch, for now his right hand achingly, softly caressed along her jaw, curved along the shell of her ear and down her neck and up again.

She wasn't so much aware of her breathing now, because it seemed to have stopped and a sort of languid warmth was entering and filling her instead. Even if she wanted to move, she didn't know if she could do it. She shouldn't be here, shouldn't want to be here, and yet she had to admit a part of her did. Why did she feel this way?

His thumb brushed below her lips. 'Your lips are ripe and lush. They give a man thoughts.'

'Thoughts,' she whispered, the word opening her mouth just enough for Bram to take advantage of it.

The coarse, callous tips of his fingers pressed down along the corner of her mouth until she wanted to open her mouth a bit more, until she felt the need to…taste him.

It was the heat from his body, the smell of his skin, the skimming of his fingers binding her to him in a way she didn't expect. Not here, not now. Never…him.

Yet he was the only man who made her feel this way.

'Aye, thoughts,' he said. 'Thoughts of what those lips would feel like, how they would taste. And this.' His fingertip traced the mole above her lip. 'This mole makes a man's thoughts change again.'

Her breath suddenly came to her again, expanded her chest until the air felt trapped there.

Bram's lips parted. 'I see this one and the others just below your ear. I can't see any more, lass, and I'm afraid to ask.'

When Bram's eyes returned to hers, she thought he might be feeling what she felt.

'Afraid of what?' she asked.

'That there might be others.'

'They're not…catching.'

'I think they are,' he answered, a shake to his head. 'I seem to be caught in them. Are there others?'

'Aye,' she whispered, swallowing her breathlessness.

His eyes, intense, heavy lidded, dropped to her lips and she swore she felt a tremor through him. She didn't think it was because he was truly afraid of her spots. She thought, maybe, that he…*liked* them. He didn't actually step any closer, yet she felt him as if he did. As if he was compelled to be closer. She thought, maybe, she understood why.

'You said…in the keep… You said you'd kiss me.'

His fine, fluid hands stuttered, and his eyes rised to hers. 'And you think this is the same as before?'

No, she didn't. He was different now. How… Why? She didn't know.

She shook her head.

'You're a bold one with your words.' He shifted until his leg was between her own. 'And, aye, I want to kiss you. However, when it comes to these matters, a man looks to a woman's eyes to know if he'll be received.'

'My eyes?'

'Aye, your eyes that are more beautiful than a blue Scottish sky and filled with more depth and emotion than any life-saving stream. Your eyes say much, Lioslath.'

His fingers continued, but they now skimmed along her collarbone. His left hand no longer brushed the back of hers, but clasped it. His thumb rubbed and pressed gently into her palm. The sensation rushed up her arm and deep into her body.

Since all she could see was him, she wondered what he would say. 'What's in my eyes?'

His hands stilled, before he dipped his chin and looked at her through his lashes.

'There's desire, lass. It's what's keeping me close to you, it's what is making me incapable of walking away. I saw it yesterday while you showed me your land. You were looking at me as if you'd never seen a man before or known what the purpose of him was. But as you kept looking at me, I couldn't help but be reminded, acutely, painfully, what a man's purpose is when he's being looked at by a woman.'

Her skin flushed at his words. Embarrassment, but something more.

His hands stilled as a predatory sound emitted from him. 'I hold by a hair here, lass. Especially now your eyes have gone all smoky dark.

I'm lost in them and I'm guessing my words affect you the way they affect me.'

She was supposed to speak, but her lips were suddenly dry and she ran her tongue along the seam. Bram's eyes fell to her lips.

'Ah,' he continued. 'But there's a hesitancy behind that desire as well. When it's there, a man cannot simply take. So I stand here and feel your short breaths fanning against me, your skin warming in the sunshine. And with your eyes swirling like they are? You're making me a beggar.'

She felt like a beggar with his voice swirling heat around and inside her.

'I cannot just take, Lioslath, though I stand caressing you with my hands. I'm gentling you. I must, though everything in me is begging for a taste of you.'

His words that gave heat were now like ice. Had he said he wanted to gentle her like a horse? To *break* her?

No! He wouldn't tame her. He couldn't tame her. A hot ball of anger coiled deep in her gut as she jerked her head away from his touch and tried to snatch her hand back.

'Thanks be to God in heaven,' Bram whispered, as he held her hand firm, yanked her to him—

Gillean!

Gillean stood behind Bram. Gasping, Lioslath shoved Bram away and he swiftly turned and released the dagger from his belt. But he paused when he came face-to-face with Gillean, who didn't move either. She, too, was rooted to the spot.

Bram reacted first.

Crouching low, he swiftly flipped the dagger's handle to the boy. By doing so, Bram changed the dagger's threat into a game.

Before Lioslath could get her heart to settle, Gillean's wide eyes fell immediately to the dagger.

'Here now, lad. This is a fine dagger, would you like to see it?'

No hesitation, Gillean's hurried steps put him before Bram. No hesitation from Bram as he explained the blade, the shape, the metal and the edge. He did it so effortlessly, as if he'd intended it all along.

As if they hadn't been about to kiss. That kiss…

Lioslath exhaled slowly. Gillean was enthralled. Was that all it would take for him to forget what he saw? Some distraction? Bram was so easy with him. An ease she didn't have. Not when she continued to feel Bram's arms and her own clutching response.

'You were kissing her.' Gillean's voice rang clear. 'I saw it.'

Lioslath froze.

Bram gave a brief hesitation before he answered, 'Almost kissing.'

'Are you marrying her?'

Lioslath wanted to run and hide. Gillean knew what he saw and Bram's distraction wasn't working. Lioslath wanted to put a stop to it, but a thrown knife wouldn't do it this time. 'Gillean, if you so much as—'

'Nae—' Bram started. The word was for her as much for Gillean. 'When you get big enough to hold this dagger, you'll know that kissing is for finding your wife as well.'

What was Bram talking about! He was making it worse. But he didn't act as though it was worse. Instead, he steadily knelt and offered explanations. Again, she was acutely aware of his ease around her siblings and her own failings.

Then she remembered Bram's diplomacy. Maybe this wasn't so much his ease with Gillean as his ease with people.

'You were in her bedroom. You kissed.' Gillean's fingers trailed along the dagger's hilt. 'Will she be your wife now?'

'Marriage...' Bram said as if he was considering it. Lioslath knew he couldn't possibly be, that he must be stalling for time. 'Just like a weapon, a man has to be careful what wife he holds for the rest of his life. A man rarely takes the first weapon he holds or the first lass he… almost…kisses.'

'Why?'

Hoping Gillean would simply accept what Bram was saying, Lioslath looked around them. They could be discovered soon. If Gillean continued talking about their kiss and another person arrived, there wouldn't be any discussion of a marriage. The clan would probably demand it.

'Well, you see how fine this knife is? How it fits in my hand now and how it doesn't fit in yours quite yet? Right now a dagger with a smaller hilt would fit you, later another knife will be better. That's why you shouldn't take the first lass or the first knife.'

'Are you waiting for Lioslath to…fit you?'

Panic gripped her. But Bram chuckled and looked back at her. There was puzzlement in his eyes as he searched hers, but there was something else there for her to see: heat. Then his eyes dropped to her lips and stayed. When he raised them again, he looked…heatedly amused. Did he take nothing seriously?

'Aye, something like that, lad,' Bram said, holding her gaze.

'She's shorter than you. Does she have to get bigger?'

Bram faced Gillean. 'Nae, women doona need to grow to fit.'

'Then how do you know when to marry them?'

'With a knife, you weigh it in your hands, both hands. A man has to be around a woman before he marries her.'

'A lot?'

'It…depends.'

'On your being in the bedroom and you touching and kissing her?'

Lioslath couldn't keep the strangling sound inside. Was this how Gillean saw them? She felt more than panic now. Terror. He made her sound like some whore for any man to work out his lusts on. Bram must correct him. Her brother couldn't walk away with that in his head.

'Aye, something like that.' Standing, Bram patted Gillean on the shoulder. Not as though he was a child, but as if they were equals.

'Nae!' Lioslath said. 'He cannot—'

'Now, Gillean,' Bram interrupted. 'Unlike us, your sister's a mite soft when it comes to weapons and marriage and the like. It wouldn't do for her delicate temperament to have this talked of. Understand?'

Her brother glanced to her and visibly swallowed. 'She'd get angry?'

Gillean might not understand Bram's talking

of her delicate sensibilities, but Gillean had seen her anger before.

'She might,' Bram said.

'Won't tell anyone!' Gillean promised.

'Good lad.' Bram patted the boy's shoulder again. 'Now it's time to make more hay men.'

Gillean ran a few steps before he stopped and turned. 'I know what I want now! In return for being quiet.'

'A knife of your own?' the laird said. 'If you stay quiet, you'll get one.'

Gillean flashed him a smile and nodded enthusiastically before he ran off.

Only then did Bram turn to her.

'You let him go,' she said. 'He'll tell.'

'And forfeit his prize of a dagger, when his older brother doesn't have one?' He looked at her quizzically. 'You haven't been around children much.'

'What is it to—'

'They haven't been around you either,' he interrupted. 'They didn't go to you for protection in your room and he's strangely wary of you.'

'What does it matter? He'll talk and everything will be worse.'

'Because you'll have to marry me to save your reputation? I doona think you care about that.'

How would this man know?

'It's nothing to wonder about. I opened the gates to save my reputation.'

'Did you? Why do you not know your siblings? Why did you avoid them in the village? Why did you not know that bribes often work with five-year-olds?'

All these questions. 'I know them well enough.'

'Do you? And why aren't you married?

'This is none of your concern.'

'It does concern me when I know your reputation isn't what motivates you here. Not when you dress as you do and walk freely and unaccompanied at all hours. I do remember that tunnel, lass.' He held his hands up as if to show his innocence. 'Be at ease, I have nae intention of marrying you.'

She felt relief. 'Because we doona fit?'

A quick smile. 'I think we would, Lioslath. And I think you know it.'

She took a step away and knew it was a mistake by the gleam in his eye. She didn't care, she needed the distance from him. 'I'll tell you what I do know, Bram of Clan Colquhoun. Never try to kiss me again. Or next time my dagger won't aim at a point behind your head.'

To make it clear what part she would aim at, she dropped her eyes before she turned on her heels and walked away.

Chapter Nine

Lioslath paced in circles. It had been hours since she had talked to Bram, hours since she saw Gillean skip away, but it wasn't enough time to ease her racing heart or her anger at the Colquhoun.

She needed the archery contest to ease her restlessness and soon it would begin. In the meantime, she was forced to acknowledge too many facts.

There was a roar from the crowd circling the hand-to-hand combat. Bram was in the centre, fighting his men and hers. Now he fought Colin from the village. Colin, who was as large as her father.

All day she watched Colquhouns and Fergussons cooperating. Between the preparations and the contests, the tension between their clans eased. Bram's insistence on these games was working.

That wasn't the only acknowledgement she

was forced to accept. Bram's almost-kiss. She couldn't fool herself. She *wanted* and waited for the kiss. It was his voice, the way he used words. They affected her.

Gillean had stopped them. And thus far he hadn't revealed what he'd seen. It appeared Bram's fame with diplomacy worked on five-year-old boys as well.

And that was where the acknowledgements ended.

Bram's diplomacy wouldn't work with her. She couldn't allow it. Cooperation between their clans would prove nothing, would only be another concession to Laird Colquhoun.

Soon the archery would begin and it would be her turn. Soon she would show him Fergussons didn't need Colquhouns. Pride. Aye, and if her stepmother were alive, she'd be punished. Or most likely locked in the storage rooms under the bedroom. But there was more driving her than pride.

Once she proved herself, the Colquhouns would leave. They needed to leave. For how long could a five-year-old keep a secret? Her clan might never have cared for her reputation before, but things were different now. Donaldo said she wouldn't stop any demands for honour. If the truth was revealed, they could be forced to marry.

She couldn't want to marry this man, and yet…that kiss. That almost-kiss. What would it have felt like? His lips perpetually curved up at one corner, ever ready for his frequent smiles. Over the crowds, she could hear him laughing. Yet she wanted to know his kiss.

The archery contest couldn't come soon enough.

Another roar. Colin was standing now, shaking his head. How did she get so near the ring? She could see everything.

Bram looked as he did the many times he trained his men. Determined and encouraging. Now he looked the same. As if he was training Colin. As if he was the laird here.

She resented it, and yet…Colin was already gleaning warfare skills he hadn't possessed before. Skills that would have been useful against the English.

Lioslath could not look away. Bram's formal clothing was gone and he was down to his braies. Nothing hid the power and training of his body. She'd seen him like this from the platform, but now she knew how it felt to be held by him, to be pulled closer. Now she noticed every nuance.

It wasn't Bram's skill compelling her to watch him, it was something darker, more elemental, like *need*. Something she didn't understand and certainly didn't want. Still…compelling.

Stance wide, Bram stood in a half crouch with his arms out to his sides. Sweat and dirt ran in rivulets along the cords of muscles that formed intricate patterns along his back and flowed down into the knot of fabric rolled around his waist. He'd rolled and cuffed his braies, which meant she could see the power of his thigh muscles as they bulged and pulsed with each step of his feet.

He was restrained and yet feral. There was lethal tension held in the grace of his body, a primal undertone to the way he moved. Like this, he reminded her too much of the wildness of her forest, of the danger and purpose it revealed to her every time she stepped into it.

He was a warrior used to fights, to training, to…pain. He was a laird used to winning.

There was no doubting who carried the superior skills, but Bram only encouraged and instructed. His familiar amusement and humour were present. She didn't know what to make of him and apparently Colin didn't know either.

They collided. Colin depended on his strength, Bram on his skill. With a swipe of Bram's foot, Colin fell. Bram, chuckling, helped Colin stand, then he showed him the move he made. Colin's brow furrowed, but there was no humour or light in his eyes. Was he remembering how her father trained him?

Colin's turn. When Bram suddenly hit the ground, there was a collective gasp from the crowd. Lioslath's breath left her. She remembered her father's angry reactions and punishments if ever he was felled. What would Bram do? He was an outsider. He would need to save face. He couldn't appear weak to anyone now.

But Colin learned more than footwork from Bram. Colin stretched out his hand and Bram took it. Patting Colin on the back, Bram invited another to enter the ring.

Lioslath spun away, but not soon enough. In that brief moment, Bram's eyes looked to the crowd and their eyes collided. She felt the gaze as much as a physical blow.

That almost-kiss. Why had he done it? She walked away from the ring. His ease with her siblings and clansmen burning through her gut, she sped through the crowd.

She wanted to kiss him, had stood still for his kiss, though she was supposed to hate him. He said the kiss wasn't about clans or differences, only wants and desires. Only about them.

But she shouldn't trust his words. Yet, while waiting for his lips to touch hers, she had felt the truth of them.

The archery competition couldn't come soon enough.

* * *

She was up to something.

Bram shook his arms. He was exhausted, but heartened. The matches in the ring had gone well. In between, he kept an eye on Lioslath. She held herself apart but gave furtive and frequent glances to his archers. He forced his attention to Finlay as he approached.

'Any more incidents?' Since this morning's feast, there had been minor arguments. Unavoidable, vexing and expected.

'A few, but the woman, Donaldo, interfered.'

Donaldo had been a thorn in his side since they arrived. A few terse words at the beginning, but otherwise she purposefully ignored him and his men. Today, she interacted with his clan and viewed him with a calculating eye. He suspected that she, like her mistress, had ulterior motives.

There would be some time tomorrow to discover what. For now, although he thought the day went well, he didn't want to assume. 'What do you think?'

'Laird?'

'What do you think of all this, of what has been done so far?'

Finlay crossed his arms. 'You haven't asked before.'

'I ask now.'

'As a clansman or a friend?'

'Do you think *I* have ulterior motives?'

Finlay's mouth quirked. 'Always.'

'As a friend, then.'

'I think you're mad. We've been here too long.'

'Aye,' he said. *He* had not stayed long enough, but Finlay was right, his men had been here too long. He walked a fine balance since the beginning of this tumultuous year. A balance that kept secrets amongst brothers only. For their own safety his clansmen could know nothing of his plan, or of the existence of the jewel.

'However...' Finlay said. There was a note of speculation in his friend's voice that sharpened his attention.

'However?'

Finlay shrugged. 'The delay may have helped us.'

Bram gave a huff of laughter. 'You always were an observant man.'

'Aye,' Finlay said, but he made no answering laugh. 'I also know how it kept you away from Colquhoun lands while King Edward made his demands on Scottish nobles this summer.'

He was too observant. 'You think I purposely avoided a missive from our king?'

'Nae avoided, but certainly delayed it.'

He needed to know what Finlay knew. He trusted him, but he didn't want his friend in danger. And when it came to the Jewel of Kings, knowledge meant danger. Bram's brothers had put themselves at risk before he could protect them. But he wouldn't knowingly extend the danger to Finlay. 'Do you wonder why?'

'You jest.' Finlay shook his head. 'It's for my laird to keep secrets if he chooses.'

'So well you know me. I would not tell this secret even if you threatened.' Then another warning, so his friend would understand. 'I could not tell even if *you* were threatened.'

Finlay nodded slowly as if his questions were answered. 'We ken it was to protect us.'

Of course his clan talked. How much they must have wondered on their laird's loyalty. How much they trusted him. He hoped it was not in vain. As long as he waited for Balliol's messages, Bram hadn't dared receive King Edward's summons.

'It did surprise me nae missives came to Colquhoun clan.'

'The English king's messengers may have had difficulties.'

'And then you came here,' Finlay stated.

'Aye, I needed a place to be where nae one would expect, but that wouldn't be suspicious. After all, I can't have all the messengers going missing.'

He'd bribed the first messenger he intercepted along the road and told him to return in the spring. When he discovered another was on his way, Bram knew the first messenger had betrayed their agreement. So the second messenger met with an accidental death.

'You're planning something here?' Finlay asked.

'I intend to mend relations and return home. I won't avoid the English King for ever.' Only until he knew what to do for his clan's survival, and his brothers' safety.

'You worry about Caird and Malcolm.'

Finlay needed to learn to close his eyes. 'What do you know?'

'Malcolm left here as if the devil was after him. He took two horses and a month of supplies. I think it's best if I doona know what he was doing, aye?'

Bram gave a curt nod. If Finlay didn't know more, he might be able to keep his head in the next year.

Finlay shrugged. 'Caird seemed well, though.'

Caird was a changed man. 'He's happy.'

'Interesting that he found happiness with a Buchanan.'

'Finlay, you need to look away and not notice so much,' Bram warned.

'Knowing she was Buchanan had less to do

with my observing and all to do with Malcolm
vehemently declaring it.'

A childhood tragedy had deeply carved Malcolm's hatred towards the Buchanan clan in
stone. Over the years, the hatred spread around
the entire Colquhoun clan, but Caird wanted
Mairead. 'And your thoughts on their marriage?'

'I, too, am happy for him.'

Caird was finally content. In the midst of all
the war and bloodshed, in the midst of his worry
over Malcolm and the burden he now carried,
his brother was happy. As was his sister Gaira.
Who was he, as laird and brother, to question
how and with whom they found their happiness?

It was a mystery how they found it, as he had
never been able to find a happy marriage, or
form an advantageous alliance.

Unerringly, as he had throughout the day,
he sought out and found Lioslath. She had not
changed her position, which gave her the perfect
advantage to avidly observe his archers.

She didn't look bewildered or trapped in the
crowds surrounding her now. She looked pleas-
ingly content.

'Did you check the archery targets and equipment?' he asked.

Finlay nodded. 'Aye, Callum and I, with two
Fergusson men, inspected the bows and arrows.
Everything is secure and of equal value.'

'See if you can check them again,' he ordered.

He didn't wait for Finlay to leave before he watched Lioslath again. Aye, she was planning something. The archery competition was the last contest. Did she intend to jeopardise or stop it in some way?

Much to his own body's regret, there had been progress today. The Fergusson men hit with their strength and his body had felt every blow. He was used to fighting his own men, who paced themselves and used skill.

But it was rewarding to teach the men and see the beginnings of trust. If his plan was to work, he needed the clansmen's cooperation. He wouldn't let anything ruin his plan. Each bruise, each crushing blow was incurred towards that goal.

It was rewarding to feel Lioslath's eyes on him as well. More than once, he'd been injured in the ring because he hadn't kept his eyes on his opponent. It was the way her blue eyes darkened as she viewed him fighting; the way they darkened when he was about to kiss her.

That almost-kiss. Inconvenient desire. Unexpected woman. And he no longer wondered on kissing her. He craved it. Her hesitancy and innocent questions left him in no doubt that she was a maiden and one he couldn't seduce. One he shouldn't be tempted by. But his body cared naught for plans or shouldn'ts.

In that moment he knew he would kiss her. In that crucial moment, there was only her, the touch and smell of her skin, the sounds she made. His only thought then was: here. Now. Then Gillean had come.

Bram shook his head. He'd knelt before the boy because his tunic hadn't been enough to hide his response to Lioslath. Even now, he forced himself to control his response to just that memory.

Lioslath continued to observe his archers balance their bows in their hands and rotate their wrists for flexibility. Like them, she, too, flexed her wrists and shifted her stance. Was she mimicking his archers? No. She was copying them.

She was planning something, but in his current state, he didn't dare approach her.

This was it. Lioslath calmed her breathing. The Colquhoun shots were completed. Five targets. Her clan had gone first. The arrows had been marked and removed. Then Clan Colquhoun went and their arrows were still embedded in the tightly woven hay against the trees. She didn't want them removed.

Before any could move forward, before any could get in her way, Lioslath strode to the first target's position. She ignored the gasp of sounds and Bram's voice above the others.

Any moment they would know their voices wouldn't stop her. Already with her arrow notched, no one dared to physically remove her. Moving quickly and concentrating, it was only Lioslath, her weapons and a point to prove. Exhaling, she released the arrow. It hit dead centre.

The sounds of protests quieted as she walked to the next. Released. A step, another release, and another. One more target left.

The eyes of the crowd distracted her more than their protests. One pair of eyes in particular. Bram's. She turned her gaze to him.

He stood taller than his archers gathered around him. A safe enough distance from her shots, but near enough for her to see all of their expressions. Incredulousness, envy, a sort of helpless fury as a woman beat them at their own game.

Like his archers, Bram's gaze held surprise, but there was nothing helpless about it. There was only a warning. His lips pressed tight and a slight flush crossed his cheeks as if he exerted himself just by standing still.

Oh, he didn't like that he could do nothing to stop her. Not without announcing to the clans what an overbearing, arrogant laird he was. Not without ruining his plans to create friendship amongst their clans. As if she wanted friend-ship…or that kiss.

She thought this through. It was the only thing that distracted her thoughts from Bram's lips and his almost-kiss. She'd told him she didn't want the competition, didn't want an alliance with him, but he'd forced it anyway. She couldn't want his kisses. Not after everything he did.

Her arrow was poised to make the final shot; she saw Bram's warning shake of his head.

She merely raised her chin. It was her turn to find amusement in this. By now there were no sounds from the crowd.

Turning to the target, she blocked Bram out.

The final target. Trickier than the others. The archer had hit centre, but a bit to the right. She'd have to skim it without breaking her own, or else not prove her worth.

Breathe in, exhale, release.

She didn't have to walk up to the target to know she'd hit it. She heard it from her own clansmen's cheers. She saw it from the way Bram's expression darkened, his eyes now roll-ing storm grey. His body, if possible, seemed larger, as if there was a force outside his very skin.

She knew what it was: rage. It was all directed towards her and she had no arrows left.

Chapter Ten

'Are you angry with her?' Gillean's voice rang out across the stunned silence after Lioslath's last arrow pierced the target. 'You look as though you're angry with her.'

Anger didn't begin to describe the feelings roiling through Bram. Wrath came close. But even that wasn't enough.

All day, he built camaraderie as the clans built props for the competition. His training in the ring taught her men fighting skills, but also ways to ease differences. His plan had been working. He hadn't failed his family or his clan. He was succeeding here.

Her single-handedly besting each archer's shots—with a fluid ease no one could mistake for luck—was the equivalent of the first cry for blood in battle.

Everything inside him wanted to violently answer.

'I think he's angry with her,' Gillean shouted to Fyfa, who ran over to quiet her brother.

Moments away from making peace here and ending the animosity. Moments away from gaining acceptance so he and a few men could stay the winter. So he could commit, but not get caught committing, treason. And she destroyed it all.

Fighting for control, for patience, he looked wildly around him. The only expression that stood out of the now deathly quiet crowd: Lioslath's victorious smirk.

He watched as Donaldo swept to her side, as Aindreas gave him a look of triumph. He watched as his own men gaped at her skill, but also at the sheer, scheming underhandedness of it.

There was no mistaking she'd done it deliberately and calculatingly. She'd never intended on mending relations. Had, in fact, set them up to fail.

Never mind he thought she felt desire, as he had when they'd almost kissed. It was the sheer shame of the matter overriding everything. His years of diplomacy had not prepared him for this. Because he forgot his one rule: listen for weaknesses and never underestimate his opponent.

With Lioslath of Clan Fergusson, he most definitely underestimated her.

Lioslath watched as Bram's incredulousness turned to fury. In that moment she knew why he was both feared and respected.

She wouldn't break her gaze, because she neither feared nor respected him. He had almost kissed her; she had almost accepted. But she couldn't accept him ever. She just wanted him gone.

'He's definitely angry with her.' Gillean's voice was the only one heard above the crowd.

Lioslath didn't even hear Donaldo's low, urgent mutterings. She kept her eyes on Bram, who was advancing towards her.

'Does she fit you now?' Gillean cried out. Lioslath heard Fyfa shushing him.

'I warned you.' Donaldo's whispers grew louder. 'I warned you not to press matters too far.'

'You knew I would do this.'

'But to win every shot and to beat his best archer? What were you thinking? He gave you a feast, which you refused. You argued in the village and then he did this competition. He could take the supplies he brought or destroy them in front of us. He could take more than the English did. You've left him nae choice.'

'I was saving our pride.'

'A poor warmth pride will be this winter. Can't you see he's mending relations?'

'For what purpose!'

'Laird Colquhoun gazes intently at you, Lioslath, and he gives us all this. Not only the supplies, but also skills. You saw what he did for Colin.'

'I think she fits him now!' Gillean dodged his siblings.

'What is that boy talking about?' Now Donaldo's eyes tracked the running children.

Lioslath froze. Gillean was too excited and knew too much.

She needed to get to him, but Bram was approaching. His men, as if by silent command, were separating from hers. There would soon be a fight.

How to stop this?

If she rushed to quiet Gillean, she'd look guilty. If she didn't quiet her brother—

Lioslath broke Bram's gaze and hurried over to her brother. 'You have to be quiet.'

'But he's angry with you!' Gillean darted around Donaldo. 'You have to fit now!'

Fyfa was running after him. Something she did only in dire circumstances. 'She said quiet!'

Gillean giggled. Where was Eoin? He could usually catch his brother.

But Donaldo suddenly grabbed the boy's arms, hauled him up and narrowed her eyes.

Lioslath knew that look. 'What do you mean, child?'

'She's always angry with us, now he's angry with her. We're Bram's family. That's why he was kissing her and in her bedroom! We're to be family!'

Gillean's excited voice carried over the stunned crowd. He declared it all. Everything. In front of everyone. Including Bram.

Donaldo set Gillean down slowly. 'Is this true?'

Lioslath could feel the stares of everyone around them, but she didn't dare look. She kept her eyes on Donaldo. She didn't need to look at Bram. She could sense his anger and something else making her fear him for the first time. There was a predatory stillness. That calculating moment when an animal tensed before its lethal bite.

And she felt as if she was the prey.

Donaldo had a calculating look in her eyes, too. With suddenly gripping certainty, she knew Donaldo would think it an advantage to marry the Colquhoun and pretend she had a reputation. Lioslath needed to stop it.

'It wasn't as it seemed,' she said.

She heard a protesting shout from Aindreas before a roaring in her blood drowned out all sound.

What had she done?

In the gaping silence she made with her final shot, she ensured everyone heard Gillean's excited announcement and her admitting Bram kissed her.

'Is it true?' Donaldo repeated to Bram.

A heavy silence fell. One in which Bram could have offered a myriad of diplomatic explanations. Instead, he gave a wide smile as if he was overjoyed. Before she could step away, he gripped her hand and pulled her close.

Acutely aware that Bram's smile didn't reach his eyes and that his grip was too tight to disengage her hand, Lioslath stood beside him.

Without waiting for her compliance, Bram faced the clans. 'Lioslath has won the archery competition.'

His voice boomed over the stunned crowd as if he was laird of the land making a formal announcement. Some clapping ensued, which was polite, scattered and quickly silenced. The spectators knew there was more to come. Laird Colquhoun was holding the hand of Lioslath of Clan Fergusson.

Bram looked down at her and dared her to look anywhere else. A dark emotion barely contained seethed behind cold grey eyes, but he addressed the crowd before she could understand it.

'It seems,' he announced, 'the lady is in

need of a prize for her excellent and remarkable marksmanship.'

A roaring began in her ears then, a prickling awareness caused by Bram using a different voice from the one she heard before. The tone now was cajoling, beguiling, humour thickly lacing around each syllable despite the coldness in his eyes.

'This is more than a competition,' Bram stated, his voice grand again. 'This is a celebration!'

A deliberate pause in which the roaring in Lioslath's ears popped and an avalanche of sound entered her tangled thoughts.

No, not an avalanche. Only one sound was hurtling towards her. Bram's voice, as he completed his announcement to the clans.

'By vanquishing our best archers, Lioslath has indeed gained a prize. And so have I. For with the strike of a well-aimed arrow, she has wholeheartedly agreed to my proposal,' he said. 'We are betrothed!'

Bram's laugh joined the merriment. But she stood the closest to him. He was laughing, but there was no humour in the sound. Instead, his laughter barrelled shards of malice towards her.

'You're my prize?' she whispered just as the frozen tumultuous truth of his announcement hit her. Her words must have kept above Bram's icy laughter already burying her because he replied.

'Aye.' His answer resounded over the festivities, over her, with the finality of a cold tomb.

Chapter Eleven

Rage seethed and scraped at Bram until he felt raw from it. It was this extreme emotion that made him rough with his orders to his clan after the congratulations were over.

Luckily Finlay and Callum took their cue from his temper and did not ask questions.

Yet even after his men followed the nightly routine, Bram felt exposed. As if everything he was striving to make of himself and his clan was a sham.

Lioslath had done it. With her dagger and arrows Lioslath had wounded him. Opening up old injuries until she exposed what he was underneath. Her stunt revealed that same young cockerel from his past who tried to prove himself and failed in the most altering way.

Since that fateful winter, he had faced far more terrible foes, had overcome unlikely odds and had enjoyed and revelled in his successes.

Never again had his family suffered and gone hungry. That bitter winter was why he played, why he laughed, why he began each day as if he would conquer it. Because since then, he always conquered.

There was nothing now to laugh about. His family and clan were in danger and he was failing in the simplest of plans to keep them safe. A plan where all he had to do was *wait*.

He wished he could simply leave and wait for news of the jewel and from John Balliol somewhere else. He wished he'd never listened to his sister Gaira about the orphans here, or felt that strange something tugging inside him at her story.

That same something compelling him to make amends to this clan as he had to his family all those years ago. The worst of jokes on him. This clan didn't want him making amends.

He traded with more powerful clans, foreign emissaries and royalty. Even in the toughest negotiations, he managed to wrest a benefit for his clan so that his pride remained intact.

Here, with Lioslath, he couldn't give away his wealth. She wouldn't even allow an apology. He'd had enough.

So with a few crucial words, he wrested control from her. It wasn't only anger motivating him, but with Gillean's words of marriage, he realised there could be another way of staying the winter. He could bargain with Lioslath, as he had with her father. Offer a marriage. A *temporary* marriage.

It would secure an alliance and give him her clan's acceptance and security. In turn she'd have his wealth and power. She wouldn't have to barter as her father had. He would simply give it to her. He'd give her lasting benefits even after he left. Whatever it took. He'd made a promise to his clan, and to his brothers. At any cost, he must keep to the plan. He could do it, too. As long as he and Lioslath didn't consummate their short marriage, then—

'You didn't ask her.'

Bram turned to Donaldo, who was standing calmly by. Her great girth like a boulder that could be moved only if she wished it. He had no intention of moving her or this clan. He would keep to his plans and if he had to go around their stubbornness he would.

'It is done.' But he had too many questions and, if the new strategy was to work, he needed information. His duty to his clan demanded it.

Lioslath was unexpected and he had underestimated her. They hadn't talked since he announced their betrothal. He couldn't go to her again without knowing more about her. Because when he saw her again, he expected resistance, and this time he would not fail.

'How did she hit those targets?' Her skill couldn't have been executed without intense practice.

'I've known that child since she was born, witnessed every joy and heartbreak. Do you think I'd tell you?'

No, she wouldn't, and he was a fool to ask. Again, he wasn't listening as he was trained. When it came to Lioslath, his thoughts were too much affected by his emotions.

'But I will barter with you.'

Surprise, and another fierce emotion, gripped him. He was desperate, but if Donaldo wanted to barter, he would not refuse. 'Why?'

'You want answers and I have a request before your wedding.'

If there was a wedding. 'What is the request?'

Donaldo smiled. 'I won't tell you that until you agree to abide by it.'

He couldn't go to Lioslath without knowing more about her, but he'd be a fool to agree to this woman's terms. He thought himself an unparalleled negotiator, but the Fergusson clan was constantly outmanoeuvring him.

'I agree,' he said foolishly. But if he was a fool, he was one with no choice. He might have announced to the clan that he and Lioslath were betrothed. By her silence she might have appeared to accept, but he needed to truly secure the acceptance. He needed all the knowledge he could obtain.

'She's skilled,' Donaldo said, 'because she's hunted for this clan since she was practically a bairn.'

A woman, hunting for a clan. It was unheard of. He'd never allowed his sisters any such recreation, and yet he couldn't deny it. Lioslath had been wielding weapons at him since the first time he saw her.

'Busby allowed this?' he asked.

'Allowed? Oh, aye. He allowed it,' Donaldo continued, 'Not in the way you probably are thinking, Colquhoun. It wasn't a pastime for her that he indulged. He forced her to do it.'

And there. That revelation changed everything.

Busby. He had given his sister into Busby's keeping, when it was clear he hadn't known the man at all. The wolves were rife in the forest here and Busby, a father, had forced his daughter into that danger. Did he want her dead?

'Why did he do this?' he asked.

Donaldo paused. 'Your curiosity goes beyond our agreement.'

Curiosity never motivated him. Many people made this mistake, since obtaining facts was a pursuit he shared with his family, but they did it for different reasons. His brother Caird pursued answers because he liked the world to be ordered. Malcolm pursued facts purely for the sheer intellectual love of solving puzzles.

But Bram pursued answers to use them in his diplomacy, to gain power, and he would do so now. 'I need to know why Lioslath gained her skills,' he said.

'You only asked *how* she gained her skills and that I answered. It would hurt her for you to know why,' she said.

'Is this your continued revenge against me? Not to give an honest answer? You doona surprise me. I expected this deceit.'

'Did you? If you feel resentment, remember it is not this clan that is to blame.'

No, he blamed himself. But it didn't matter if he would get no direct answers from her. He knew where his responsibilities and duties lay, and though it was meagre, she gave him some facts, which was more than he had before.

'What is your request?' he said bluntly, his sense of diplomacy gone.

'Before you marry her, ask Lioslath why she cut her hair.'

In the dark, Lioslath continued to pace the empty stables. It was the only place she could go and be alone. It was late and the Fergusson revelry was mostly quiet. Now she paced, wishing for Dog, wishing for distractions. And waiting. Waiting and knowing Bram would find her and she had nowhere to run.

She was trussed like some game, waiting for her wedding, waiting to be hoisted over the firepit, as though she was some sacrifice, and her clan celebrated. Celebrated a betrothal she hadn't agreed to. Did she even want it?

Bram brought nothing but misery to this clan, and yet…they celebrated a union and she still wanted his kiss. What did she know of people? Nothing. She didn't even know herself.

Weak. Vulnerable. She hadn't felt this way since her father journeyed to the Colquhoun clan, when she openly returned his smile as he looked down at her from his horse. Eyes sheening, she brimmed with some unknown happiness as Eoin exclaimed how funny she looked, as Fyfa returned her smile, her sister's eyes dancing at the thoughts of a new mother. One who would care about clothes and ribbons.

Now she turned before she hit the back wall. She didn't need the light to know where she was. Alone. Exposed again.

Except this time she wasn't brimming with happiness, just the vulnerability, just the weakness.

Two emotions she ruthlessly hid after her

mother's death. After her stepmother, Irman, requested she sleep with the horses. Irman, who told everyone Lioslath preferred the horses over her own family.

Her father had believed Irman and ignored her in favour of his new family. Worse, he abandoned her, yet kept her close. A constant reminder she wasn't wanted.

When she became part of Niall's family, she found her home amongst the trees and with her love of hunting. If she hadn't found joy, she had at least been content. Until her father's death.

Her role with her clan hadn't changed immediately. At first, only Aindreas and Donaldo made demands of her. Insisting she didn't have a role with the clan, she fought them. After all, what had her clan done for her when her father treated her so cruelly?

She exhaled and spun again. The horses were getting restless with her pacing. So she stopped, though she didn't want to.

She didn't want to claim responsibility for her clan either. And it hadn't been resentment towards her clan that she had felt those many months ago. It had been reluctance to claim a role she didn't have the skills or the knowledge to do.

Yet what else could her clan have done except ask her to take up the role? With cruelty and bitterness her father pursued his follies and the Colquhoun lass. When her father died, her clan was as lost as she.

Since then, she tried to be what her clan needed. She thought by winning the archery contest she could be what they needed. Someone fierce to drive away the Colquhouns. What she'd done was bind herself and her clan all the more tightly to them.

Marriage to Bram. Did she want it?

It was all her fault. Donaldo warned her that she might go too far. But she wanted to go far, to get them off her land and to lick her wounds in private. The English had left scarcely weeks before Bram crested the hill. Her clan was still reeling from the catastrophe of loss when Bram arrived to heap on more.

By then she felt broken with the dictates and the demands and the disappointments. By the lack of control.

And there…there was her pain. Because it was not only the truth that Bram took every bit of her freedom. It was that her clan, by their silence, agreed.

Bram orchestrated her father's death, arrived too late to protect them from the English, and yet her clan celebrated a permanent union between them.

Could she marry Bram, Laird Colquhoun? It

was only her decision now. Her clan had made theirs.

'I thought you escaped through the tunnel.'

Bram's voice in the dark. Affecting her before she could brace herself against it. So she stumbled as she whirled around to face him.

The tunnel. As she had in her childhood, she used the tunnel to escape. To walk, to keep walking, but it became late, and without Dog's protection, she couldn't stay in the forest. She couldn't face her clan either, and so she came to the stables instead.

'I thought you'd be here sooner,' she said, grateful her voice didn't betray her turmoil.

A small chuckle that held the edge of his anger as he entered the stables. 'You were expecting me.'

Words. The same words he used that first fateful night in her bedroom. He sounded so at ease again and her frustration increased as he easily navigated the uneven surfaces and the low rock and wooden corrals.

'Aye, I was expecting you, Bram of Clan Colquhoun,' she repeated. 'I was expecting an apology and for you to announce the betrothal was only a game you played. A…trick.'

He smiled then, though she couldn't possibly see it. Even guessing it was there made the tension inside her coil tighter. Which was better than feeling vulnerable and exposed to the distinct tenor of his voice.

'Interesting, since I came here expecting an apology from you, and you have to know, in matters that I intend to win, I do play games.'

His voice held a bite, but still it was playful. She was in turmoil, feeling vulnerable and exposed, and he was *enjoying* this.

'I never understand you,' she said. 'You were furious mere hours ago. You gazed at me as if it was I who trapped you into marriage. I just—'

'Thought to show off? Those were impressive skills you hid, lass. Maybe you didn't hide them. I seem to remember weapons in your hands before. Care to tell me of them?'

'Nae.'

He shrugged. 'Pity, since I hoped to keep this discussion friendly.'

'Friendly!'

'Aye, after all, we do need to come to an agreement.'

'I'll agree to nothing.'

'Not even for your clan?'

Her clan. So many sacrifices she made for them since her father's death and they expected her to do it again. And why wouldn't they? It benefited them for her to make such a profitable marriage. Aye, she was trussed like game for the firepit, but Bram was here to talk, which meant he wasn't as sure as he sounded.

'What game do you play?'

'You shot the arrow, though you knew we needed the competition to ease relations between the clans. You aggravated them again.'

'I agreed to it and the competitions happened. There was nae agreement on a winner.'

'As I realised too late. I think it is a matter of perspective who plays games, Lioslath.'

She could feel tension wavering just under his surface, though he remained calm. His calmness infuriated her. 'You announced our betrothal in front of everyone. Whatever power I had was taken away from me.'

'Is that it? Is it control you want?' He looked over her shoulder and out the window before his eyes returned to her. 'You have to know, I cannot force you to this.'

Now she truly didn't understand. The Colquhoun controlled all situations. He didn't relinquish control. 'Are you *negotiating* with me?

'Why can't we make such an alliance as your father had with my sister?'

She heard him stepping closer. 'After everything, you think I'd…barter with you?'

'I think it would be beneficial for us to marry, lass. After all, your father thought so.'

Was that all this was about? 'If it was beneficial, why didn't you make it when you arrived or write about it in the missive? Why wait for that moment?'

A stillness to him. A pause. Her question surprised him. It surprised her as well. She could just refuse him. By asking questions, she almost sounded interested. Her clan had made their decision; she still had to make hers.

'Does the timing matter?' he asked.

It did, and yet what could be done about it now? There was nothing practical or useful about wondering why. What mattered was now, but she had to clarify.

'You want to marry me the way my father married Gaira?'

'Exactly.' His words sounded pleased.

'For…sheep?'

'You have to know it's for more than that. If nothing else, then for the needs of your clan and your siblings. You do know about them, aye?'

Even in jest, she could not talk about her brothers and sister. Not when the truth was that she knew them very little.

'Why are you alone?' he continued. 'Why weren't you surrounded by your siblings and clansmen when I made the announcement?'

The clans cheering, she had tugged her hand out of Bram's and swiftly walked away. No one had followed her and she hadn't expected them to.

'They were there,' she said. 'And so was I.'

He shook his head as if to deny her words. 'They were there, but not with you. Why do you know so little of your clan and siblings?'

His persuasive voice no longer teased, but softened, as if he did wonder about her feelings. As if he pitied her. She would have none of that.

'You constantly talk,' she said. 'More than any man I know and yet you say nothing.'

He thinned his lips, but his expression was rueful. As if he tried to hide his anger and humour. When she was angry, she was angry and she stayed that way. His mercurial behaviour, his constant humour, bewildered her.

'It's my years of trading,' he said. 'It's a game of saying things and never revealing anything. Most doona notice.'

Games again. She hated them. They were useless.

And now they were in the dark. Alone. Never again did she want to be in this position. He was only reminding her why she hated to be indoors. This time, she didn't have Dog or a dagger.

She didn't know or understand this man at all. A marriage was significant, important. Between them it was grave. But while he made the announcement, he had laughed.

'I doona play games and I won't marry you.'

'So easy to refuse me?' A disappointed sound

emitted from Bram. 'It's an advantageous alliance between us. Your father thought so and I give you my word I will give you more wealth and security than I offered him.'

He sounded persuasive. 'You mean this. You *are* negotiating with me! I doona understand. You made the announcement. I can hear some clansmen continuing to celebrate.'

'Ah, so you stand in the dark believing it is done? What if I told you I announced our marriage, but I wanted to bargain with you? A bargain where you hold the upper hand in the negotiations.'

He was giving her the power to refuse or accept him. After everything this year, she wanted that control. Was it enough?

'You have the decision in this, lass,' Bram continued. 'I'm requesting the agreement I had with your father be between us. Except this time, there will be more than sheep. You'll have the entire Clan Colquhoun behind you.'

Could she do this? Could she do what her father had intended for his clan? He had had such pride in securing a Colquhoun bride, and supporting the clan again. Now her clan expected her to secure a Colquhoun husband.

'Lioslath?'

She didn't want to make this decision only for her clan's needs. If Bram meant she had the upper hand, then she could barter for more. Her clan benefiting wasn't enough, but what of her siblings? 'I saw you today, with my brothers.'

'Aye, a fine mess Eoin made when he fell atop the prepared vegetables.'

'I think Gillean intentionally tripped one of his poles.'

'Of course he did, and a right telling-off Fyfa gave in return.'

'You provided that food, but weren't angry. You…helped them.'

'Ah, so you do think of them.'

Always. Constantly.

'Your eyes soften when you think of them. Would you agree to my proposal for them? I would provide for and support them as well.'

Her siblings were her family now. If only she knew how to be with them. Bram made it look so effortless today, laughing along with Gillean, at Eoin, covered and flopping about in smashed turnips and cabbages.

He had disengaged Eoin from the stilts, given him a kind lecture and sent him on his way. In one moment, Bram understood both her brothers' antics and Fyfa's desire for order.

But could she marry him for her siblings? She felt as though she was making that sacrifice again, but this time she was contemplating the fire.

No, this couldn't be about her clan or her siblings. There had to be more than that. She…deserved more than that. Her whole life had been to please others.

'You've gone quiet again, lass. Maybe I need to add more words.'

He did. She wasn't done contemplating his proposal and felt just as restless and uneasy as the horses.

'You'll have whatever wealth, whatever protection my clan, my sword and…my body can give you.'

Bram's voice, his hands. The way he used both. She was trussed over that firepit and yet it suddenly felt as if another fire licked at her. It was Bram and the way he made her feel. Never before had she felt this way. But…was that true for him as well?

'Is that why you almost kissed me? Was marriage your intention all along?'

Another chuckle. 'You should not negotiate, Lioslath. Ever. You reveal too much to me.'

'It's dark. There's nothing for you to see.'

'I can feel you stepping away from me. It only makes me want to step closer. Especially when you make that little sound and talk about kisses.' He paused. 'But nae. That is not why I almost kissed you.'

'You laughed then.'

'But only at myself.'

'How am I to believe you?'

'Is that what you worry about with this marriage agreement? The potential that we fit?' He looked down at the floor and scuffed the fresh hay there. 'Would it help to know I think about that kiss as well? I've thought, too, of the...difficulties that brings if we are to have a marriage agreement like your father's. But I'm willing to keep to their terms, if you are.'

Lioslath waited for him to finish his thoughts, but he didn't. And yet there was a part of her that believed what she did understand.

Despite their talking of it, he wasn't expected. Could she be unexpected for him, too? Like his voice, and how it sounded to her when he said he wanted to kiss her. There was something in the tone that told her he still thought of kissing her. She thought of it, too.

Despite the thought that she hated him. The fact she couldn't depend on him. She knew she waited for and wanted Bram's kiss.

Oh, she knew he set it all up and her clan paid the price. She knew, too, that if she allowed him control, she would pay some price. Still, his marriage offer was enticing.

He...enticed. Could she take what he offered and not pay? Could she sacrifice something for her clan and yet gain something for herself?

She didn't know, and he stayed quiet, even as he stepped closer to her. Closer yet. Did he want to kiss her now? How was she to guess when he used only trading words? 'Terms? Difficulties? You talk too strangely.'

He did. Bram knew he did. Blind anger made him announce their betrothal. Reasoning showed him he could use it for his advantage.

Yet there was one thought permeating all others. He declared their betrothal, but he was negotiating for a marriage, which would be a tighter connection with her.

No. Not a tighter connection to her, but to the plan.

A marriage would secure his stay here for the winter; a private agreement with Lioslath would ensure it remained temporary and that he could leave in the spring.

Lioslath knew he asked for the agreement as her father had. A temporary marriage, to give the appearance of a strong alliance. As long as they did not consummate their marriage, he would be free to leave.

And there was another reason why it had to be merely for show. Because of Gaira, and Robert, her husband, who ensured Gaira's safe travel back to Colquhoun land. Robert was a good, honourable man, but he was also the same English knight who killed Lioslath's father. Lioslath didn't know and he couldn't tell her.

Bram needed no long-term connection with the Fergusson clan. He ran his hands over his face and through his hair. His coming here, his negotiating, his feelings for Lioslath. It was madness. All of this was madness.

But he needed the agreement and he couldn't find reason or sense in all this. Had it to do with her? He wasn't one for keeping emotions. He learned long ago not to be ruled by them. Now, with her, he possessed too many of them and they battered inside him.

Anger for being thwarted. Worry for his family. Desire.

Because even now it was there and it had nothing to do with a plan or a purpose. It had to do with that almost-kiss.

He couldn't see her now, but it didn't matter. It was enough to hear the way her breath hitched. Even at this distance, he caught the faint scent of her. She smelled like the trees surrounding her home. When she was in her bedroom, he caught that pine and fresh crispness, and it was just as compelling as her beauty.

She smelled as he needed her to smell. A need he didn't know he possessed until her.

So when he took steps towards her, he depended on that elusive scent and the slight breathless gasps indicating her frustration and anger with him.

But he wanted more. He wanted to see her. The way her pale skin flushed with that almost-kiss, the way her lips parted to take in a breath. The way they did now as she made these... sounds of confusion.

Because he kept walking closer. He knew he did and he knew she had nowhere to go, so that eventually—

This was wrong. His desire for her over everything would make it difficult staying here. Difficult enough that he shouldn't flirt, shouldn't tease, shouldn't need to be closer to her.

This wasn't a planned seduction so she'd marry him. This feeling he had for her was unplanned and uncontrollable. Yet that certainty wasn't enough for him to stop walking towards her. No, the only thing that did that was the sound of her clumsily hitting the slatted wooden wall.

She had nowhere to go. And neither did he. He had no choice now. He didn't have Lioslath's acceptance of a temporary marriage, though he'd given her sound reasons. Maybe if he knew more about her, he could negotiate differently, but there was no time for contemplation. Donaldo's demand burned in his mind. There was only one thing left for him to try.

'Lioslath, why did you cut your hair?'

Chapter Twelve

Surprise pulled the ground from beneath Lioslath's feet. To keep from falling, she dug her fingers into the rough slats behind her until splinters poked each fingertip. The pain was enough for her anger to anchor her. To brace her for a discussion she'd never intended to have with this man.

'Who told you?'

Her hair. She didn't care about the quality and condition of her clothing. She didn't care that she slept in the stables and probably smelled of hay on a good day and horse on a bad. She didn't even care what hunting had done to her hands and fingers. No, all of these things she could dismiss, but not her hair.

'I doona ken,' he whispered.

She didn't care if he understood. It was her loss and she understood that all too well. He didn't deserve to know. 'Someone told you. Who was it?'

'You're angry. Why?'

'I'm not angry. It's just hair. Stop with this… false concern.'

Lioslath pressed herself against the back wall and hated herself for it, but she wanted to flee this conversation.

'Not to you. It's not simply hair to you,' he whispered. 'What happened?'

Too much. She somehow told him too much. No one asked about her hair because they all knew why she'd cut it. Her clansmen had lived through the same nightmare she had. A nightmare she didn't want to relive by telling it to the almighty Laird Colquhoun.

'You were forced,' he said.

He would push and keep pushing. His siege taught her that. So she pushed back. 'Forced? Nae, I cut it myself. It used to be down to here.' She pointed to the small of her back, though he couldn't see the gesture. 'Long, straight, just as thick. Just as unruly. All mine. So I hacked and hacked because all I had was my hunting knife. My hunting knife that I had been using to skin a sheep.'

Sheep wool and blood—her own blood as she cut herself with a dulled knife. It had all flown around her like some macabre cloud and she hadn't been able to stop. Just as she couldn't stop remembering now. She could practically feel the blade again as it sliced tiny cuts on her neck. Almost feel her body freeze and burn with terror as she yanked at the locks that stubbornly remained.

'Why did you only have your hunting knife?' Bram asked, his voice sounding distant. 'Why did you hack it that way?'

'Why?' Every word, every remembrance felt like some punishment. Not even her fingers gripping and stinging from the splinters made a difference. The grief inside her spilling out in front of this man was more painful than tiny cuts in her hands. 'Why ask me? Why torture me more? So you can simply hear my pain?'

He exhaled as if she'd suddenly slammed a fist into his stomach. 'I hear it now,' he said steadily, controlled. Without a doubt.

Compassion. Pity. Never from him. Her fingers released from the wood and she started to slide to the ground.

Bram was there. His arms wrapping around her as she leaned onto his chest and the solidness of his thighs. He cradled her and she clutched him with stinging palms and fingers.

What had she done? Nothing. Nothing but revealed a weakness to an enemy. Again.

It was he, it was his voice in the dark; it was

his vibrancy that kept her off kilter. But her feelings had to be fleeting. Just this moment. No more. She didn't think she could take any more. 'Let me go. Leave.'

'The English,' he said, instead of letting her go. 'The English have already been here. That's what happened to your crops. The scorch marks, the razing. That is why you have nae supplies.'

Of course he'd guess. 'Surprised it wasn't all our mistakes and failures at turning a profit that's made the Fergusson clan so poor? Or maybe you're not surprised that Fate despises Fergussons? After all, we continue to be an easy target for your manipulations.'

A brusque shake of his head. 'So I was right. They came...but you didn't know it. You were caught unawares and in haste you cut your hair. Why?'

Though he didn't deserve to know, though he didn't deserve for her to open the keep's gates, she told him anyway. 'Aye, they came in summer,' she said. 'I hacked my hair right here in the horse stables and hid it deep under the hay to throw away later. My clothes were already covered in blood and wool, but I brushed them with manure in case...they wanted to take more. Then I went out to meet them. I went out appearing like the son my father wished he'd sired.'

Her hair, so black like her father's, but thick

and down to her waist like her mother's. In memory of her mother, she kept her gently waving hair unbound. There were no paintings of her mother, no tapestries, no needlework. Any softness her mother added to the keep were taken away by her stepmother. But Lioslath kept her hair.

Then when the English came, when she heard the cries of her people, she knew what she had to do. To become a young man, because her age and her position and her sex could never protect her family otherwise.

She couldn't even cry as she cut it. She couldn't cry because she couldn't risk any tear tracks. To disguise herself even more, she wiped dirt on her face and smeared horse dung on her hose until her nostrils stung. She couldn't protect her clan if the English ever thought her a woman.

He wrapped his arms more tightly around her and she allowed it. She had no strength in her arms to push him away.

'They came,' he said. 'You had nae defences, nae power. That's why you're angry about my being late, about my not being here.'

Bram could feel Lioslath's tiny breaths for control. Her fingers kneaded his sides. As if she was clawing her way out telling him…or remembering.

'It was useless to tell you this. You can see we survived. I… We didn't need you. Let me go.'

He fought to clutch her tighter. The English. The English had razed Fergussons' crops to the ground. Burned homes and winter supplies. Lioslath and her family survived, but she had to endure the destruction of her home…of everything. And he hadn't been here to protect her.

The English were pouring through Scotland now to make their accounts. Sheriffs were taking taxes. Villages were being rebuilt as Scotsmen signed King Edward's Ragman Rolls to proclaim their fealty to him.

Lioslath said Fate hated them and he was starting to believe her. The English could easily return here.

Of course they would return here, since they easily acquired supplies and incurred no losses. Maybe they'd wait, but they would return. If they came before next autumn, the Fergusson clan wouldn't have any supplies to give them. Then people would be razed to the ground. Lioslath would be—

Bram had been a fool to agree to Donaldo's request. And now he knew why the woman had demanded this of him.

If their alliance was temporary, when the English came again he wouldn't be here. He would be on Colquhoun land or maybe somewhere hiding because he couldn't stay stationary. Not when he'd committed treason so many times over. In the form of Robert, the English king's favoured knight who lived on Colquhoun land. And then the Jewel of Kings, which was in his brother's keeping. And now he purposefully avoided a king's summons.

This clan needed the wealth and protection of the Colquhouns, but he wasn't the man to do it. But who else did they have? No one. The thought that his actions made them more vulnerable burned in his chest.

If Donaldo wanted revenge for him hurting Lioslath, she succeeded. Between his desire for Lioslath and now this protective urge towards the Fergussons, it would be difficult to leave. But he must do it. Never again would he fail his family.

But he could not fail Lioslath, who trembled in his arms. Each tiny movement shook through him. And he *feared* they would expose and wound him far worse than her arrows and dagger.

He had a duty to his family but also a promise to her. With a king wanting his head, he could fail one or the other.

In the meantime, by staying here he fulfilled the plan and could at least offer some protection and supplies to sustain the Fergussons. They... She needed more than that despite her demands he leave. But he must compromise. Compromise? Holding Lioslath, knowing he couldn't offer her more, felt like a sacrifice.

But all of his meagre offerings and perilous planning could only be accomplished if Lioslath accepted a temporary marriage. He had to push her for an answer. Guilt racked him, but duty demanded more.

'Lioslath, lass, your answer. A marriage just like your father's. That's all. It won't be any more than that. I won't ask for any more than that.'

When she eased away from him, he let her.

'Not now,' she said.

'You told me of your hair. You know I can help.'

'Tomorrow,' she whispered. 'I'll give you an answer tomorrow.'

Bram rolled his shoulders as the last of the thatch he lifted above his head was taken by his clansmen on the roof.

All day the clans worked together, tearing down the hastily made repairs, reworking patches and discussing what needed to be done and when. It was punishing work, rewarding work, and the sun would be setting soon.

Still, there was no answer from Lioslath.

He worked harder than all, knowing Lioslath could say no, that he'd be forced to return to

Colquhoun land, that she would be more vulnerable when the English returned.

When he spied Finlay exiting the keep, he excused himself to intercept his friend. There was much to discuss and they needed to be alone.

'How fares the keep?' he asked when they were far enough away.

Finlay walked beside him. 'The platform fell so suddenly, Callum will have a bruise on his back for a month. He couldn't get out from under it fast enough.'

To know it was down was no relief. Not when he knew it could have fallen with Lioslath hurling debris at him. He thought the Fergussons were terrible carpenters. Instead, they desperately made repairs in case it rained. He arrived too late to protect this clan and he pushed Lioslath too much regarding the marriage. He did not deserve any reward as he ripped and made stronger repairs, built new beams. Still…it gave him satisfaction mending the wrongs here.

'The one we're building will take a couple of days,' Finlay said.

'As long as it's secure.'

Finlay looked around. 'There is much work to be done here.'

'Aye, and it will get done.' There was more than repairs to be done here. The Fergussons lacked skills, swords and defences. Lioslath had a...vulnerability he didn't understand. He continued to feel her trembles.

Finlay exhaled. 'I need an answer.'

'As laird or friend?' Bram said, expecting this conversation. He dreaded it nonetheless.

'Perhaps both,' Finlay said.

'I cannot answer all your questions.'

'Aye, I understand, but in this… Your betrothal was a surprise. I need to know if the weeks here have been nothing but a courtship.'

Carefully worded insults. 'You know me better.'

'I hoped you'd say that. But we've been here for weeks and the men are restless.'

'So they look to you to discover my intentions?' As laird he was used to factions. 'Merely a few more weeks until the repairs are done, then you and the men can return.'

'Or stay if we like?'

Bram's chest swelled at the blind friendship Finlay offered. 'I did not want to lose our friendship.'

'You have not lost it, but it seems we have lost our laird with this betrothal.'

Finlay frowned and there was tightness to his features Bram could not ease. He deeply regretted not telling his friend of his plans. That this marriage was temporary and he would return to Colquhoun land. But the knowledge could put

Finlay in danger, and it did Lioslath's reputation no good. At the end of the betrothal, it had to be her to break if off. It was the least he could do. That was, of course, if Lioslath accepted.

'I have purposely kept things from you, Finlay—'

'I doona like it,' Finlay interrupted.

'But I will continue to do so as a friend. You know we withheld from Dunbar, but I did not do it without knowledge by a certain person of power. I am not a traitor, but other matters have transpired since—'

'Nae, I doona want to know. You could never be a traitor.'

Bram breathed out slowly. He had been about to confess and didn't realise how much he needed to. The truth burned inside him, and the sun was beginning to set. The day was almost over.

'Thank you,' he said to Finlay as he sought a glimpse of Lioslath in the fields. She was there, on her hands and knees, gleaning along with her siblings and clansmen.

All day he waited for her answer, while she ignored him.

Finlay gestured around at the work to be done, at the din and disrepair. His face held a sense of bewilderment. 'Is this what you truly desire?'

This clan needed him. So did his own. But he was the master of manoeuvres and he would find a way to take care of them both. His clan's safety warred with Lioslath's trembles. He would find the balance somehow.

As if she knew it was time, Lioslath straightened and met his gaze. Her eyes held his in a determined wariness as she said a few words to Donaldo.

If possible, she was more beautiful to him. Especially now, when daytime was merging with the night. When it lit the dark of her hair with sunlight but shadowed the brightness of her eyes. Had he ever seen a woman look as she did? Had he ever heard of a woman protecting her clan as she had done?

Simple desire, complicated plan. And too many lives at stake for him to fail. Was this what he desired? To take care of a woman who despised him? What would it be like to have her as a wife? One he could not touch, and now with her troubles, one he craved to protect?

It would be hell.

'Wholeheartedly,' he lied.

Finlay tilted his head. 'It's good to have you back.'

'Was I someplace else?'

'I know that gleam. It was missing until you took her hand and announced your betrothal.'

Control wrested, but only enough to save face and to protect Lioslath. But if she didn't agree to the rest of his plan, it would all come tumbling down. He almost laughed. Even his plan was temporary.

The winter was such a short time and he couldn't stay. Yet he felt like growling as Finlay also gazed at Lioslath steadily walking towards them.

Her unwavering gaze only increased his need of her. What would it feel like to kiss her properly? To see her summer eyes darken before he pressed her body to his?

He choked his thoughts. Regardless of her answer, he would never know. If she declined his offer, he'd have to walk away. If she accepted… He shuddered. They agreed it would be a temporary marriage like Gaira and Busby's. That marriage wasn't to be consummated. He made the terms of their marriage and Lioslath accepted them. If they did marry, there would be no knowledge of Lioslath's body, or of how her lips tasted.

'She's stunning, Bram, and this land is fertile. It has nae leader and is only waiting to be conquered.'

Aye, control for his own clan at the expense of the Fergussons.

'Yet you announced a betrothal and view her too greedily,' Finlay continued. 'Could you be waiting for her answer?'

A low chuckle, since his friend had found the empty chink in his plan. 'Finn, you're too observant.' Everything hinged on Lioslath accepting his betrothal. Everything depended on her accepting a quick, decisive marriage. She showed him a vulnerability, but still she challenged him. He wrested control, but in appearances only.

'Though she walks ever closer, she doesn't look as if she'll agree.'

He waited, to find if he could wait. The irony was not lost.

'You are too patient with this clan,' Finlay said.

Bram felt as if he was standing outside his own skin. Patience. He had none. He wanted to protect her, though by staying, even temporarily, he could hurt her worse. He was a traitor in the eyes of his countrymen and the English. Marrying Lioslath could endanger her.

'They deserve our care and protection.' And he must fulfill his duty to his clan. Few knew his whereabouts. The risk was low.

A few steps more and Lioslath would be here. His chest burned until he realised he held his breath. Exhaling, a calm descended upon him and he smiled. For he knew, in any heated negotiation, appearances counted.

Lioslath stood in front of him now. He could

see Finlay give her a courteous nod before he walked away.

Moments. A pause.

'I've come to give you my answer, Colquhoun,' she said.

Chapter Thirteen

It was evening. Late. The hall, the courtyard, noisy, despite the hard work of the morning, and the preparations of the afternoon. It had happened so fast, so fast, and yet it felt inevitable. Lioslath didn't try to hold in her shaky breath. She had married Bram of Clan…Fergusson now.

A simple decision and one not made easily. In the end, she knew what she had to do. She had to accept Bram's marriage offer. It took every bit of her resolve, but she did it.

She was relieved when Bram answered her acceptance with only a curt nod. His words and voice, for the first time, mute. She wondered about that. She wondered, too, about the slight flexing of his fingers and the fisting of his hand as if he wanted to hold on to something. But then she left without another word and that had been that.

It didn't bother her. It allowed her privacy and

her own thoughts again. That was until she was descended upon by Donaldo and Aindreas, who wanted their answers.

But she'd done it. She secured an alliance that would help her clan for generations. She accomplished more than her father's agreement of sheep and she'd done it without stabbing Bram. As much as she could, it was a marriage on her terms and for herself.

Slow, steady steps as she followed Bram to her...their...bedroom. There had been a solemnity to the wedding and it carried on between them now. Except Bram was even more taciturn than when he gave his vows. As if once they placed their hands in each other's and pledged in front of her clan, he could no longer touch her.

Her hand in his was the only contact throughout a hastily prepared and eaten meal. Hasty preparations, but none of it dimming the fact that a part of her knew she sacrificed herself this day. But if she felt sacrificed, she knew she'd been steadily, abruptly, walking towards the firepit since April.

Since her father's murder, she'd been forced to interact with her clan. Forced to change the way she lived. From sleeping in the stables to having a bedroom in the keep. From only hunting to deciding the evening meals. From observing her siblings play and laugh with her father to them now hovering around her. Her agonised acknowledgement that they wanted to climb on her, too. Always fearing she'd drop them, she walked away before they got too close.

Then the English came and she knew she couldn't hold herself apart any longer. Had to do what her clan needed her to do. She had to represent them. There simply wasn't anyone else.

Yet, as much as this marriage felt like a sacrifice, there was something more she felt than that. Her feeling had nothing to do with this man she followed to her bedroom. Although the desire to kiss him was there. Constantly there.

While they pledged to each other, she had felt the warmth of his hands around hers, seen his breath expand his fine clothing, felt each word he spoke in that deep voice of his.

It was dark in the Hall and candlelight dimmed the brightness of his hair. And for once, she wanted to see its vibrancy. If nothing else than to distract from his eyes that never left hers. For they warmed her more than the candles surrounding them and the firepit she felt certain she dangled over.

But she had done it. Married Laird Colquhoun, pledged her body and life with him, and she'd done it for herself. There was a part of her that longed to belong. That didn't want to feel the grief and separation of her mother's death any more.

As much as she tried to argue with herself, she couldn't help the feeling that with this marriage, she wouldn't be held apart. Bram played with her siblings and they appeared to like him in return. Maybe in this, too, her clan could also heal and become whole again. Because for better or worse, they were all she had, and in this marriage, she was giving all of herself.

When they reached the narrow corridor, Bram gestured for her to precede him. It wasn't much, but enough to bring her attention fully to the man she pledged her body to.

Her body was very conscious of the man she followed. Of the feel of his hand across the small of her back, the slight brush of his arm against the side of her body. Of the warmth of his nearness, at the smell of soap and…him.

Her awareness increased when he spoke. It was his voice. Nothing more than a few words indicating courtesy, but he was close and she felt the low timbre like a caress.

She married him for political alliances and to heal her clan. But with the awareness of him, the certain breathless hitch from the heat of his hand on the small of her back and lower, she knew she agreed to marry him for this feeling she had when she was around him as well. Only him. And it was that, that made her agree to his proposal.

Otherwise, how could she do it? If this marriage was a sacrifice, she wanted something for herself as well. She wanted to belong, wanted protection for her family and clan. And she wanted that kiss he promised.

When she fully walked into the room, she turned as Bram closed the door with an audible click of the latch.

The room had no fireplace. So the room held a chill, but a newly placed drape of leather was over the closed shuttered window, the holes in the roof had been patched. Furs were thrown onto the floor and at the foot of the turned-down bed, made more comfortable with the sheen of fine linen and a newly stuffed mattress. Near the two padded chairs gleamed a small table laden with a large platter supporting a pitcher, cups, and small rolls and butter for their taking.

While they pledged themselves to one another, someone came into her bedroom and supplied it with luxuries, with comfort as was befitting a laird.

Already there were changes. Small, but they were a beginning.

Now the largest changes would only come by…bonding with this man. At that, heat flared just under her skin.

The room was well-lit exactly as Bram requested and he could see Lioslath's wariness and unease. Her emotions were sweet despite their agreement. She was as nervous as if this marriage was real.

In a sense, he supposed their temporary marriage, with its boundaries that must not be crossed, was real enough. At least outside their bedroom it was necessary to pretend it was real.

Inside their bedroom, they knew what was at stake. Unlike most newly married husbands, he didn't expect to share a marriage bed.

However, alone the way they were, it was difficult to remember any of their terms.

She was even dressed as if this marriage was real. More stunning and beautiful than he'd ever seen her. Where they found the dark green gown he didn't know. But it fit her. Skimming her curves in the maddening way that mesmerised him as he watched her walk. The dark colour accentuated the paleness of her skin and the blackness of her hair. Dark, so her eyes rivalled the brightest of days.

Candlelight flickered until she looked like a night with stars and the first bright sun after winter. She stunned him with her beauty and grace. She stunned him when she placed her hand in his as they became married. He swore he trembled. Trembled! And felt her own hands mimic his. After that, he hadn't been able to touch her any more. Couldn't look at her without starting to believe this marriage was real as well.

It had been a negotiation. Nothing more. Certainly, at her agreement, he felt a sense of victory. He'd felt this way in the past when discussions were heated, when opposing forces made any bartering for power or goods difficult. But something flawed his satisfaction: he didn't understand her agreement. 'I didn't think you'd agree to this.'

Despite his reasons, she had at first denied him. She had every right to deny him. A temporary marriage was a paltry offering for the wrongs he committed here.

Lioslath's expression was all too fleeting for him to understand. 'You did not act as if I had a choice.'

Walking to the pitcher on the table, he answered, 'You had a choice.'

'The arrow again? That was merely me demonstrating your needing to disappear. It was not an invitation to a marriage announcement.'

At the time he announced it, he hoped shock and anger would keep her quiet. And they had. He'd never forget the look on her face. The bewilderment and something too painful as she scanned her clansmen before she stormed away, her footsteps not as steady as he'd seen them before.

'You had a choice afterward. The conversation we had was in private.' He knew at any time she could have refused. Instead, she had agreed and he didn't know what to make of it.

He poured the ale and took a sip, pleased it was the strong brew he supplied. He would be needing it tonight. Even though Lioslath's back was to him, her lure was not hidden from him.

And they were alone. The first of many nights until they could terminate this marriage. Pouring another cup for her, he approached her, but she did not turn around.

To touch or speak? A test for him then. His hand around a cup, he trailed a finger along the curve of her arm. She didn't startle, but he felt her shiver before she turned around.

He handed her the cup. 'Deep in your thoughts?'

When she took it, he made sure he released the cup slowly so their fingers caressed. A momentary entwinement he was reluctant to release, but she did.

Taking a swift step back, releasing their touch, but not the way it felt. As she took a drink, her eyes remained wide on him.

It was a test and he knew she felt what was

between them, too. Desires that could never be fully explored in a temporary marriage.

That almost-kiss was like an eddy of anticipation within him. So why did he test whether he could touch her and hold himself back? Because now he knew she felt desire for him as well. It would only make this night torturous. Even so, if he could, he'd touch her again.

Her eyes lowered as did her cup. 'You worked hard today. Your hands…they're cut,' she said, her voice regaining its calm, though he knew his wouldn't.

His work in the fields and in the village had been swift and decisive. The idleness of those weeks gave him plenty of opportunity to plan. He enjoyed the hard work; he enjoyed even more her watching him. Too much. Complicated desire.

He'd never seen a woman work as hard as Lioslath did. Crawling on her hands and knees in the fields as she gleaned along with the children for any usable grains from the blackened dirt. She worked until he saw sweat and dirt pour down her face as he knew it poured down from his. Her face fierce, her body determined, but he didn't know what was in her eyes, because he didn't notice she watched him as well.

He flexed his fingers and felt the sting there.

'It was worth it. I meant what I said. I mean to keep to our bargain.'

'Our marriage,' she said as if it was a question.

He nodded and watched as she took another drink. She was nervous.

Other than the anticipation humming through him, at the need he knew he could not release, he felt calm. In control again.

This temporary marriage would keep him hidden from the English king's messengers and he would amend his grievances with this clan. As long as he didn't consummate this marriage, as long as Lioslath stayed a virgin, he could return to his keep by spring.

In the meantime, his clan was protected by Caird and he knew Malcolm would uphold his duties to the jewel.

So it was the time spent with the woman here that would be his trial. She drew him to her. The weeks of watching her on the platform, the way the moon revealed her in her darkened bedroom. The way she moved. Her flashes of temper.

Then there was the almost-kiss. The way her body felt against his, the widening of her comprehending eyes. A comprehension he couldn't explore. He didn't dare.

He welcomed the company of women and had grown used to them. He could control his actions with them, giving and taking pleasure. Lioslath wasn't like the others. Already he knew she was different.

It was his need for her and his anger at her opposition to him. Extremes he'd never felt before. Over the past months, he battled with dangerous forces he didn't understand. With politics that taught him how much he was a pawn in someone else's game. With…grief in Irvette's death. Through it all, he could find balance. He kept his sense of fairness, of diplomacy, and he found humour when the odds were against him.

With Lioslath, there was no balance. With her, he only wanted more; he wanted it all. He wanted to kiss and hold her. He hoped he could control his desire for her, hoped she'd help him when he could not. For he feared he could not.

Especially if she got that crease between her brows when she was troubled by something he said. That look made him want to laugh, to kiss her, to fall onto his knees in front of her and… He stopped his thoughts and wished instead for more ale.

If only he could have claimed the kiss before they made their agreement on this temporary marriage. Maybe he would not be so plagued!

All too aware of Bram's eyes searching hers, and still feeling Bram's touch, Lioslath flexed her fingers around her cup. He gave such a simple caress against her hand. Yet she was acutely aware it was his hands, the long, tapered fingers, the calluses from his training and labour, touching her. There was nothing simple about the way they felt.

She watched his interactions with the clans. The way his body toiled. But through all of it, she watched the way he used his hands. Capable, determined, with purpose. The hands she'd soon feel against her body.

After all, it was their marriage night. It was simply she didn't know how to go about it. She couldn't understand what he did now, standing away from her and drinking more ale.

She didn't know anything about him. She knew of his clan's wealth and power, but for the rest…?

'Would you tell me about your family?' she asked.

'This is unexpected,' he said.

'We're married now,' she said.

'True, but I thought you already knew,' he said. 'Your father never told you?'

Her father confiding in her? She couldn't imagine it. 'I know of Gaira, but he didn't tell about the rest.'

Bram took a drink. 'What do you want to know?'

She didn't know; she just expected him to talk. He was used to people asking questions and answering them in turn. She barely asked her question.

Bram lowered his cup and tilted his head as if he was assessing her. Did he think this was a negotiation? A barter? She shrugged.

'We'll start from the beginning, then,' Bram began. 'My mother died giving birth to my youngest sister, Irvette. My father died some years later. He was always eager and one day he was reckless with a horse.'

A small smile against his lips. 'My youngest brother, Malcolm, is like that. Looks like our father as well, although his hair is darker. The rest of us have the traits of our mother.'

An odd twinge happened near her heart as Bram recalled his mother. She looked at the vibrancy of him, his constant laughter, the ease he had with everything…and yet he knew pain and loss in his life. How could he find laughter so easily?

She lifted the cup to her lips, but it was empty. When he gestured for her to bring it to him, she hesitated to hand him the cup.

She was right in the hesitation. He didn't only slide his fingers this time, he enfolded his fingers over hers as he poured the ale. His entire concentration was on the liquid pouring into the cup, but hers was on their touch.

When he released his hand, she barely stopped from protesting. To hide the sound, she said, 'The rest of your family?

Bram took a step back, his fingers now moving around the cup like a caress. 'That would leave Caird, who's a few years younger than me, and Gaira.'

Gaira, his sister. She didn't want to talk about Gaira. 'What of your other sister, Irvette?'

His hand jerked around his cup. 'You truly know nothing? I thought my letter told you.'

'Your letter was of my father's death and your coming.' She didn't want to talk of Gaira returning to Colquhoun keep and his intention to come here. Not tonight. But she could tell from his expression that he didn't want to talk of Irvette. It wasn't only the pull of his brows, it was the pain filling his grey eyes. Then she knew.

'You lost her, too. Did she die when your mother did?'

'Irvette's...gone. Your father never mentioned it? Maybe he didn't have enough time.' He shook his head and the pain eased a bit. 'Irvette died at the massacre of Doonhill.'

Grief and loss laced the tenor of Bram's voice.

'She died, along with her husband, at the massacre. Their daughter, Margaret, who we call

Maisie, survived along with some other children.' He looked into his cup. 'It feels…odd… telling you this story.'

'Why?'

'Because your family is such a large part of the tale.'

Again, he was mistaken she was part of a family or part of a clan. She was surprised he hadn't realised it himself. She thought nothing escaped his observant gaze.

'Tell me,' she said. 'If you want to.'

He turned, and it looked as though he wanted to take her hand before he let his own fall to his side.

Odd that she felt that loss. To cover her reaction, she walked to one of the chairs and sat. He sat in the accompanying one and turned towards her.

'When Gaira…separated from your father, she rode to Irvette at Doonhill, but it was too late. By then the English had destroyed everything, killed everyone. Gaira found Maisie in the valley and three surviving children in the forest above. She returned with them to Colquhoun land.'

'She travelled that distance with children?'

'Aye.'

She hadn't known. All this time, she imagined Gaira as someone weak. Why else flee her father and the hard work waiting for her at Clan Fergusson? When in fact, such a journey from Doonhill to the Colquhouns' would have been dangerous. Gaira couldn't be soft or weak or anything she imagined her to be. But talking of Gaira and her journey was painful for other reasons and the grief on Bram's face was still there.

'Irvette. You miss her still,' she said.

'Every day. Malcolm and I talk of her, but Gaira most of all. She's raising Maisie, who has so much of our sister in her. It's joyous and heartbreaking to see her grow.'

'And Caird?'

'Still won't talk of Irvette. He rarely talks as it is. But with Irvette? Absolute silence. We all tried, but he's never been open or talkative like the rest of us. Malcolm once accused him of not caring. Caird swung fast and hard, and took us all by surprise. By the time I reached them, Malcolm had left the keep.' Bram jerked and some sound came out of him before he took a long drink. 'He even left Colquhoun land for…a while.'

She tried to remember Malcolm, and what she had been able to see of him. He had scars and they weren't that old. Had they occurred after he fled?

'No one's accused Caird of not caring again,' Bram continued. 'That swing was lethal and

Caird never loses control. Although—' he tilted his empty cup '—I think that may change.'

Lioslath took a sip and thought back to the day she'd seen the Colquhouns talking with Bram outside the gates. Caird had been the man with hair that looked red only in the sunlight. 'He was the one here with the curly-haired woman.'

'That was Mairead. I think my brother has met his match with her.' Bram went to the pitcher, which must have been empty, since he set it and his cup back down. Then he eyed the bed and small room. The light was dimming as some candles sputtered out. There weren't any sounds from the Hall or courtyard.

'They were close… Are they married?'

'You observed much in those weeks,' he said.

'Little was left for me to do.'

That brought his eyes to hers. 'Aye, well. We have this agreement between us now.'

'This marriage?' she said. 'Aye.'

He looked around him again as if he was lost for words or actions.

'It's night,' he finally said, glancing at her and then away. 'Are you tired?'

She should be. She drank the ale, but none of her nervousness was gone because he'd touched her hand, he'd talked and his voice affected her. 'Nae.'

He went to the pitcher, which was still empty,

but it seemed to surprise or irritate him again. 'We should talk more.'

'Why?'

'Because the night is long. Because I didn't think it would be like this with you.'

'Am I to understand you?'

'You're making a crease between your brows, Lioslath. It's very trying to a man who's denying things.'

She shook her head. 'What is there to deny?'

Bram looked away when Lioslath's lips remained softly opened on her last word. A single word should not be so tempting. And it had nothing to do with denial. It had everything to do with the colour and shape of Lioslath's lips and everything else about her in the dark green gown. 'Tell me anything. Talk to me of anything. Anything at all. What is your family like?'

Lioslath sat deeper in her seat. Her stricken look cut through his desire. Fool. He asked about her family. Of course, she would think of her father. This was not the night to discuss her father.

'Your siblings, what are they like?' he asked, sitting down again.

The pain eased around her eyes, but not the tenseness around her shoulders. And she took another sip of her ale. 'You've seen them.'

Aye, he had seen them with her. Like today when she gleaned and ploughed the fields with them. How she frowned perplexingly or startled when they tried to play with her. Minute actions, but all as if she didn't know what to do with them.

She had that look, too, if she was approached by her clansmen or if she suddenly looked around her. As if she realised she was surrounded by people and was wondering where they came from. He never thought himself curious before, but when it came to her, he...was.

'What do they like?' he asked.

'Like?' She shook her head a little and set her cup down on the table. She was perplexed, but he didn't know if it was the question or him asking the questions.

Patience, he reminded himself. Even if the marriage was temporary, there needed to be some understanding between them.

'What do you do with them?' He sat forward and rested his arm on his legs. 'You have lived here all your life, haven't you?' he teased.

She looked away. 'Aye,' she whispered.

He hurt her again and the night was not even half over. He remembered Busby. He had been a strong man, prideful...vengeful. Talking of her family would not benefit either of them this evening.

Still, he didn't understand why talking of her siblings or clansmen hurt her. Her brothers and sister obviously loved her. Her clansmen were loyal to her. He needed another distraction. Maybe another subject.

'What do *you* like?' he asked.

Lioslath looked around the room. She felt like standing or pacing or doing something with her body so she didn't feel so trapped by Bram's questions. It felt as though he was prying, and yet she asked him similar questions, and he offered answers. She knew it was reasonable for him to ask something of her. But she didn't know how to answer questions of her family.

'What do I like?' She liked to have food, a roof over her head and a dry bed to sleep on, but she didn't think this was what he meant. Games. Play, which she didn't do. But there was something she did. 'I like hunting,' she said.

'Like when the men bring food to the keep for preparation.'

She didn't like his smile, or him thinking she didn't actually hunt. 'Nae, not like that.'

He straightened. 'You're saying you *like* to hunt? It's just—'

He sounded too incredulous. Did he think her a liar? 'Did you forget how I beat all your archers?'

His lips thinned.

'Now you're angry again,' she said.

'Nae, I could not doubt your skill. I thought…
maybe you were forced to hunt.'

'What would give you that idea?'

He shook his head as if answering an internal
question. 'Forgive me. What do you like about
it?'

The freedom of it. How her skill gave her
pride again, when her whole life she felt worth-
less. But that was not what she wanted to tell
this man she married.

'It's…the way the air feels in the morning…
the stillness. Except, the forest is never still because around the next tree there will be—' She
waved her hands, not knowing what that fast
feeling was that coursed through her.

'Excitement?' he offered.

'You're making fun of me.'

'Nae, did you not know I like to hunt? I know
that feeling, lass. That one that makes your blood
hot and cold at the same time. It's called anticipation.'

She anticipated food or the day breaking.
Could a feeling be anticipation as well?

'What else about hunting do you like?' he
asked. 'Was it always like that?'

'Nae, I came upon it by accident, but I
quickly… It felt like what I was supposed to do.'
Avoiding the emotion of it now, she talked of

learning the skill, the different equipment she favoured and the times wildlife would surprise her.

As she talked, Bram became very still. His eyes turning from dark to almost light and filled with a sort of pleasure that skimmed over her. She was dressed, and yet, with the heat in Bram's eyes, she felt suddenly bared for his touch.

'I doona think I like this talking,' she said.

He seemed surprised she stopped. 'It leaves us little choice if we do not.' He gave a small smile. 'Otherwise all we have is…anticipation.'

The gleam in Bram's eyes reminded her too much of their almost-kiss, but at the same time, she could tell he teased again.

'I think it will only lead me to throwing a bucket of dung at you.'

He laughed. 'I didn't know you had a sense of humour.'

She would never understand his amusements. 'I meant it.'

He stopped suddenly, as if her anger and confusion stunned him. 'That's what I feared. Especially since you look the way you do.'

Donaldo had spent hours on her appearance. Of course, she would have ruined their efforts by now. 'How do I look?'

'I was hoping the ale, and the labours of the day, would be enough. How do you look? You get this crease between your brows and it just about—' He sighed then, as if tortured, as if facing what he could not. 'We need to negotiate, Lioslath.'

Chapter Fourteen

'Negotiate?'

Maybe it was the dimming candlelight, but his usual smile didn't seem so easy for him. 'Regarding our agreement,' he said.

'I married you. Why would we need to negotiate?'

'Because I need to change the parameters of our bargaining.'

She didn't know what he was talking about.

'We're alone, love. We've talked. We're not tired. We've drunk all there is to drink and I'm not eating those rolls.'

'Is this because I doona know how to talk? It's true, I do like to hunt—'

Bram sat forward with his arms resting on his knees again. It was a restful pose, but his heels subtly rocking belied his underlying restlessness. She was beginning to feel that way, too.

'I know that now. I heard it,' he said. 'Saw

it with your skill and how you glowed with the pleasure of talking about it. If you only knew what that means to me, that a woman would feel the way I do about it.' He stopped moving and laughed, but it seemed to be pointed at himself. 'And that's a problem, too. It's not your talking, lass. You see…I want to kiss you.'

'Kiss?'

'The want, desire, longing to kiss you hasn't disappeared simply because we're married. You see, it's your hair, your eyes, the way that crease happens between your brows when you're confused. Like now.'

'Those things make you want to kiss me?'

He straightened and sucked in an unsteady breath. 'Aye, just like that.'

'We're married.'

'Given the parameters of the agreement, I have nae right to ask for more. But I was a fool thinking anything different, so I have to change them.'

'Change the…parameters…of our agreement?'

'Exactly, but I won't do it without your consent.'

'To kiss me?'

He pressed his lips together and nodded as if he couldn't get the words out.

'I didn't think it mattered what I wanted,'

she said. She agreed to marry him. What more needed to be discussed?

He shook his head. 'It does matter. It must in our agreement, or we wouldn't be keeping to our bargain. Although I would have argued about it before, I'd say what the wife wants in a true marriage should matter anyway.'

'On the kissing.'

Abruptly, Bram stood and turned in the little room before facing her again. 'Aye, the kissing… amongst other things. I desire you, Lioslath. It's your hair that rivals the night and your eyes that shame the sky. It's your moles, your spots and that crease between your brows. All these and so much more. Too much more. You fought the English. You *like* to hunt.' Another self-deprecating laugh that turned into a true chuckle. 'I can't believe I'm saying any of this at all. Doona you want to kiss?'

If they had to negotiate for kissing, she did not understand what occurred on marriage nights. She certainly didn't know he'd ask for a kiss. She held still for him in the field and she married him. Ever since the competition she thought of that moment. Of how he felt to her then. And even before, like when he carried her from the kitchens. He was warm and she wanted to bury herself in that warmth.

She wanted to kiss him, but how was she to

tell him that? She felt awkward asking about his family. How was she supposed to talk about kissing in a socially acceptable way? Was there a socially acceptable way to talk of kissing? Bram seemed to think so.

'Your silence drives a hard bargain,' Bram said, his voice breaking into a silence she didn't know she created. 'I've said what I like about you. Isn't there anything about me you like?'

As if to show what he was talking about, he rested his hands on his hips. His legs were slightly apart, his face almost grim, the constant laughter still in his eyes. He stood as if for her inspection.

Now she truly knew nothing about wedding nights. Nothing.

She knew of his diplomacy and trades. Everyone did. Maybe he was so good at it because that was simply how he thought. All the time. Like now on their marriage night. His talking seemed all too direct. Blunt.

Lioslath's confusion eased a bit. She wasn't used to talking, let alone talking of wants or desires. But if they bargained, they'd have to be direct with each other. That she could do. So what did she like about him?

His hair was still that blazing red that wasn't anything she'd ever seen before. So offensive when she first saw it, but now it fitted him and she couldn't imagine another shade. His eyes were always reminding her of storms. From the broadness of his chest that tapered to a narrow waist, his body was without an ounce of give, just as formidable, just as forceful as his personality. And his legs looked…sturdy.

'I can feel your eyes on me, lass,' Bram said, his voice lowering a tone as if in warning.

'You asked me if I find anything pleasing about you.'

'Nothing came readily?'

'Nae.'

He tilted his head back a little. A grimace, a wince before he released his hands from his hips and took a step away. 'I deserved that, nae doubt.'

'Doona move.'

He stopped as if surprised and looked over his shoulder.

She stood. 'I'm still considering.'

Bram turned and held still. If possible, he held more still than before and there was no sense of humour in his eyes. Instead, his eyes were somewhat…heated. 'This negotiation is becoming difficult.'

'You're merely standing there. How is that difficult?'

'It's your eyes, Lioslath. Your eyes are going all over me.'

'Nae one can feel someone's eyes looking at them.'

'I could feel yours if they were on the other side of the ocean.'

'Are you jesting?'

''Tis romantic sentiment. I'm wooing you.'

'We're married.'

'Aye, but it appears you doona like anything about me, so I have to use words.'

'Why?'

'Because I can't keep to my bargain.' He clasped his hands and rolled back on his heels. 'I know I've made our agreement difficult because I'm asking to renegotiate our terms, but I made a mistake. You standing there like that, and knowing what I now know, I realise that I made a mistake. If you keep looking at me like that and not stating your current position on our terms, I'm going to break…'

Bram threw his arms in the air. His hands, long, lean, strong even in his frustrated state, noticeable to her before he put them again on his hips.

'Nae man could keep to…' His voice trailed off. Words stuck in his throat. Or at least it seemed like it when his eyes went wide and he stared at her.

'Your eyes, love. They're on me.' His voice

was low, almost hoarse. 'Are you still considering if there's something pleasing about me?'

'Aye,' she said. His hands, his fingers along his hips. They drummed his agitation and there was a certain strength and grace in the way they moved...

'You're looking where nae maiden should be looking unless—'

Did he think, did he *believe*, she was looking at— 'Your hands,' she blurted out. 'I like your hands.'

'My hands.'

He felt closer to her, although she hadn't seen him move. 'I like your hands.'

'Lioslath.' A different question to his voice, as he truly stepped closer until she could touch him. Until he could touch her. 'Is this your counter? My hands, are you adding my *hands* to this... marriage?'

She was aware of the heat from his body, but she was also aware of his size and indomitable strength. Too much strength and too close. The awareness inside her was almost painful. Far more than when she held still for his kiss.

'Aye,' she said. Of course she added his hands to the marriage, as well as the rest of them. Were they to negotiate on every body part? She already pledged her body, but now couldn't remember if he pledged his.

'You…drive a hard bargain, Lioslath. You do. I have underestimated you. Again.'

But Bram didn't care. In this, he couldn't care. She agreed to new terms. Agreed to something physical between them. And she added his hands, which were suddenly sensitive to the very air around them. Greedy to feel the softness of her skin, the heat and the give of her curves. His hands. Not even touching her, his hands felt the palpable heat of anticipation.

Oh, she surprised him. She was complicated, like his desire for her. They must have a temporary marriage, he warned himself. But one that might no longer be hell. He was allowed to touch her, to find pleasure with her.

'This may be more difficult than before, but I'm a desperate man. You've made me desperate with your—'

'Crease between my brows?' She could feel it herself with this strange conversation.

'Aye, exactly that, but I accept your terms.'

Bram took her hands in his, slowly walked back until they reached the bed and sat her down next to him.

She didn't remove her eyes from the way he held her hands together almost casually. But it didn't feel casual. Not the way Bram was fluttering his fingers around hers. Her hunting had scarred and roughened them, but held by his they looked small, almost delicate. And they felt that way as Bram's thumb pressed and caressed along her palm.

'What is it about my hands you like?' he asked.

The scrapes and cuts he earned today were already healing. Scars so deep, they must have needed stitching. Calluses from the sword and shields. From the different ways he trained over the years. From throwing thatch on rooftops, from carrying benches into courtyards.

'They're…capable,' she said.

Bram's fingers caressed again, long sweeps of his fingers as his thumbs pressed and swept over her inner wrists.

Then he released her hands, but she didn't release hers. She felt and heard the hitch to his breathing as she started to trace his fingertips. She couldn't say anything and apparently neither could he. But other sounds filled the silence. Like the cadence of his breath, which increased and matched her own.

As he held his hands in front of her, it didn't feel like Bram's teasing approach to her in the forest. There, she'd been certain Bram wanted to kiss her. Now she wasn't certain at all what he would do. Bram was doing nothing but holding his hands out to her.

Before she knew what she would do, she

leaned down and kissed the back of one hand. Then the other.

She felt the tension in him now, alive, and against her. Felt the little shiver go through him at her kiss and her own body mimic his. She felt it increase as he turned his palms upwards. Waiting. Feral. Like her forest with its beckoning wildness. It compelled her to him. She might not know about marriage nights, but she knew how she felt and she wanted more of it, wanted more of Bram.

He was beckoning and dangerous with his warrior-roughened hands, and she kissed the centre of each palm. Slowly, wanting and yet startling at the heat of them, the smell of leather, ale and Bram. Heart thundering in her chest, she straightened to see Bram's hands slowly furling. As if enclosing her kisses in his palms before he rested them against his thighs.

'Lie down.' Two words roughly said. As if the words escaped before he could stop them.

'Bram,' she whispered. 'Will you...? Are you lying down with me?' She wanted that now. Wanted to kiss more of him. Feel his kiss. Why hadn't he kissed her yet?

He quickly looked away and roughly exhaled. Inhaling, he bent to throw off his boots. 'You've added my hands to this marriage, Lioslath. Do not worry, but do not ask for more. I will not break our bargain.' Reaching to her shoes, he quickly untied them and threw them to the corner as well. When he straightened, his eyes went past her to the bed. 'Lie down, lass. Please.'

She didn't know why she obeyed him now. Maybe it was his talking of bargains and she knew he didn't break his word in negotiations. Maybe it was his voice, or how he held still for her touch. He was always moving, she didn't know he had that stillness in him.

'Aye, that's it, place your head there. Like that.'

Bram might have said he'd use only his hands, but he used his voice as well. She knew it because she moved just as he had told her.

'I'll keep to your bargain. You've added my hands to this marriage. But it'll be you directing them.'

She started as he placed a hand under hers and then somehow linked his fingers with hers.

A huff of breath left him, a sound deep, primal, his fingers flexing, her fingers flexing along with his. When his thumb moved, so did hers.

'Take my hand, Lioslath.'

She lowered her eyes again, riveted by her hand over his. She had the control, and yet he supported her.

'Bram…' she said, certain she didn't know the way of this.

'I cannot do more than this. Not tonight. It's the way you look, lass. It's that spot above your lip, the ones I can see behind your ear. It's the fact I need to ask for more, but I know I can't offer more tonight or I'll break our agreement. But…there's a need. I feel it in you. I see it in your eyes. It's there for me, too. So take my hands. Make them capable. I won't do anything more.'

She didn't understand his need for agreements. But she understood the urgency behind them. It was the way he used his words. She wanted him to keep using them. 'Tell me how.'

'Oh, lass, you can't—' He breathed in deeply, lying down next to her. On his side, she felt the width of his shoulders and his legs against hers. Such little points of contact, but they were enough. Too much. They held hands and that was too much.

'Where are your moles, Lioslath?'

What did spots have to do with his hands? 'Along my body.'

'And your legs?'

'Maybe.'

A shudder from him. 'Lie on your side. Like that.'

She did and felt him adjust along her back. His

breath was warm against her neck. His legs were kept away from hers, but the bed was small, and she felt those as well as his arm over her. The unfamiliar weight anchored her to the bed. She liked him anchoring her to the bed.

'Do you know what you need? Do you know what you want?'

'Nae.' She knew nothing of husbands and wives. She certainly didn't know of this odd languidness flowing through her from Bram's touch. Or her crisp awareness of the room surrounding them with dimming candlelight, of the bed's softness, of Bram pressed behind her, of the cadence of their breaths.

'I'm rearranging your gown, lass, just a bit, just enough.'

He drew her gown's layers slowly above her knees. But it wasn't only her skirts he touched. She felt his fingertips caressing along her leg as well, the back of her knee, along the outside of her thigh. 'Is this what you want?' he whispered. 'Here, like this?'

It was and wasn't. The feeling of his fingers she touched, kissed, had started a feeling…but rearranging her gown wasn't what she wanted. She wanted more. 'Nae.'

A soft ragged chuckle as he clenched her skirt again and tugged a bit more. So she felt more.

Cool air against her legs, the heat of his body

behind her and the rough and unfamiliar cadence of his breathing.

'Bram, what do you do?'

His weight shifted against her. She felt the ephemeral brush of his lips against her hair as he pulled her closer. Like this, she was curled against him, her clothing seemingly covering her, but her legs lay open; his hand between her thighs like a secret.

'Do you want to know what my hands are capable of?' His voice at her ear sent shivers through her.

'Aye,' she whispered in the dark. She did. Whatever it was she felt, she wanted to feel more of it.

'Then take your hand and place it over mine.' She moved restlessly. 'My hand?'

'Aye, rest your hand on top.' He laid his hand flat against her thigh, and she tentatively rested her hand on his. She felt the slight shudder that went through him, the low growl of sound he made that somehow she understood.

Only then did he move his hand. Yet this time it wasn't only Bram's fingertips, but her own against her skin. Unexpected, frightening…and yet somehow complete. In the darkening room, she watched his hands and hers. Watched as they skimmed higher on her leg to where she wanted him to be and yet…

'Open your legs for me.'

She couldn't.

'Just a bit, just a little. Only my hands, nae more.'

Had they bargained for his hands? If so, she didn't know how it came to this. Her hand on his felt wicked; her widening her legs even more so. It felt wicked, but wanted. And so she did.

'That's it.'

More grazing touches. The skimming became sweeping caresses. His palm rough with calluses was gentle, urgent. Her hand on top of his trembled.

'More,' he whispered, flattening his palm along her thigh. Closer until he swept his roughened fingertips against her curls; until his fingers dipped a gentle swipe against her.

A sound from him, a sudden movement of his hips against hers until he stilled. He stilled, but everything inside her was restless. Her breaths, coming in fast, sounded desperate in the quiet. She felt a want before, but this was an ache. Worse than an ache. She curled her hand on top of his, desperate to be released, desperate to continue.

'Nae, keep your hand on mine. Feel what my hand can do.'

His voice, his words. So she did.

His fingers glided easily between her folds.

She kept her fingers against his, but she couldn't think of her hand when all she felt was the heat of his, the rough calluses, the gentle slide.

'What you do to me,' Bram whispered.

'What I…do to you?'

A broken chuckle. He rolled his hips deliberately against her. 'This is what you do to me.'

She shuddered at his low words, at the feel of him. She tried to remember how he looked, hands on hips for her inspection. Had his body been like this? Hard, unyielding against her curves. For a wild broken moment, she wanted to look.

'I'm needful, I'm hurting and you lied about spots on your legs. They're there, lass, they're there. But this is your bargain, not mine. Please let me.' He adjusted his fingers, opening her up even more. Her own fingers curled against his knuckles. 'Place your fingers between mine.'

'Between?'

'Entwine them.'

If she did that, she'd be touching herself… while he touched her. Incapable of words, she shook her head.

'Do you want to know what my fingers are capable of? Show me how you need to be touched.'

Trying to change their positions, she moved her hips. But he anchored her with his arm, which was holding her gently, firmly, reassuringly. Just as his fingers swept down and held still.

She couldn't stand it. Not when he swept his fingers over her, not when she felt his ragged breath that matched her own. Not when she felt this…need. Caressing the back of his hand, feeling the hot heat of his palm against her, his long, blunt-tipped fingers already there, she lowered her fingers on top of his.

'Aye, lass, aye…' he breathed.

Unable to continue, she couldn't move her fingers, couldn't lower them. It was too much. Too much. He held agonisingly still. Beckoning. And, oh, so feral. 'Please,' she said. 'I can't. I want…'

Then his fingers entwined with hers and swept the glistening skin he exposed. 'Like this?' he whispered. Wicked words. Urgent words. 'Is this what you need, my fingers like this, my hand like this?'

Shivering with need, she nodded. Barely perceptible, but her answer was there. And he answered in turn. She felt surrounded by his need. By her need escalating under his stroking fingers. Entwining and tightening between her fingers. More gliding, purposeful caresses as one finger pressed just at her entrance, then her world broke apart.

* * *

Bram ached. An agony he had never known and he didn't want to take away. Not when Lioslath slept in his arms. Not when a part of her resisted him even now. It was the way she held her body away from his. A defiance and tentativeness he didn't expect, but should have.

He'd seen it himself. How she held herself proudly apart but still longed for her clan and siblings. And just now the way she couldn't hold herself apart any more and he couldn't either.

And it was… He couldn't think of the pleasure now.

He also couldn't feel satisfaction on keeping to their terms. No doubt, he'd experience a marriage night like none other. One that was heaven and hell. She linked her fingers with his and lovingly kissed his opened palms. All of that could never be unfelt. Though their marriage was temporary, he knew how he felt about this night was permanent.

His arms flexed to pull her close and he restrained himself. This was the first night of many that could not be consummated. It wouldn't do feeling this closeness with Lioslath. And yet it was there. He blamed it on that almost-kiss.

Chapter Fifteen

'Wake, Lioslath,' he whispered. 'I've come to take you hunting.'

'Hunting?' She sat, not in eagerness as he hoped, but in wariness, and then her wariness became suspicion. 'Nae one takes me hunting.'

This didn't bode well. 'Doona you want to go?'

'Why?'

He should have been expecting that question, but he wasn't. Nor was he expecting the look she gave him as well. But he couldn't blame her. After all, it was early and things between them were in a constant state of push-and-pull.

'I want you to show me.'

'Show you what?'

She gripped the blankets tight around her. As if she wasn't fully dressed, as if she was bared to him. Then he couldn't smile at all as his thoughts went from spending the day with Lioslath in the forest to…spending the day with her indoors.

'How you hunt,' he said.

'I thought you believed me.'

'I do. I know you hunt and I want to share it with you.'

'Is this because of last night?'

Last night, this morning, it didn't matter. Her confession and truths from the stables continued to disquiet him. But last night, and how she responded to him, shattered all the protectiveness he felt and wrapped it tightly with desire. Untried, he thought their hands entwined and touching her skin would overwhelm her. But each response she gave only fed his own until she cried out in pleasure and he was consumed. Theirs was a temporary marriage, but a part of him would never be free of her.

In the months ahead, with more nights like that, how would he feel? Wasteful to think such thoughts, since nothing could be done, no matter how he felt. He had a duty to his clan and they, too, needed his protection.

Yet Lioslath was more than he could have known. He underestimated her. In every sense. Her beauty; her resolve. Her bravery in facing the English alone. So alone. How could this woman have ever been left alone?

Especially this morning. Her hair stood on end and was completely flat on one side. He felt like tunnelling his fingers through it, kissing her soft lips and staying exactly where they were all day long. Those repeating thoughts were just as dangerous as anything else. He needed to leave. Immediately. 'I'll be outside.'

'What makes you think I'll come?'

'Because you have skills, love, and you'll want to show them off.'

Lioslath didn't know how she felt as Bram, chuckling, left the room. She didn't understand his easy laughter. She didn't understand his wanting to hunt together. It surprised her. After him expecting her to be the clan's mistress and lady of the keep, he offered this instead.

Confusing Colquhoun, but she did know how she felt about hunting. The familiar excitement, the yearning and the absolute necessity of it.

She got out of bed as Dog sauntered in for a greeting. He hadn't liked her moving to the bedroom since her father died and she didn't know how he felt about Bram sharing the room. But he licked her hand, so she did her favourite thing with him. Took each of his ears and rubbed up to their tips. She luxuriated in the softness of them when the rest of his fur was bristled like his personality.

When he rubbed his head against her arm, she leaned down and rubbed her head with his. Oh, she missed him, missed their time together.

When he suddenly stilled, she let him go. He was wild and she needed to get dressed.

The sun was not up, but the darkness was already lessening and she hurried to find Bram outside the passage. His clothing was various shades of brown and he tied his hair back. He couldn't hide the colour, but like this, he almost blended in.

No, he couldn't blend in, merely standing with his back to her, he had a presence that couldn't be ignored. How was she to tempt birds to her lime sticks if he was nearby? Then he turned to her and smiled, and she wasn't irritated by his easy ways. For once, she felt as though she understood that smile; for the first time, she felt like smiling, too.

'Did you bring food?' she asked. It was customary for the hunting party to bring a breakfast and she had forgotten.

'Nae worries, I have food. Where is your dog?'

'At home or in the woods on the other side of the fields. He knows not to come with me today.'

'How?'

She shrugged. 'Most likely because you are here.'

Bram looked away, a crease between his brows as if what she had said troubled him.

It didn't bother her that Dog wasn't with them.

She wanted this time with Bram. Their marriage and the way he made her feel was a surprise.

His reaction, silent, stunned, when she told him of the English's arrival was a surprise. Then last night in their marriage bed. She knew there was more to consummate their marriage. Knew he had not found the same pleasure as she.

But they didn't know each other well. She thought, perhaps, he was being patient with her. If so, he was more considerate and kind than she had thought him.

He teased her about taking her hunting today, but she couldn't help thinking it had to do with her telling him of the English raid. That she shared something painful with him and he was giving something back.

No one had done that for her before.

Maybe today, they could understand each other more. She appreciated his patience, but she still wanted a kiss.

Why hadn't they kissed? For a moment this morning, she thought he'd wanted to, but then he laughed and wished her to ready herself. She couldn't dress fast enough. She was outside, free and no longer idle. She was here to hunt and she wanted to show him what she could do.

They reached the outer edge of the forest. They'd have to travel far into the trees to get any decent hunting in. They'd also need to be quiet, so she stopped. 'What food did you bring?'

He reached into the satchel at his side and pulled out a fresh loaf of bread and strips of boar.

'I doona suppose Cook gave you that loaf?' she said.

'Didn't see her there.'

'She won't be happy when she learns of this.'

He took a bite of bread. 'I won't be happy until she learns how to make bread.'

'What's wrong with it?'

'You're picking out stones from it.'

She shrugged. She was just happy to have food and plenty of it. Because it was getting late in the season, she worried about the hunt today. So far she'd been catching thrush and pigeons to fill their empty stores. Now she knew they'd need something more. Maybe a red deer.

'Bread's not made with stones and burnt on one side. Cheese isn't supposed to fall apart like it does here and broth with soup is to have flavour. It doesn't have to be this way.'

She was glad to be hunting, but she didn't want to hear Bram's complaints. Was he supposed to complain, when this was his clan as well as hers? 'I doona care for...keep matters. Besides, this clan's cooking is now yours. We doona have the—'

'Nae, lass, you misunderstand me,' he interrupted. 'My concerns have nothing to do with Fergusson resources. Although stones in the bread can be avoided with the proper milling, sifting and baking. I aim to repair that this winter, but not because of me. It's for you. And I know you doona care for matters involving the keep. You're barely inside enough to see cobwebs let alone be concerned about them. But that isn't my point either. What I want to say is there is better bread, there are better things, *for you.*'

To cover her sudden unease at Bram's kindness, she took a drink of water. She was unused to such consideration, although…she was beginning to believe she deserved more. That Fate didn't hate her or her clan. Bram was making her believe, but experience taught her to be cautious.

His offering kindness and talking of her deserving more was almost worse than his complaints. 'What would I know of better things? This is the way life is, this is the way bread is and siege warlords from different clans telling me there's something different won't change anything. Especially one who thinks life is easy.'

'Life isn't easy. It's never easy. But how we look at it, how we approach it, can be.'

Could it be as easy as that? No matter what they shared in the stables and again last night, it seemed sudden, so how could she trust it? The loss of the past year, her anger at Bram for her father's death, her need for revenge when he didn't come to protect them. Her clan hurting, hungry, desperate. How could a simple marriage and him taking her hunting suddenly ease her pain and anger of the past year? It *was* too easy.

She shrugged. 'We need to set traps along these runs before we go any deeper into the forest.'

Bram had never met anyone so difficult and he couldn't concentrate on the traps they were setting, not when Lioslath purposefully ignored him. Not when she knelt in the damp forest floor to secure each vine.

He was riveted. It was how she closed her eyes and breathed in the pungent foliage and mist swirling around them. She loved her home and the lands surrounding it.

He had insulted her again with his food comments. It wouldn't matter that he did it because he hadn't liked her picking stones from her bread. But it did matter that she believed she didn't deserve better.

'Let me do that one,' he said, when the vine wouldn't secure to the anchor.

'I can do it,' she said, as the contorted stick snapped.

He'd spent enough time with Gaira to know not to say anything, but he could do nothing about his expression.

'Are you laughing?'

'Nae, but would you allow me to tunnel just here?' He pointed with his foot to where the ground was well-packed. She'd found a good animal trail.

Standing, she handed him part of the woven vine. He found a sharp rock to dig deeper into the dirt so the stick wouldn't snap.

'I'd think you'd be better at this than you are,' he teased.

'I am,' she retorted. 'I proved that at the competition.'

'Nae, I mean the tunnelling part.' He had to look up at her to gather her expression. Guilt and unease on how to reply, but there was hurt there as well.

'I understood it,' he said, softening his words. 'You've been maintaining it to get away from your family, true? That's why you wanted to keep it as a secret.'

'Do we need to talk of this?' She handed him a new stick to pound into the ground.

They didn't ever need to talk of it. Come spring, he'd be gone. But it didn't stop him wanting to know. 'I have family, too. I didn't have a tunnel, but there were times I wish I had.'

She sighed heavily and looked away. 'I doona use it to get away from my family now. I laboured to maintain it because my stepmother would lock me in the room beneath the floor-boards.'

He hadn't known. With legs and knees shaking, he stood and brushed the dirt off his hands, ready to provide comfort and to hold her. But her eyes, now alight, weren't on his.

'Here, hold these,' she said. She handed him her satchel and bow and arrows before walking quickly to a tree, grabbing the lowest branch and hauling herself up.

Often a member of the hunting party climbed a tree to spy the choicest sport, but he hadn't expected her to do it so swiftly. He couldn't dismiss her skills now, when he wanted to clutch her to him and she was spotting fresh game tracks.

'Where are they?' His breath hitched as she leaned out from the last branch.

'Off to your far left,' she whispered.

He didn't look where she pointed while she shimmied down the trunk. When she was safely in front of him, with one arm he pulled her close.

'The tracks,' she whispered.

Bram noticed her heart flutter. Oh, he liked her short hair. Liked that they could share the forest.

He didn't like the stories she kept telling him. 'Lioslath? I didn't know the tunnel—'

'I doona want to talk of it,' she said.

'Why did you tell me?'

'You told me of Irvette…and we're married now. But I can't say any more.'

He didn't want to let go. There was heartache in her trembling voice. But he, too, wanted them to share a carefree day.

'I want this day, too,' he answered. For now, it would be enough.

Taking a couple steps away, her eyes not meeting his, she pointed. 'There's fresh deer spoor. I thought it was too late in the season, but I saw the herd beyond the next hill. The wind's in our favour and they are all mature enough.'

'How mature?' Mature red deer had prongs.

She shrugged again. 'Enough. Better for us.'

Better for them meant very mature and definitely dangerous.

Her hunting was unexpected. Everything about her was. Even in this brief time together, he could see she didn't take care of the manor, or the food, or the general household. With her hunting, however, she came alive…shined.

'How did you become skilled at this?'

'Hunting?' She shrugged. 'Aindreas's father taught us. He's an excellent tracker.'

He suddenly didn't care about hunting or tracking. 'Aindreas. You've done this with him?'

'Aye, I wouldn't go after large game by myself.'

'Dressed like that?'

'Of course I wear these.' She gestured to her clothes clinging to her thighs. She passed him and headed further into the forest. 'Have you ever hunted in a dress?'

He didn't like that Aindreas had been here with her like this. Didn't like that Aindreas had seen her haul herself up a tree or slide down. She was his wife.

Temporarily. All of this was temporary. He had duties to protect his clan. He had to return. It didn't matter even if he could stay. She didn't want him. She married him only because her clan needed her to. She wanted him gone and showed him so several times. Yet he felt uneasy, knowing that when he was gone, Aindreas would still be here.

Balance. He had to find it again…as he always found it. Through humour, through distraction. 'Actually I have.'

Lioslath stopped. 'You have what?'

'Hunted in a dress.'

There formed another crease between her brows and he grinned to see it. 'It was rumoured I hunted all my life, even when I was in my mother's womb.'

She almost smiled then and he wanted to see more. He shouldn't want to see more.

'So you're saying you like it here?' she asked.

'Being here amongst the trees? Aye.' He

kicked the dirt, needing the distraction from Lioslath's almost-smile. 'You come here often as well. Have you taken your brothers?'

'They never asked,' she said.

'Never asked? When Gillean wants a hunter's knife and Eoin asks my men how they earned their scars?'

She turned her head quickly as if she saw something he could not see. 'We need to hunt and I need you to be quiet.'

When she walked deeper into the forest, he let her. She was avoiding his questions and it was probably for the best. He had questions for Lioslath, but with this marriage, he didn't deserve answers. He didn't want to think that maybe she needed distractions from marriage nights like him. That wouldn't help matters at all.

When she reached a copse of trees with low shrubs, she stopped, and he exhaled. Loudly. She gave him a look and he grinned.

'You stay here,' she whispered.

'You will not stay with me?'

Bram was teasing her again. Teasing, even after he asked about her siblings and her tunnel. Grave matters she didn't want to talk of today.

Though he teased and laughed, she was beginning to believe he understood her. It was his liking the forest and hunting. It was his understanding her need for the tunnel, and her need

not to talk about it. There was an accord beginning between them she didn't expect and which
she couldn't trust. Not yet. Wishing for a better
life for her and her clan, she married him. But
she'd been disappointed too many times in the
past. She needed time before she would depend
on him.

So she tried to ignore his steady gait and the
way he watched her. She also tried to ignore
when he made his jests or when he was purposefully too loud.

But she couldn't ignore his voice, which sent
shivers down her, or the way he asked her to stay
with him, which reminded her of last night and
his anchoring arm.

'You're going to remain here,' she said. 'And
be quiet and still.'

He was right that she wanted to show off, but
it wouldn't happen if she simply stared at him
until she admitted his voice affected her. 'You're
either hunting with me or not. Either you're dependable or you can go home,' she said.

'Oh, I'm dependable,' he said. With a too-
confident grin, Bram leaned back against a tree.

Lioslath strode to another tree, where the
wind was in her favour, and she adjusted herself until she was comfortable. It could be hours
before anything approached them. There was

nothing more they could do but stay quiet, stay still and wait.

Waiting had never been an issue before. Now, however, it held some…expectation. A feeling of anticipation that shivered over her skin. She didn't have to guess why.

It was Bram, who was as still as the tree he leaned against. It was the fact that before she left he brushed his hand against hers. That simple caress had unerringly spread to the rest of her, too. She swore she felt it now.

He tied his hair back at the base of his neck. Between that and the dampness of the morning, she didn't have to worry about its colour giving away their position. His clothes, too, for once were of a dark colour, which surprised her. Ever since he'd arrived at the keep, he'd worn coloured clothes. As if he wanted to impress her with the Colquhoun wealth.

She hadn't thought he owned clothes like the ones he currently wore. Dark, the fine weave cutting across his form like a second skin. He seemed comfortable and they suited him more than his stiffer clothing. If so, why had he been wearing the other clothes all these weeks?

She preferred him looking this way. She preferred what he showed her of himself. Indomitable, too easy with his laughter, but also his patience and kindness.

She…desired him. It was there in her shortness of breath, in how her eyes constantly strayed to him. It was in her heated blood as she remembered last night.

It was in his watchful gaze. There was a certain core of quietude within him that held his vibrancy steady.

The trees were like that. Holding still, strong, but cradling a burst of life within. She could breathe with her trees. And she was finding with Bram, when he was outside with her, she could breathe with him, too.

Watching Bram watch her, she almost missed the movement to her left as the deer entered the little copse.

Disjointed, relieved her thoughts had kept her still, she aimed and let the arrow fly.

Chapter Sixteen

'Tell me what happened when the English came,' Bram said.

Lioslath's hands jerked and she cut the rabbit instead of its skin. It had been hours since she felled the deer and they returned to the traps for the other game. Hours, and Bram hadn't talked and neither had she. They had fallen into a comfortable compatibility as if they'd done this all their lives together.

At ease, he appeared content to be here with her. She couldn't fully contain the feelings bubbling inside her. Feelings she hadn't had in so long she hardly recognised them. And they were happening so fast. After so much pain, she thought this marriage was simply another sacrifice. It was like bracing herself for the pain of the firepit, and instead feeling Dog's tongue against her hand.

But Dog never asked her questions she didn't want to answer.

'The English?' she said. 'I told you.'

'There's more, though, isn't there?'

So much more, but she thought she'd have a reprieve in the quiet of the forest.

'I know nae one was killed and I can see the damage, but I doona know how *you* fared.'

He wanted to know her feelings? Their torches burning brightly, the English had swarmed the village like darkness. At any moment she had been sure they would burn their homes and slaughter her entire clan. But they kept the torches burning brightly while they harvested the fields, while they drank their ale and stole the winter supplies. Torches burned for days, until they were tossed upon the fields, ensuring nothing would be left.

'I... It is too fine a day for that,' she said finally.

'There's more you didn't tell me of the English and your hair,' he said softly. 'I know it isn't vanity that makes you cut it still. You work too hard to care for appearances.'

She didn't like that he noticed her severing the growing locks. She didn't want to explain why she needed more time before she saw it long again. 'Working has a purpose and there's always been much to do here.'

'And appearances are not useful?'

She knew she wasn't beautiful and hadn't cared before. For some reason, she cared now. 'Nae, they are like your games and play. Useless. They doona feed families.'

'Ah, but your hunting is a game you play. You enjoy it, like I do my games.'

Play. She hadn't done so since her mother's death. She didn't want to think of her mother's death. 'This is a foolish conversation.'

'And you are stubborn. You have more to tell me and are avoiding the conversation.'

'There is nae conversation. We have more of these to skin and hang in the tree before we get to the deer,' she said. The deer they'd dragged until it rested at an incline away from where they stood. Later, they'd hook the tendons behind its hooves to hang it from a tree.

For now the rabbits kept them busy. But she could feel Bram waiting. It made her hands unsteady. Already she had difficulty skinning the little beasts.

'Lioslath.'

Relentless. Relentless since the day he crested the hill and she needed to turn his thoughts elsewhere. 'We have work to do. Why can't we just work?' She glanced over at him, but he appeared engrossed in his task. She knew he was pretending.

'It doesn't make sense! Why talk of my hair, when we're doing this? Why bring this up now? When there's—'

'Your head's bent at your work. I can see… Lioslath, you have moles behind your ear.'

Her spots. He noticed her spots. Kept noticing them. She thought he might be relentless when it came to those as well.

She turned back to the rabbit while Bram became quiet. Too quiet. Her hands fumbled at her task until she gave up and threw the rabbit to the ground and washed her hands and knife with the skeins of water. 'I doona want to talk of my hair.'

But she knew the mistake the moment she repeated it. By protesting again after Bram's silence, she revealed her feelings about cutting it.

It had to be last night and today with their hunting together. Her noticing how he looked amongst her trees, as if he belonged. She never revealed her feelings. What would he do with them?

What had he done with them so far? Wary, she watched as he finished his rabbit and picked up hers to finish as well.

Idleness. She became idle and this Colquhoun was doing the work. It only increased her agitation. So she stood, paced, but it didn't ease her. Bram was waiting for an answer as if he knew it was coming, and she was beginning to believe he was right.

'It happened so fast,' she whispered past the tightening in her throat. The words not a relief, but a slice across a non-healing wound. 'I think I cut myself more than the hair.'

She thought her explanation would be enough, but then she saw Bram wince. Was he thinking of her cutting herself? The blood hardly mattered. She'd been in agony over her hair.

He finished the rabbit and stood. 'It hurt you in other ways,' he said, arranging the rabbits on a log.

He wasn't looking at her and yet he knew. How could he know her so soon? Was it as simple as watching her for all those weeks as she had him? Maybe he wanted to understand her the same way she wanted to with him. Could she tell him?

He brought her to the forest to hunt and they were married. They were supposed to talk of feelings and their future together. Since their marriage, it seemed as if Bram was willing to let go of the past. Of how she treated him. Of their heated words. Shouldn't she, if she could, do the same? But she'd never had someone to talk to before. 'I'm not used to talking.'

'I know,' he answered, as he grabbed the

skeins to wash his hands. 'I've seen it. Just…
can you forgive me if I forget?'

'Forgive you because I doona talk?'

'Forgive me because I ask questions of you.
It's… I forget. It wasn't supposed to be like this
between us.' He shook his head and smiled at
her. 'My questions are improper given our agreement. I have nae right to know and you needn't
tell me.'

Lioslath waited for him to continue, but he
didn't and that wasn't what she expected. Bram
would never simply capitulate.

He asked about her hair and then stopped himself. He did want to know. Was he being patient
or kind? Was this sharing part of his telling of
his family and his grief over Irvette? He'd said
it wasn't supposed to be like this between them.
Maybe something about what she was feeling towards him had taken him by surprise, too.

'My mother had long hair,' she said. 'It was
glorious. Not this colour. I got that from my father, but the way it waved down to her waist.
Mine…was the same as hers.'

The only indication that she surprised him
was his sudden stillness. Then he asked, 'What
was she like?'

'She was good and kind. Loving.' She continued her pacing, realised her legs felt as her hands
did, that they were shaking as if they couldn't

stay within her skin. 'The clan loved her, as did
my father. She was determined and liked her
own way, but always gentle and soft-spoken. The
keep was a home with her in it.'

It was all she could say as the words choked
in her throat and her eyes burned with unshed
tears. She looked around for something to keep
her busy, but there was only the deer left and that
would require his help. She felt weak, vulnerable. Even with his kindness, she wasn't ready
to reveal her weakness.

Bram wouldn't push for more, but he wouldn't
turn his head and allow Lioslath to gather her
emotions. He could barely contain his own. So
much pain in her life, but how could she not
know the truth? He had to tell her.

'I have nae doubt your hair was glorious,' he
said. 'And I can imagine it rivalling any night
sky. Yet…I like it now.'

'As short as a man's?' she said. 'It's shorter
than yours. The curl is almost gone. It's why I
cut it again. I doona trust if it'll be the same as
hers any more.'

Difficult, stubborn, and she deserved more
than his first feeble words. The question was
whether he could give her more. He held her
last night, but hadn't found the pleasure she had.
Even if he did, he would feel the same. Tightly

coiled, protective and longing with the need to kiss her.

'I find your hair beautiful, Lioslath,' he said.

She turned to argue, but stopped when he held up his hand. He needed to say the words and she needed to listen to them. Though he was barely containing his desire for her, he stepped closer.

'I find it beautiful because it means I can see how expansive your eyes are. Like the sky.'

Her eyes widened at his words. Oh, that pleased him. Too much. He had a duty to his family. He had a duty and a promise to her that they would not consummate this marriage. He could not desire her this much.

'Your hair would fall and conceal too much of your eyes, or the crease you get between your brows when you're cross with me. I love every expression you reveal and wouldn't wish anything to cover them,' he continued.

Her eyes widened more until he felt he was drowning in the sky she showed him. 'I love your hair because I can see the curve and line of your neck, like a path to those spots behind your ear. Those spots have prompted questions I have nae right to ask, but want to taste all the same.'

'Taste?'

His desire for her only increased with every moment, and now...with one word, he was vanquished. 'Aye, and I need to add to our marriage agreement again.'

Lioslath spun with Bram's words. They were flattery, aye, but he meant them. There was no teasing light in his eyes or coaxing words. In truth, he looked tortured as he said them and now he looked resigned. Should a man talking of his wife's appearance look resigned?

'I doona ken this bargaining you do,' she said.

'How could you not?' Another step. 'We have a marriage agreement, like your father's. I mean to keep it. Yet the talking and hunting was not a distraction. In fact, it may have made it worse. But I hold hope, since you changed our agreement terms first. So I'm countering. I want my lips, my mouth, my kisses added to this marriage.'

She felt too…open for this conversation. After the hunt and their unexpected accord with each other. Revealing the truth of her hair and the loss of her mother had been too much. This was… overwhelming.

'Is this a game you're playing?'

A small smile. 'Does it feel like a game we play?'

'Nae,' she said. How was she to know of games, or bargaining, or any of this? She agreed to this marriage as a sacrifice. But thus far, they only shared pleasure and now he talked of kisses. Oh, she wanted those kisses.

'You're right, this is not a game, but there is something...' Bram swiftly looked down, away, his frown deepening, as he pursed his lips before he looked to her. 'Lioslath, will you let me add my kiss to our marriage?'

He jested. Kisses were already part of marriage. Maybe Bram was simply fond of bargaining.

'Nae,' she whispered, although what and why she was denying she didn't know. Maybe she didn't want any more of Bram's bargaining and talking.

Because if that alertness was in him, it was doubly so in her. He might be enveloping her with his words of kisses and his voice holding the promise of them, but she was clenching them tightly to her until the air she breathed disappeared.

'Nae? Yet you've added my hands and this is only a bit more.' He tilted his head. 'Was it too much last night, with my hands? *Our* hands.'

She didn't know she was walking backwards until her back met a great oak. But Bram did and he put his hands against the massive trunk to cage her there. Her eyes absorbed every one of his features. The way the trees' canopy deepened the grey of his eyes and the shadows of his eyelashes. There was a hint of colour around the sharp slants of his cheekbones as if he exerted himself, though he stood very still.

'I'm being...practical. The forest is impractical.' It was. She wanted more than his kisses and that couldn't happen here.

It was the way his lips moved when he whispered, 'Impractical?'

'The ground is wet, Bram.'

Bram's eyes slid to her lips; his words a hoarse whisper. 'Ah, you can't know what you do with your words.'

It was the way his very breath and voice caressed her. She wanted more. When had her anger at him turned to this? It seemed everything that had begun between them led to this. As if Bram's relentless siege and endless demands led her here: her back against a tree with nowhere to go except where he wanted to take her. And where she wanted to go.

'What do I do with my words?' she asked.

His lips hovered along her temple and down her cheek. 'Make a man imagine things. Things that would make him want you more.'

'My words have never had such a response before.'

A soft chuckle near her jawline made her body shiver and her skin tighten. 'Ah, see, even that answer tempts a man.'

She might not know where he wanted to take her, but she had gone somewhere when his hand entwined with hers, and she knew there was more. Like kisses. And yet he talked.

'Tempts you?' she said.

'Aye, and right now I'd kill any other man who was tempted by you.'

His hands skimmed across her shoulders, down her arms and along the backs of her hands at her sides. They continued their whispering caress as they retraced their path back up. Each soft, repeating stroke embedding the heat and want and intent deeper in her.

When his roughened fingertips glided over her bare neck, a sound escaped her lips.

'Why do you do this?' she said. Why was he still talking and bartering when she wanted more of his touch, more of him. If he felt the need to do it, she needed to understand. Then she would kiss him.

'I'm feeling the softness of your skin and craving more.' Lowering his head, he gave more almost-kisses. His lips, ephemeral yet penetrating, hovered along her neck, across her collarbone and up to the other side. 'Add my kisses, Lioslath. You can't know what you do to me with your denying.'

His words continued. A litany. She felt every

one. 'Do you feel like I do when I hear your voice?'

A pause. 'My voice?'

'Aye, it seeps and unfurls inside me.'

'My voice does this?' he asked, but his voice held a different note now.

'Aye.'

She felt his half-smile against her. 'Ah, lass, I do feel like that, but the fact you do *and* you're giving words to it?'

'Words to it.'

'Those kinds of words give satisfaction to a man. Words I could use, love. Words I intend to use.' The barest skimming of his lips. 'Add my kisses.'

Talking, bartering and negotiating. Still. His touches remained light, though she felt the feral heat of him pressing against her. The air between them felt like a cruel caress, too soft to ease. And her own body ached for something stronger, solid. Him.

Shuddering, he pulled away. Grey eyes besieged by need, breaths stuttering through starved lungs. His light touch now digging, releasing. Kneading.

She watched as his eyes darkened even more. Felt as if her own must be darkening, as if her vision was blurring, until all she could see was the continued asking locked inside Bram's eyes.

'Stop talking,' she said. She still didn't understand, but she'd had enough of his bartering. They were married and she wanted his kiss.

'Lioslath, please, the agreement.'

Frustration and desire roiled and collided inside her. 'Aye, Bram, I accept. Please, your voice, your hands…your kisses.'

Hands suddenly cupped her face, fingers tunnelled through her short hair, his heavy body pressed her to the tree. The ache inflamed and pierced until she parted her lips to let in more air, to release a cry, and his lips, finally, met hers.

It was a kiss too long denied. Too overwhelming and yet not enough. She protested it being not enough. He answered her sounds with his own.

But his kiss only continued to coax as his fingers released her hair, as his palms slid to the nape of her neck. Her breaths stuttered when he grazed his teeth along her lower lip, when he enclosed her upper lip between his own and gently sucked.

Her own needs demanded the feel of his hair still tied, and the heat and slickness of sweat on his neck despite the coolness of the morning.

She pulled until he pressed even more against her, but it wasn't enough. She wanted harder kisses, hungry kisses. They were in the forest and she wanted more of everything.

'Lioslath?' he said, her name a rough sound.

His lips hovered over hers. Close, but not nearly close enough. She dug her fingers into his shoulders.

'Do you ache, lass? I can give you more kisses,' he whispered. 'Just more kisses, just more touches. Let me show you.'

She wanted nothing else.

Tilting his head, he kissed the mole above her lips. Then along her jaw and down the lines of her neck.

She arched her neck to give him more access and he released an approving sound. With both hands, he skimmed the backs of hers and up her arms. There, his fingertips traced patterns along her collarbone as he lingered more kisses along her neck and jaw. He repeated a pattern her body understood even when she couldn't.

Then his fingertips lowered, his palms cupped against her thin tunic so she felt her breasts swell to reach his palms and her nipples hardened before his thumbs flickered and pressed over them. All along, his mouth increased the pressure of his kisses.

Oh, his kisses. She knew the compulsion for more. Her own body was giving in to it. She was no longer leaning against the tree, but towards Bram and his kisses and his hands. Her own hands finding balance and heat and need as they gripped his sides.

There was no warning when Bram suddenly sank to his knees before her and her hands found his shoulders for support.

Want and need swirled in the grey depths, but also…amusement.

'What do you do?' she asked again.

'I'm kissing you. As only I can here. As only I'm allowed to do. We can't do any more. And this…even this may prove too much for me.'

'How are we to kiss like this?'

Bram's hands were now on the outside of her thighs. The heat of his palms arced up her body until she restlessly shifted to bring his hands more central.

Amusement and desire darkening and flushing his face, Bram made a choked sound and leaned his head against her stomach.

'There's another way,' she whispered, realising now what he meant. 'There's another way of kissing.'

His amusement increased as did the curve to his lips, which looked almost wicked to her now she knew what he intended.

'You can't, here,' she gasped.

'Aye, it's possible. Will you let me? Let me touch you, kiss you, here?'

His voice, his kisses, and just where she ached.

'Aye, please, Bram. Now.'

As if he feared she would pull away, his hands wrapped around the backs of her thighs, his thumbs grazing the curves of her bottom.

She gasped as his heated caresses continued their path, till they were between her legs. His fingers just...*there*.

'I'm liking this hunting outfit, Lioslath. Been liking it because it reveals the shape of your legs, and the shape of your—' He stopped, but she knew what he meant as his thumbs swept upwards and she flushed.

She couldn't speak, not when he indicated with a slight pressure for her thighs to widen. Not when she complied.

'That's a lass.' His fingers caressing, his words encouraging. 'Again.'

She widened her step again. She was fully clothed and felt bared to him, knowing she would be entirely bare to him soon.

'There, aye.' His eyes never left hers as he slowly stroked his hands around her thighs and up to her hips. There he loosened her hose until they fell.

Her short tunic and widened stance were no barrier to his eyes or to his hands, to his fingertips trailing from the fallen hose and up along her inner calves and around the backs of her knees.

Gentle, so gentle, and yet she was acutely

aware of the roughness of his calluses, and the strength restrained behind those fingers.

She understood now why his hands fascinated her. They were capable of speaking to her body, like his voice, enfolding her not with sounds, but with touch.

Her body knew this. It knew as Bram's fingers trailed closer and stopped. She knew as she felt the urging to widen her legs even more.

'I mean to kiss you,' Bram coaxed. 'Kiss you till the ache goes away. You'll let me now, will you?'

Was he asking permission? 'Why ask? Why… stop?'

A bemused curve came to his lips as she surprised him. 'I didn't want to startle you.'

'It's all…startling.'

His eyes dropped to where she was bared, his fingers trailing around, coiling the heat even tighter. Making her ache…more. 'Aye, it is,' he whispered reverently.

'For you, too?'

'I cannot describe.' His fingers were no longer skimming, but stroking. His palms, no longer hovering, but caressing and giving heat. 'Let me show you.'

Bram kissed. Tiny encouraging kisses that were strange and wondrous and needed. So wanted and yet…and yet— 'It's not,' she gasped, 'lessening…the ache.'

Bram's hands caressed around and between her opened thighs to stroke her there.

'Please,' she demanded. She felt the gripping fluttering of his fingers, the heat of his hands on the backs of her thighs and the increased pressure of his rhythmic kisses.

Lioslath fell against the tree, giving herself to the support of his hands and the bracing of his arms along her sides.

She gave herself to his kiss, to his mouth, to his tongue, her ache only increasing. Increasing again. She felt his lips, the wickedness of it. Wickedness that tightened the ache until she cried out when it broke within her.

Bram didn't want to stop. Not his hands, nor his kisses. Not the feel of Lioslath against him, nor her taste. But when her trembles turned to shivers and he felt her tentative touch on his head, he eased away.

'Lass, love, what you bring me to.' He hurt, but it was the sweetest, most pleasurable ache. A pleasure he would share again and again, and they could. He continued to kiss along her thighs, felt the tremors in her lessening and his own increasing. Increasing to something he could barely contain. 'What I want to do.'

Lioslath couldn't catch her breath and the ache

she thought was unbearable increased. It was Bram's kisses, his words, his breaths in short bursts spilling against her bared legs.

She touched along the parts of him she could reach. His shoulders, the backs of his hands as they caressed along the width of her hips.

'Then why doona you?' She slid her fingers to lock with his as if to restrain him there, when she truly wanted to press his hands and slide them against her.

But he stilled almost as if she did restrain him. 'I can't. Not here.'

The forest was still wet. 'Then let's return to the keep.'

'We can't return to the keep. Not yet. Not when you have me like you do. I doona trust myself. I'd go too far.'

She didn't understand this conversation. She didn't, but they were married, so she needed to understand it. 'Aren't we supposed to?'

He jerked, as if she suddenly released restraints on him. Then he stilled, so still she couldn't see his breaths. And his stillness held him away from her until she felt the cold morning mist.

Then he removed his hands from her sides and his mouth from her thighs, but he didn't straighten her clothes or stand. He stayed crouched before her.

'Nae, we aren't supposed to,' he said, his voice just as cold as the mist. 'We're never supposed to. Not like that, not fully... If we do, I cannot leave.'

It was as if he pulled her suddenly out of her precious canopy of trees and into the most unforgiving sunlight. The harsh rays burned her skin, burned *through* her as she remembered every single word he told her when he proposed marriage. Her insides burned to ash as she remembered every single word of their conversations since then. It was wrong. She had to be remembering wrongly.

She pulled at her clothes, her fingers clumsy. But her anger was dagger sharp. 'You're leaving.'

'As we planned, as we discussed. As soon as the clan is secure, after winter, I will go.' A little frown. 'I told you this, that we'd have a marriage like your father's.'

'My father married your sister.'

'Aye, a temporary marriage.'

Surely it was a cruel jest. So much damage had been done. So much pain. So much permanent loss had been caused by that marriage. 'There was nothing *temporary* about it.'

'You didn't know? How could you not know?' Bram stood, his breath shaky. 'I thought you understood! It was a marriage for a year only. A marriage in name only. It was perfect for your father and perfect for us as well.'

She searched his eyes for his familiar amusement, for some sign his words were a lie. It was happening so fast, but everything was happening so fast. And she was clumsy, unused to people, unused to sophisticated talking. She forced the words out. 'Nae, this isn't true. You…you *jest*.'

'Nae! You get what you truly desire, protection, my wealth, and then I will leave. You get me off your land. You've wanted nothing more than to have me leave. You wouldn't, couldn't, want a marriage in truth!'

'You…you cannot mean this.'

'Aye, I mean this and so did you. We agreed to a temporary marriage like your father's. It's the only reason you so readily agreed, surely. You agreed because you want me to leave, to disappear, haven't wanted me here at all. So my staying—'

'Is temporary.' She bit out the words. Her insides, burnt to ash, were blowing away to leave her empty. If she stood here much longer, listening to his words, to this agony he caused her, she knew there would be nothing left of her at all.

Her marriage wasn't real. All the expectations for the clan brimming inside her today were temporary.

She was temporary.

Humiliation fumbled her fingers on her hosiery ties. Shame had her tightening the fabric until it bit her skin. She sacrificed herself to save her clan and it was all for naught. Before there was nothing left of her, she tried to push past him.

But fear stopped her.

Chapter Seventeen

His body thrumming with desire and burning with anger, Bram blinked hard against the terror in Lioslath's eyes.

When the hairs on the back of his neck prickled, he understood the danger they were in.

The forest was quiet. Too quiet. Which meant there were larger and far more dangerous creatures than them nearby.

'Lio—'

'A wolf, to my left in the shrubs.' She pressed herself firmly against the tree. 'I can't see the others.'

Wolves hunted only in packs.

The deer she shot lay far behind him on an incline to gently drain the blood from its body. They could have laid no better lure for the wolves.

It wouldn't take long for the wolves to realise it was only them to protect the horde of free food. Anything they did to protect themselves would appear like a threat when the leavings were so good.

At least Lioslath's back was to the tree; he only had to protect her front. To do so, he needed to release his sword.

'He's only inspecting us,' she said. 'I still can't see the others.'

Neither could he, which meant they were most likely surrounded and some could be creeping behind the oak.

'My dagger's there by your foot,' she whispered.

He'd have to crouch to get it. If he did, he might appear docile or fearful. The only advantages they had were their size and the wolves' innate desire to avoid them. If he appeared weak in any way, they would be killed before he could turn his sword to pierce them.

'It stays.'

'Nae.'

Did she think she'd defend herself? It was a good hunting knife, but it could only be used up close. He'd die before he'd let them get that near to her.

Then he saw them. Two wolves, one on either side of them and circling the tree.

The one on his right was brown, gaunt. Its

head was bent low and its eyes were fixated on the deer behind Bram.

The one slowly approaching on his left was magnificent. He was a bright silver grey with streaks of white. Impossible for him to hide and he was a wolf in his prime. The only way he had survived to his age was through battle. The moment Bram turned to brandish his sword was the moment he and Lioslath would die.

'We're surrounded,' Lioslath whispered, the wolves coming into her vision.

'Stay still,' he whispered.

'You have a weapon.'

'We let them take what they want.' The deer was prize enough. As long as he and Lioslath were never perceived as a threat, they wouldn't be attacked.

'I can see them now. You cannot. They're looking at us. They'll kill us.'

'Only if we move,' he said. 'If we let them take away the food, they'll leave us alone.'

She shook her head; her face adamant.

Fear. He'd never thought he'd see fear in her eyes. Starving, half fainting, she defied him from the first.

'I know wolves. These ones won't leave. I need my dagger.'

Her hunting skills surprised him. But he had no intention of giving her freedom now.

Her back was protected by the great oak. If he could turn around, he'd be able to protect her front. It was his duty and right as her husband to keep her safe. It was all he intended to do.

Slowly, he released his sword from his side and heard a sharp growl from the wolf in the low shrubs.

Lioslath's eyes darted to her dagger on the ground.

'Stay still,' he ordered.

He knew when the wolves reached the deer, their unearthly silence now marred with voracious growls.

Lioslath shifted and he leaned forward to block her the best he could. Her eyes stayed riveted to the scene before her. His eyes stayed on hers, but he heard the wolves behind him. The crunch of leaves, the menacing breaths of communication between them.

Moments passed as Bram felt the sweat trickle down his back and his sword hand tightened with nerves. He flexed his fingers.

'They're taking the meat into the trees.' She enunciated each word. Her eyes met his, and he saw the beginnings of relief. Then he heard the increasing growls and Lioslath's eyes widened.

'The deer seems to be…seems to be snagged on something.' Her voice shook. 'They can't take it that way. The grey is beginning to drag it towards us. The other one doesn't want to.'

There was no way he'd be able to keep his back to two fighting wolves.

'The brown one keeps looking at us.' Her eyes pleaded with Bram. 'I need my dagger.'

'Nae.'

'If we doona move, they'll attack.'

'We'll move out of their way.'

'With your back turned?'

No more arguments. Hunching his shoulders and keeping his head down, Bram slowly turned.

The two wolves instantly lifted their heads; their long snouts pulled back to bare their blood-reddened fangs. Their muzzles and sides were now bloodied from the deer stretched between them.

The wolves were much nearer than he thought. A cold intelligence gleamed out of both their eyes. The grey had two different-coloured ones. There was nothing other than curiosity in him until he saw Bram's sword, and then his eyes went to Bram's again.

'Seen one of these before, have you?' Carefully, he hid the sword behind his back. If the wolf attacked, he'd lose precious seconds, but there wasn't another way to convey he wouldn't use his weapon.

After tense moments, the grey bit the deer to

drag it towards their tree. The other wolf tugged it the other way. The wolves' growls increased until the third wolf gave a piercing howl.

When they swung their eyes towards the agonised sound, the wolf collapsed. No longer hidden by the shrubbery, the pregnant female wolf started labour.

The grey bounded away from the deer and Bram rounded with sword out, to protect them, but that wolf paid them no heed.

Too late to realise he'd taken his eyes off the brown wolf.

He attacked. Instantly, Lioslath hit the ground. Before she could reach her dagger, before Bram could complete the downward thrust into the wolf's neck, it clamped its jaws on her lower leg.

Lioslath cried out. Bram roared and sliced through the wolf's neck. He swung around to the other two before the wolf crashed to the ground.

The grey stood sentinel over the female. His fur was on end, his ears were flat, his snarl was vicious. But he did not leave his female and neither would Bram leave his.

He pointed his sword towards the grey before he darted his eyes towards Lioslath. Awake, in agonising pain, tears streaked down her cheeks. Her eyes were angry and accusing.

All his fault. 'I have to get you out of here.'

'Not yet.' She clenched her teeth.

Too much pain. He didn't want to move her, but there could be others. 'We must.'

Bram knew the grey would not attack. They both had their females to protect and the third, now dead, had instigated the fight. In the law of the forest, Bram was within his rights to defend.

Keeping his eyes on the grey, he swiped his sword against his legs. He would lose the use of his sword arm while he carried Lioslath, so he would use the dripping of wolf blood to warn any others they'd pass.

When he resheathed the sword, the grey returned his attention to his female.

And so did Bram. Clutching her leg, Lioslath seemed diminished. Blood poured from the gash on her leg.

Kneeling beside her, and tearing off his tunic, he said, 'This is going to hurt.'

'It hurts now,' she bit out.

Noticing her hands trembled in pain, while his in fear, he ripped and tore his tunic into jagged strips. 'Is it broken?'

'I can't tell.'

Too much pain. Laying his hands and cradling her leg, he felt along it. The bone was straight, but he felt no relief. They had far to travel. He could harm her merely by carrying her, but he couldn't leave her here to seek help.

Carefully, he tightly wrapped the strips around

her leg. Lioslath's whimpers through pressed lips sliced his insides more than any sword could. Then he knotted and bound a longer strip around him and her leg for support while he carried her.

He glanced at the wolves, who waited for them to go. He couldn't get out of here fast enough.

'I'm lifting you,' he said.

Her breath coming in quick pants, she gave a curt nod. Fluidly, he rose and blackness claimed Lioslath.

Chapter Eighteen

They hadn't reached the outer homes before the villagers gave an outcry.

It was the children who reached them first. Eoin's and Gillean's eyes were wide with fear. Fyfa's eyes darted to him as much as to her sister.

He knew what they looked like. Wolf's blood splattered across their faces and torn clothes. Lioslath, unconscious, draped in his arms. Her head was at an unnatural angle as he supported her leg. Her skin was pale with a deathlike sheen.

'She's alive,' he told them. 'I need Donaldo.'

'I ran to get her,' Fyfa answered.

'She's bleeding!' Gillean reached out.

'She'll live,' he assured him. 'Thanks, lass, for getting her.'

'What happened?' Eoin asked. 'What happened to you?'

Donaldo was running and pushing fast through

the forming crowd. Then she was in front of him with her arms outstretched. He shook his head and tightened his hold.

'Wolf attack,' he said, ignoring Fyfa's distressed cry. 'It wasn't broken when we left, but I doona know now.'

'I know what to do,' Donaldo said. 'Eoin, Gillean, fetch boiling water and ale. Get others to carry it to your sister's room. Then I'll need two…nae, ten of the flattest boards and branches you can find. About this big and wide.' She demonstrated. 'Fyfa, get me some strips of old linens and fetch my pouches of herbs and pestle!'

The children hesitated, their worry turning to alarm at Donaldo's demands.

'We've got your sister and she needs your help,' he said. Fyfa tugged on the children until they ran.

Donaldo swept towards the keep and he followed behind her.

'How long has she been asleep?' she demanded.

'Since I lifted her.'

'Stayed awake during the attack?'

'Enough time to argue and blame me.'

Donaldo smiled knowingly.

'You're right to be prideful and I deserve her blame and a great deal more than that.'

'Aye, since you aren't harmed as well.' Donaldo eyed him speculatively. 'The wolf's dead?'

'Aye, I'll fetch the pelt later.'

'I'll be wanting it.'

'For healing her?'

'Nae, for refraining myself from battering you on the head.'

He nodded.

'At least you didn't smile,' Donaldo said. 'This bodes well.'

He didn't think anything boded well. When they reached their room, he laid Lioslath on the fresh linens. They would be ruined with her blood, and Lioslath would yell at the waste of that later. When she woke… If she woke.

Would she live?

There was a commotion behind him as Cook and Aindreas brought in buckets of steaming water and pitchers of ale. Fyfa hurried behind them with pouches of herbs and a mortar and pestle.

Lioslath was so pale against the linens. The starkness of the blood was a violent reminder of how he almost lost her. How he could still lose her.

It was all his fault.

When Donaldo laid her hand on his arm, he realised the boys had returned, and his hovering over Lioslath blocked their access to her.

'You need to let us tend her now,' Donaldo said, reaching for the pouches of herbs. 'She'll be fine.'

'Her leg is swelling.'

'It's straight for now. We'll keep it that way.'

'If it's broken...' Lioslath's long strides through her home, her purposeful walk as she meandered around the trees in her beloved forest. He couldn't stop the images.

'We'll see to it, Colquhoun. The rest is in God's hands.'

God's hands now, but she had been in his protective care first. 'I have healing herbs. Concoctions from home.'

Donaldo looked as though she wanted to argue, but she gave a curt nod. 'Bring them, then. I'll smell if they're still good.'

Still good. What if nothing was good enough? Lioslath was alive, but if she was crippled, if she couldn't walk again without pain... That had nothing to do with God and everything to do with his failing her.

He didn't deserve to be her husband.

'Go now. If you be wanting me to use the herbs, I'll need them.'

Everything in him protested. He wanted to stay, though he'd made the suggestion to fetch the herbs. No, he wanted more than that, he wanted to erase what he had done, what he had failed to do.

He could no longer pretend that what he felt was merely lust or attraction or a simple accord with Lioslath.

He loved her.

'Go, Colquhoun,' Donaldo demanded. 'And get the pelt before some other animal does. Or I'll have you attacked by another wolf simply to ensure I receive my pay.'

It would be the best skinned wolf there was in all of Scotland. He'd see to it.

It was night before Bram returned to Lioslath's side. Donaldo rose from the chair in the corner and walked towards him.

'Aindreas found you.' Her voice was pleased.

'Unerringly.' Even in the dark, his bruises and swollen lip had to be obvious, but he gave as good as he got. Aindreas might love Lioslath like a brother, but he was a protective brother. The fight and cooperation skinning the wolf afterwards had been a necessary conversation.

'You couldn't prepare the pelt by yourself,' Donaldo said. 'I knew you'd need help.'

'And to settle matters. You'll be pleased to know your pelt is prepared and protected. Has she woken?'

'Nae, but the herbs you gave me are good. You'll have to tell me of them later.'

They were Oona's herbs, the Colquhoun healer who was almost as old and stubborn as Scotland itself. If only he had Oona's counsel as well. 'You're not wanting to talk of the herbs now?'

'Nae, I have something else to say.'

He knew what was coming.

'You're a fool.'

No doubt. Donaldo's great arms were crossed. Her eyebrows arched. All she missed was her toes tapping.

He had been foolish, making assumptions, demanding things his way. He could have lost Lioslath. Just like that and he would never have known what she meant to him. All of it because of his arrogance. He never approached any discussions without checking the accuracy of his facts.

'We entrusted her to you,' Donaldo said. 'She's special to us, though...I thought, perhaps, she needed to find her own way. Everything changed when her father died, but she didn't recognise what we wanted from her. In that I was foolish as well.'

Her admission surprised him.

'There was too much damage done,' Donaldo continued. 'You ken? Her...inability with us.'

Her inability. Every single day he saw her inability and her longing to connect. But he dismissed it as something he imagined. Because how could she be alone, when she was surrounded by people who were loyal and loved her? How could someone as beautiful…as brave…as she be hurt? 'Why is she like she is?'

'It was Irman, Busby's second wife, who sank her hatred too deeply.'

He knew about Busby's marriages. He knew about the children. Yet he had never enquired further. Why would he? He approached Busby for trade, for alliances, not…feelings.

'Lioslath's mother died when she was six,' Donaldo said. 'Busby soon married Irman. Even after her death, Lioslath's mother's kindness and generosity were everywhere. It was apparent that Lioslath was well-loved and Irman didn't want her to have such power. Lioslath was often punished, and she learned to stay away from the keep. When Irman became with child, she forced Lioslath to sleep in the stables with the horses. She explained it would be temporary while the babies were small, but nae room nor bed was ever built for her.

'When Irman died in childbirth, it was too late.' Donaldo shrugged. 'Still, Lioslath tried. I think she tried for us and for her mother's much-remembered gentleness. With her hunting and the care of horses and sheep, Lioslath did tend the clan. It wasn't enough for Busby. He thought Lioslath should have stepped into the role of her mother. Yet she didn't. Too much time had passed and she couldn't know how to by then.'

Images of Lioslath in the stables, hacking her hair with her hunting knife, consumed him. No, there couldn't be anything gentle about that.

'Busby changed when he married Irman and became worse after she died. Lioslath's inability to suddenly become the lady of the manor angered him.'

He knew of Busby's desperation. Had been able to sense the bitterness, but Donaldo's confession let him know how badly he failed Lioslath by making the alliance.

'It was safer that Lioslath hid, because Busby was uncontrollable by then,' Donaldo continued.

Safer for a daughter to stay away. And yet Lioslath defended her father. He knew nothing at all about this clan. Knew nothing of the woman he married. Because he hadn't cared about anything else but his own pursuits.

'Before the attack.' He shook his head. 'I didn't understand it...' He pulled up, changing the subject. There were matters he needed to say to Lioslath alone. 'Why didn't you tell me of the English?'

'We have our pride and you were so certain all the poverty and misuse was our own fault.'

He'd been such a fool. 'I mean to set it right.'

'With the missives to your clan?'

He tried to protest, but it came more as a shocked laugh. He should have known Donaldo was still watching him.

He gambled with the two missives he laid in Finlay's safe hands. Two letters written hastily before he went for the wolf pelt. One letter to be shown to his brother Caird and the elders. And a separate, private, letter to his sister and her husband, Robert.

Caird wouldn't be surprised or protest his being made laird. As the one brother who most adhered to rules and promises, he was the logical choice.

As for Gaira and Robert's letter? Dread and resolve filled Bram's heart when he wrote it.

He regretted requesting that Gaira and Robert travel the dangerous distance here. Yet it was the only way for Lioslath to understand and she deserved the truth. He loved her and wanted their marriage in truth. He needed her trust.

So she had to know what happened last April. She had to know who had murdered her father. It had hurt her that it had happened. He feared it would hurt her worse once she knew the truth. But he had no choice.

'Donaldo, does nothing escape your eyes?' he said. 'You should work for the king.'

'The king couldn't afford me,' Donaldo said, as she walked to the door.

'Nae doubt you'd request more than a wolf pelt for payment.'

'Oh, I'll be asking more than that from you. But for the rest, I'll simply wait.'

'In the meantime, if I come to the wrong conclusions?'

'You're a fool, Laird Colquhoun, but as for your actions? They are already on the correct path.' Donaldo opened the door. 'You merely need to walk the rest of the way.'

As Donaldo closed the door behind her, Bram brought the corner chair to the bed. If he had to walk any direction on the right or the wrong path, if he had to rethink everything he'd ever learned, he would do it. But he knew with absolute certainty he wouldn't be separated from his wife.

Later in the night, and so quiet that only the dust from the floorboards stirred, Bram's path was still unclear to him.

How had it come to this? A fool, Donaldo called him, and he agreed. But a fool who needed Lioslath's hand in his. Even though she couldn't feel how tightly he held it or how his own trembled.

Now her pale skin had a grey cast, made all the more alarming against the blackness of her hair. The shocking light of her eyes was hidden behind her closed lids, so nothing detracted from the graveness of her injury.

How had she come to this?

He didn't mean the wolf attack. That wasn't the true danger. *He* was the danger. Too much of what had befallen this clan was his fault. He came here to make amends and to fix one mistake from the long list of mistakes over the past year. Now…Lioslath might be crippled and could lose her leg. He had no doubt it was because of him.

She often accused his diplomacy skills of being merely manipulation. She was right.

He was laird, born into the responsibility and the power. His clansmen swore him fealty and in turn he protected them, listened to their disputes and offered aid when needed. He listened; he was patient. In fact, he prided himself because both provided him information in order to…to ensure his own victory.

He splayed his fingers so her hand rested openly in his. So tiny, and yet…so fierce. He'd seen her hands fling refuse buckets, seen her fingers grip a dagger's handle all in defiance of his...

Manipulation.

Was every horror that his family suffered this year caused by his need to control the outcome? Could he have ill-used his sense of responsibility and power for his own gain? He couldn't doubt it.

For at what point did his laird's responsibility extend to forcing Gaira to marry Busby?

His sister cried and yet he still decreed it. He could have simply talked to Gaira. She was headstrong, but she only ever did things out of love. Instead, he dictated her fate and forced her to marry Busby.

There were many southern clans near to Irvette at Doonhill. Yet he chose the most desperate of clans. They wrote and discussed their positions and terms, but he'd been patient, listened, until the odds were in his favour. Then when Busby's back was against the wall, when Gaira ran away, he threatened him.

His manipulations extended to Clan Fergusson as well. He thought he hadn't wanted to bring more grief to them, but in fact, by laying siege, he weakened them. Lioslath was forced to open the gates, forced to take the supplies, forced to hunt with him.

The marriage. He believed she understood, but had all the words been said? Had he purposefully assumed? In case…in case saying the words would give her power to refuse the marriage and force him away?

He flexed his fingers against hers and looked for signs she was waking. He was desperate for signs she was waking. Because this was what he had to face. Had he forced his marriage because he wanted her at any cost?

He wanted her and he wanted her still. Her fierceness and beauty stunned him from the beginning. If he manipulated the marriage, it hadn't felt as if he approached her with any sort of calculation. Nothing he felt about her was planned. From the moment he saw her in her bedroom, he had no thought, no pattern and no plan. He only…wanted.

He fought the wanting of her, his duty demanded it, but it had been futile. They…fit.

He brushed at the strands of hair clinging to her forehead. She was so hot and damp with fever. But was she worse? He didn't know. At least he had Oona's herbs and Donaldo was willing to use them. He only hoped they were enough.

They had to be enough. God could not take more away this year. His sister was dead, his honour was in tatters, his brothers were in danger. It was enough. It would stop now.

He paused and shook his head. He was being

arrogant again. Thinking he could control this situation the way he did everything else.

For now, he would ask for forgiveness. He'd do it now while she slept. And when she woke, he'd say it again.

Asking Lioslath for forgiveness was only the first step on the path he needed to take. A path that continued to be unclear to him.

He swept his thumb across the back of her hand. Watched the flutter of her lashes and her shallow breathing. He wanted her to wake, wanted her to rest. He wanted—

No. The path wasn't unclear to him. For the first time in his life, all was undeniably revealed to him.

Lioslath was his direction.

She had been since the moment he had seen her in the dark of her bedroom. She had been like a night star to him and he'd been navigating himself towards her ever since.

Chapter Nineteen

Light filled the room when Lioslath woke to the heavy warmth of Bram's body pressed against her side.

He was asleep, but the tangle of his hair was the only softness to the unforgiving angle of his jaw and hard slant of his cheekbones. His lips were bruised and swollen and a dark circle formed just under his eye. Brawling wounds that didn't hold her attention. Even asleep there was a vibrancy, a determination, to him. Determined and ruthless no matter the cost.

She was the cost.

Over and over, she paid for what others wanted. Irman, her father. When there was no one to protect the clan, she had been there. She cut her treasured hair so her clan could have someone stand for them. So she could be the son of the laird, who didn't tremble, who looked their enemy in the eye and gave them her entire inheritance.

Then Bram crested the hill and dominated her life. Demanding more when she had nothing else to give. Demanding…marriage.

But the most damning of all was her own actions after Bram's announcement. For then, Lioslath realised she did have something more to give than her broken soul and her childhood memories. She had her body. And in marriage, she pledged her body and the rest of her life to Bram.

Bram, with his voice, with his hands, his lips and warmth, showed her how, despite everything, her body could feel.

In this marriage, she believed she sacrificed enough. That because she finally gave every part of her, body and life, whatever Fate or God had against her clan, her family, would be appeased. That since she gave everything, some good might be found.

But she was wrong. Oh, how wrong, when Bram knelt before her and told her their marriage vows were false.

Now there was more to pay. As she watched Bram with her brothers and sister, watched him argue and laugh with her clan. Somehow, in the time after her marriage, she gave Bram the last of her there was.

Hope.

She'd been holding hope inside her. Hope she didn't even know she had. So precious she hid it from herself. Like a miser who buried a coin and forgot about it.

It'd been hope encouraging her sacrifices. Hope, that by cutting her hair, she could help her clan. Hope, that by her marriage to Bram, her clan would prosper again.

Hope, that by pledging her life to Bram, she wouldn't be disappointed or abandoned. Hope, that by pledging her body, there would be children. Ones who knew they were loved, who knew they'd never be left behind.

The hunting together had been hope for a new beginning. Until Bram knelt at her feet, his legs sinking in mud.

Until he told her in his beckoning voice that their marriage was a lie. He hadn't laughed. He hadn't. But as he knelt before her in her precious forest, she felt as though he told some terrible joke.

When the wolves attacked, it hadn't mattered. Not to her. There was nothing they could do to her that hadn't already been done.

She shamed and humiliated herself. Her attempts to help her clan, her family…herself. Bram's declaration blindingly showing her she never, ever, could.

She swiped at the threatening tears. Her leg

throbbed, she needed the privy and she was hungry. Harsh reminders she was alive. That no matter how dead she felt inside, her body still made demands.

Except to move would require moving her false husband, who slept against her. His large body was in a chair, the upper half of his torso and arms sprawled on the bed, one lying heavily across her middle.

She saw only determination and vitality when she woke. Now that it was brighter, she could see the darkness spreading and yellowing under his eye, the swelling of trapped blood from the split in his lip. He looked...exhausted.

It didn't matter, she needed to move. She didn't want to wake him, to hear his voice, to see his storm-grey eyes. Not this close, not today. Not now.

Carefully, slowly, she slid his arm until she could be free of him.

As she made her way to the privy, she abruptly stopped. She feared why she worked hard not to wake him and it had nothing to do with avoiding him, and everything to do with how exhausted and vulnerable he looked.

After every betrayal, she worried for him. Realisation ran cold along her spine. She knew then some part of her might never be free of him.

* * *

'Why didn't you wake me?'

Bram was behind her in the corridor as she stood outside the privy, having not been able to return to the bedroom. The agony of her steps was insurmountable.

Strong arms encircled and lifted her. The pain and pressure in her leg lessened, but her ire increased. 'I'm hungry. Put me down.'

'Didn't it occur to you to wake me?'

His arms felt like a vice around her.

'Let me go!' She knew she sounded hysterical, but against him she felt his voice as well.

He eased his hold and let her down on the floor, although he didn't let her go until she found the wall's support. Only to realise she should have asked to be put on the bed. She couldn't make it to the bed.

Something flitted across his eyes. Bafflement. 'I am here now. When you need something, ask.'

'I'm to depend on you now?' she said, as his bafflement darkened into something like pain.

'Aye, I want to be someone you can depend on.'

His voice, his words, played tricks because he sounded truthful. She had to be hearing him wrong. It was just that he looked almost vulnerable now. His hair was in disarray, dark circles were under both eyes and a crease marred his cheek. He'd been in a deep sleep when she left and it must have softened her to him.

He wasn't dependable. Never could be. Only yesterday he confessed his intentions to leave.

'What happened to your face?' she said instead.

'Aindreas and I came to an arrangement.'

Aindreas had defended her. How much did he know? Probably the entire humiliating story. She wished she could have swung at Bram herself. 'You deserved it.'

'It's why I let him hit me.'

She opened her mouth, closed it. Aindreas had skill, but Bram was older, more…honed. Either Bram was surprised when Aindreas struck or Bram spoke the truth. He had purposefully taken the fist.

She shook her head. She didn't care why Bram thought he deserved pain. She couldn't care and her leg hurt.

'Take me back to the bed,' she said.

Without a word, Bram carried her to the bed. Then he laid her carefully down as if she was precious to him. She knew otherwise.

'We have to talk,' he said.

'We did that yesterday.'

'I was a fool yesterday.'

Lioslath felt like a fool now. Bram strode to the window and threw open the shutters, but his hands remained tightly gripped to them. The light was changing. It would be morning soon, people would wake and another day would come like every other. Nothing would...could ever... be different.

'How is your leg?' he asked, his voice hoarse.

'It hurts,' she said.

He nodded his head, not in understanding, but as if he was answering some other question.

'I should have allowed you your weapon.'

She was wrong. The day was different from yesterday. Bram, Laird Colquhoun, was apologising.

'I saw you use your bow and arrow,' he continued. 'I saw your skill at the competition. You could have killed that wolf between breaths.' He shook the shutters in his tight grasp and she waited for them to be torn from the wall. 'I fear your leg might not heal.'

He spoke to her of feelings? He had no right.

'It isn't your concern now, is it?' she said.

He didn't let go of the shutters, but he turned his head to pierce her with his grey eyes. 'You will take care of it. You will rest it.'

She hated rest, but most of all she hated his ordering her. 'After yesterday, you think you have rights to order me?'

He sighed. 'You are in pain.' He suddenly released the shutters and strode to the table by the bedside. 'There's a drink here to alleviate it.'

She took it without question, drained the bitter contents before handing him the cup. 'There,' she said. 'We're even. You caused me pain, you've alleviated pain. You can leave now.'

He shook his head. 'You need rest for the pain to subside, but I cannot leave until we have some understanding.'

'I understood you fine yesterday.' He wanted to talk more? She wanted to throw a dagger at him, to demand Dog to attack. 'Now understand me clearly. You aren't wanted here.'

'I should have been here sooner,' he said as if he hadn't heard her. 'I intended to be here before you received my letter telling you I was coming.'

'I doona want to hear your excuses, Colquhoun.'

'It's too soon, but this cannot wait.'

Relentless. Determined. Always. She felt the sigh inside her and forcibly held it back. 'Dunbar. You want to talk about Dunbar and how you're a traitor.'

'I want to talk about why I wasn't here for you,' he said. 'Why I wasn't there for my brother at Dunbar.'

'It hardly matters now. What's done is done.'

'It isn't done. I didn't go to Dunbar because King John Balliol ordered me not to go.' He held up his hand. 'Wait. It's a long tale and one I never intended to tell. One I swore never to tell.'

She hadn't expected a confession. So she grabbed the easiest emotion she felt when she was around him. Anger. 'So now you break a promise?'

He waited a breath, two, but kept his eyes steady on hers. So steady she tried to concentrate on the pain in her leg instead. But it wasn't her leg making her gasp, it was Bram's steady gaze and his words. 'I break a promise to a king, so that I honour one to my wife.'

'Your wife!' Into those two words she sank every bit of bitterness she felt.

He looked as if she threw a dagger and it hit his heart. 'Not yet, Lioslath. Not yet. I need to tell you more now.' His eyes left hers to look over her shoulder as if he was seeing something else now. 'Early this year, before spring, Balliol ordered me to remain on Colquhoun land. He had two messages from two different directions being delivered to me. Once I received them, I was to protect them. Most important, I was not to leave the land ever, even if war broke out, and I'd forever be called a traitor.'

Dunbar had been that war. The only Scots who survived were those who fled to Ettrick Forest. There, John Balliol lost his Scottish crown.

Despite herself, she asked, 'And these messages?'

'I didn't receive them when I should have, but I know what they are now. Everything was revealed when Caird and Mairead arrived here on your land.'

He exhaled as if the pressure inside him was sudden and he needed to release it. She almost didn't want to hear it then, but she couldn't leave.

'They weren't messages at all,' Bram said. 'They were treasures. The messages had to do with…the Jewel of Kings.'

It had to be the pain in her leg and Bram's apology confusing her. 'Jests again, Colquhoun?'

'I'm not jesting. I'm talking about the Jewel of Kings. You know what it is?'

'A legend. Whoever holds the jewel, holds the heart of Scotland. Whoever holds it can be… king of Scotland. But it's merely a tale for little children.'

'Its legend goes beyond Scotland and extraordinarily it exists. At great risk to himself, Caird brought it here to Clan Fergusson so that I, as laird, could determine what was to be done. I knew instantly that it was what Balliol wanted me to receive.' Bram shook his head once, twice. 'I think Balliol wanted me to be called a traitor because of the jewel. So nae man would suspect I had it.'

'So you have it with you now?'

'Malcolm has it.' Bram's regrets about Malcolm ate inside him. If only he had protected his brother when he was young, Malcolm wouldn't have seen his friend killed. If only he had told his brother the truth about Dunbar, he wouldn't have recklessly fought that day. Malcolm had to have the Jewel of Kings so he could set things right and believe again. It didn't stop the regret and worry plaguing him, though. 'There's more to tell, but not for now.'

Despite everything, she wanted to know more. He was claiming the Colquhouns held the power of Scotland after an English king declared Scotland was his.

'With John Balliol, with this Jewel, why did you come here? Why did you even marry me?'

Bram tumbled the cup in his hands before returning it to the table. 'When I wrote that letter last April, I meant only to be here for you and for your family. To make repairs and return to Colquhoun land.' When he raised his head again, a look was in his eyes, a vulnerability, she thought she'd never see. 'But with Dunbar, with the jewel, my brothers and I devised a plan. For me to remain here for the winter, to avoid King Edward's messages and to wait for more information on the jewel.'

'So the marriage was a way to hide from King

Edward, to wait for news of the jewel and commit treason.'

'Staying here was part of the plan. Being married to you wasn't.'

Pain sliced through her. 'Does it make a difference? If the marriage was temporary, planned or unplanned, is there any difference to me?'

Brows drawn, Bram gave a shake of his head.

The marriage, her hope for her family, was all false. Bram only married her to secure his stay here. To ensure his great political plan would work. Bram truly was the great negotiator if he bargained his life, his clan's future, for a legend.

And all of it was too great of a secret. Bram told her as if he trusted her, when she could now so easily destroy him and the entire Colquhoun clan. Then she realised what she truly wanted to know.

'Why did you tell me these things?'

'Because I'm staying. I want this marriage in truth.'

Chapter Twenty

❦

'You're awake, you're awake!' Gillean burst into the room. He was followed quickly by Eoin and Fyfa.

Lioslath jumped, ready to tell them to leave, when Donaldo entered with a large tray of food and drink. Dog was at her heels, his head low and his eyes darting as if he was afraid something might harm him at any moment.

Dog. She narrowed her eyes on him and he bowed his head even lower, but he came to her hand hanging over the bed's side. Cool muzzle, hot breath and she could breathe a bit easier. Breathe, but not much else.

'Eoin, step away from her legs,' Donaldo said, as she set the tray down.

Lioslath tore her eyes from Dog's. Fyfa's hands were in front of her, her face serene, but her hands were tightly clenched. Gillean had…branches… in his hands. What were they doing here?

'I'll go now,' Bram said.

He couldn't just go. He couldn't go when he had said what he did. Marry her in truth? 'Nae.'

'There's time.' He walked to her side and, as if he couldn't stop himself, he brushed one finger along her cheek. A tender caress as if they were truly married. It made her equally angry because she couldn't stop him and flummoxed because she didn't know what she would do if she could.

Then he made it worse, by leaning in and whispering in her ear. Everything inside her was acutely aware of him even as her eyes darted to the rest of her family, who were pretending to ignore them.

'They love you,' he whispered, and the words went straight into the empty place inside her. With him this close, this intimate, she could do nothing to protect herself. 'They love you, will wait for you, and they won't go away. And neither will I.'

Her entire being was covered in goose pimples as his words caressed over and inside her, though Bram didn't give her a backwards glance as he stepped out the door.

Fyfa released her hands. 'Oh, it's good to see you, sister.'

'It'll leave a scar. A huge clawing scar. With *wolf's* teeth marks!' Eoin looked at her leg as if he thought such a scar was a miracle.

'Can I see it? Can I see it?' Gillean danced around the bed, the young branches waving and releasing the scent of the trees.

'Your sister needs peace,' Donaldo informed them. 'Not you jumping around the room, Gillean. And I'll need to re-dress the leg, so you can't stay here.'

'But we want to see it.' Gillean brandished the branches as if they were a sword.

Branches. Not flowers or weeds, because they knew she liked the trees, the smell of pine and damp oak leaves. It stunned her. They knew what she liked.

'It's not sensible for you to see it,' Donaldo said. 'Now that you see she's well, you'll have to leave.'

But her brothers and sister wanted to see her injury. More important, Lioslath knew they wanted to see it.

Fyfa needed to see it because she was worried. Under the linens, her leg was swollen. It was alarming and serious, but as long as she cared for it, it would heal. Yet how could Fyfa know how to tend wounds, as a future clan's mistress must, if she didn't learn now?

Eoin wanted to see the teeth marks. She knew there were long, jagged marks where the wolf tore into her skin and raked its claws along her thigh. Hideous, extremely painful, but she earned them like battle wounds. Eoin was six. He was obsessed with battle wounds.

As for Gillean's excitement, he was curious as any child would be. She was in agony as the tincture Bram gave her was wearing off, but Donaldo was here with more. Her siblings wanted to see her injury and how could she not show them?

'They can stay,' she said.

Donaldo's warm eyes flashed to hers and the world became suddenly blurry. She was crying. The first tears since her injury, since Bram hurt her. Between Bram's words and the wolf's claws, she was broken inside and out. But by some miracle, she understood her brothers and sister.

She knew it couldn't always be this easy. She was lying down and helpless, and they weren't confusing her with their playing. But their looking at her broken leg was exactly what she wanted them to do and what they wanted to do. A small step, a giant step. For once, she understood them.

By their astonished faces, they realised it, too.

Lioslath woke. How long had she lain like this in this bed, with Bram keeping watch over her? Weeks. The agony in her leg was gradually dimming. She walked with the aid of a staff and could get to the privy. And whilst Bram wanted to carry her, she wouldn't let him. She wanted nothing from him.

There were days when the pain was worse. The claw marks on her leg were red, stitched and swollen. The boards and wrapping constantly itched, but her leg wasn't broken. Though Bram treated her as if it was.

He was always there in the middle of the night when the tincture would wear off. Always there to adjust her wrapping or position her in the bed. Always. Just as he was now.

Bram slept on the floor. Dog stretched nearby, his front legs almost touching Bram's. They were companions now and she didn't know who was more protective of her.

Because the pain increased after that first day. There were days of agony that only dimmed with the herbs. Then there had been no more discussions of marriage, no more whispers in her ear when her brothers and sister visited, when Donaldo came to help with the dressing, or Aindreas with his concern and laughter to cheer her.

And Bram laughed with him. There seemed to be some understanding between Aindreas and Bram now, which made her more uneasy than Dog's acceptance.

It had been weeks of healing while her pain eased with help.

Now her pain was dim and she hadn't the tincture yet. She was recovering. Recovering, but she wondered if anything would ever return to normal.

Bram had done so much for her clan, said so much to her. Leaving several times a day, telling her of the improvements and the setbacks. The recent rains made it difficult for building, but the weather remained mild, so they could plant. They began reinforcing the tunnel, which wasn't a secret any more. He listened to her terse advice as if she was his council. As if she was his wife.

He apologised every day for being foolish when it came to her. She could forgive him for being late to Fergusson land. But for a king, but for a legend, he would have been here. He could no more be held responsible for Dunbar than the English who ravaged her home.

So for those things he had no control over, she forgave him. But for his offers to her father, for the false alliances, for his manipulating her as well?

Never.

She'd seen this pattern of apology too many times with her father. His schemes. His reckless hatred; his quick apologies afterward. Her father had disappointed her over and over again, but Bram had done something worse than her father ever had.

Bram had taken her hope for a better future

for her clan, for herself, and destroyed it. She could never trust him, never depend on him. Now she'd do anything to ensure he left Fergusson land. She'd keep throwing buckets, daggers, and shooting arrows. She'd shut the gates again. But he would leave.

She was done toiling for meagre results. Done sacrificing herself for bitter disappointments. It was Laird Colquhoun's turn to abandon his aspirations and ambitions here and return to his home. It was Bram's turn to fail.

Heavy knocks on the door.

Bram leapt to his feet and almost tripped over Dog, who gave a low huff in warning. He glanced at Lioslath, who didn't hide her smirk as he wiped the sleep from his eyes and face.

Knocks again. More insistent.

'Come in,' Lioslath called out.

'Are you in pain?' he asked, as Donaldo charged into the room.

'Nae, not today,' she said.

'Riders with carts are cresting the northern hill,' Donaldo panted.

Carts full of supplies for Clan Fergusson. Exactly as he ordered. Bram knew who crested the hill. It wasn't an enemy, but Lioslath wouldn't see it that way. 'Prepare as much food as you can,' he said. 'They'll be hungry.'

Donaldo's gaze darted to Lioslath before she nodded and let herself out the door.

'Who are they?' Lioslath asked, although she had to guess.

'Colquhouns,' he said, which wasn't a lie. Not any more at least. He pulled on his hose over his braies. 'They bring more supplies, wool, extra horses. Some winter barley and wheat to sow. There's still time for planting.' He pulled his tunic over his head and wrapped his belt around it. 'It's warmer here, so they brought oats, though they may not seed. For the rest, the ground continues to be soft, we could have crops by spring.'

Lioslath's face darkened. 'Colquhouns,' she said. 'More of them.'

He knew she wouldn't be pleased. He pulled on his boots, tied the back of his hair. After the attack, Finlay had ridden out with five of his men to deliver the missives to the Colquhoun clan. A handful of Colquhouns remained here to make the necessary repairs before winter. Though there were fewer here, they still weren't welcome. He was still not welcome.

He sent the letters to Clan Colquhoun weeks ago, and he knew he had only a short time to win her trust before they arrived.

So he exhausted himself in preparation, but it hadn't been enough. For a fleeting moment, he wanted to try again, but what hadn't he already told her to make her trust him again? Wildly, foolishly, he craved something to give them a chance. He knew he had destroyed everything between them that day in the forest. He knew once she saw who the riders were, she wouldn't forgive him this time.

'Love, we need to get you dressed,' he said, helping her from the bed.

'Stop calling me that.'

'What?'

'Lass or love. Signs of affection. There is nae affection between us and I do not want these Colquhouns to think there is. Especially since you'll be riding home with them after the seeds are sown.'

'We're married. I'm not going anywhere.'

She tensed under his hands. She was mostly dressed, her chemise thick, luxuriant, but not as soft as her skin.

He dressed her now and allowed himself the barest of touches. It was all he could do not to kiss her.

Instead, he carried her down the few steps and reluctantly released her. 'Nae matter what happens next, remember I'm here to stay.'

'I want to remember none of this.' Even using her staff, Lioslath was forced to use Bram as support through the courtyard. By now she could see the two riders. A broad man with brown hair whipping against his face as he looked to the woman riding beside him. A tall, willowy woman, with flame-coloured hair that almost matched Bram's.

Gaira was here.

Everything froze inside her. Everything, except more hurt and pain. Except the accusation in her words. 'What have you done?'

He didn't answer her, so she was forced to look to him. Forced to see his grey eyes plead and demand. But the conflicting emotions in his eyes held nothing to the determined agony in his voice as he answered.

'Remember, Lioslath, we're married. You put your hand in mine, but I'm the one who won't let go.'

Chapter Twenty-One

Gaira was riding through the gates. Fergusson gates. Her hair, so similar to her brother's, was multiple plaited. Her clothes were plain, serviceable, more like the clothes Bram now favoured. The clothes and hair were unexpected. Everything was unexpected. And very, very, unwelcome.

'You shouldn't have done this,' she said.

'Steady, Lioslath.' Bram placed his hand against the small of her back. For comfort or to ensure she stayed still? 'I only did what was necessary.'

'You had nae right to ask your sister here. What are you manipulating now? I do not want to see your sister. I'm through negotiating with you.'

A muscle ticked in his jaw and she knew she had hit her mark. 'Nae negotiation, nae manipulation. Nae more with you.'

'And I am to believe that?'

'I hoped you would by now.' Grey eyes stormed with a light she didn't want to guess at. She was seeing it too often now. Guilt again for her injury? No. This was an almost desperate emotion. Difficult to recognise on Bram. For how could someone like him be desperate? Conquerors were never desperate. Great negotiators would never have their backs against the wall.

Jerking her gaze away, she observed the man dismounting. He was a hair shorter than Bram, but broad throughout and walked with the lethal grace of a man used to training. He would have looked deadly except when his eyes met Gaira's as he helped her dismount. Then they smiled as if they were welcome, as if this was a friendly visit.

'What do you think to gain from this? What do you hope to prove?'

'Everything, Lioslath. I'm showing you everything. My only hope is you'll accept it.'

When they approached, Gaira gave only a quick glance to her brother before she said, 'I can see from your expression my wanwitty brother surprised you with our presence.'

Gaira turned to Bram. 'Some day you'll dictate the life of one person too many.' With a wave of her hand, she continued. 'Lioslath, this is my husband, Robert of Dent.'

Dent. Dent wasn't Scottish. The man stood close by Gaira's side, his arm around her as if he was giving her support or protection. As if he was waiting for a reaction.

It didn't take Lioslath long to feel a reaction. Lioslath felt the blood leave her face before she felt the sudden weakness in her leg and she leaned more heavily on her staff and Bram.

Shards of ice. Flames of heat. Anger. Grief. This was Gaira's husband...and he was English.

Gaira had travelled from Doonhill to Colquhoun land with four children. But she hadn't been alone on the journey. This man had stood beside her. Robert had been there when her father came for Gaira.

'It was you,' she said, no question in her voice, only accusation.

No surprise in their expressions. She was facing the woman who caused her father's pursuit and the man who ended his life. And she didn't have a blade in her hand.

'Aye,' Robert said.

She tried to tug her arm out of Bram's. Instead, he clasped his hands with hers and wouldn't let go. She couldn't yank her arm free or she'd fall.

'We should sit,' Gaira said. 'I need to sit.'

Gaira wanted her to go inside, to be trapped. As if her leg wasn't enough of a hindrance to her freedom. Especially now that she wanted to run amongst her precious trees and never see any of them again. Then she saw it, subtle, barely there, Gaira's hand hovering over her flat stomach.

Lioslath answered the only way her mother would have wanted. 'Aye, we'll go inside.'

They walked awkwardly through the narrow door into the Hall, where the table and benches from the feast had been set up. The Hall had new rushes and was freshly scrubbed. The table and chairs made it look passable. So many changes since she agreed to marry Bram.

Gaira sat as if the roughly hewn bench was a great seat with cushions and leaned a bit against Robert, who sat by her side.

In the tenseness, the silence had its own sound against the barren walls.

Lioslath wanted to leave right then, until she saw the kindness and wariness in Gaira's eyes. So she waited. However, if they wanted her to talk, it wouldn't happen. She could barely contain the emotions inside her as it was.

'I suppose I should be the one to speak,' Gaira said, turning to Bram. 'What have you told her?'

'Nothing I should have.'

'Ach, it's a start you realise that much.'

Gaira glanced at Robert before beginning. 'Bram, as laird, demanded I marry your father. I didn't know about it until Busby stood in front of me ready to pledge to the marriage. I was shocked and hurt, and I allowed it.'

Lioslath was glad she sat as she felt Bram tense next to her as if taking a blow. Lioslath didn't look at him. Couldn't look at him. Not when faced with the absolute truth. She knew Gaira spoke the truth.

Bram had forced his sister into marriage.

'Why didn't you tell my father this?' Lioslath asked, though she knew, she feared, the answer.

Gaira braced herself as if this was the answer she dreaded to give. 'Because your father was large, because he hadn't said a kind word, because...I feared him.'

Gaira had feared her father. A woman who had travelled with four orphans over enemy lands. If Gaira had feared her father, he had given her reason to fear him. Lioslath felt the stabbing pain of acknowledgement.

Bram adjusted next to her as if he wanted to comfort her. She didn't know how she would react if he touched her now.

'And you?' Lioslath addressed the man with his arm wrapped protectively around his wife.

As if Lioslath would attack. But Lioslath couldn't attack and it had nothing to do with having no weaponry. It had to do with the truth being told.

'Busby attacked me in the village square on the way to Colquhoun land,' Robert said.

So he fought back. Robert was shorter than her father, but she didn't doubt his skills. She knew a well-trained knight when she saw one.

Gaira squeezed Robert's arm. 'Robert was at Doonhill, but not part of the massacre. He helped me get to Clan Colquhoun with the children. At the village, he was paying for supplies. If it wasn't for him—'

'Gaira,' Robert said as if warning her, as if she said too much.

Yet he hadn't. Lioslath was recognising the truth. The journey was far, dangerous even with help. It was a miracle they survived.

She felt more than pain now because she knew there was more here and they intended to tell her. They would brutalise her with the truth and she couldn't take any more. Not here, not when she was trapped inside. 'Nae more,' she said.

'Lioslath,' Bram said.

One word, her name, and yet it held so many possibilities and none of them she wanted to hear right now. Not while she was inside, feeling trapped with grief, with loss, with a truth she never wanted to know.

'Bram, Robert, you should go,' Gaira said steadily.

'Lioslath,' Bram repeated as he stood.

Only then did Lioslath raise her eyes to him. 'Go, Colquhoun, or I will shut the gates on you again.'

Lioslath didn't know how long it was before Gaira finally spoke. 'You aren't angry with me.'

She wanted to be furious at Gaira, but how could she be angry at a pregnant woman who didn't wear fancy clothing or have several servants waiting on her?

Gaira wasn't what she expected.

But Bram was. Controlling his family and hers as well. All this time and he had known who the killer of her father was. He *had known*. She hadn't thought herself capable of getting hurt more by him. How was it possible she continued to be hurt by him?

'I was until I knew who was truly to blame,' she said.

'Did my brother ask you to marry him or did he demand it?'

It was a question Lioslath wasn't expecting, but she knew the answer. 'He announced it before the entire clan. Perhaps demanding is the only way he knows.'

'Ach, he can be a daupit eel-drowner!'

Lioslath blinked.

Gaira gave a laugh. 'I've known him awhile.'

'I'd say you know him well.'

Gaira tilted her head and, for a moment, Lioslath could see the family resemblance.

'Aye, and I can tell he's changed,' Gaira continued.

Not that Lioslath could see. Constantly manipulating people, even now. 'I'm sorry he brought you here.'

'Are you? Or are you simply sorry you're meeting me?'

'Does it matter?' she said. 'You shouldn't have come when you are pregnant.'

Gaira smiled and waved her hand. 'I didn't want to say anything, since this meeting was about you, not me.'

'You almost fell over in my courtyard.'

'Is that why you invited me inside?'

'The only reason.' She had been blindsided by their arrival. But now that she had time to reflect, she knew she'd have eventually invited Gaira in. Bram already told her of Gaira's bravery with the children. 'But I do have questions.'

'So…before…he told you nothing about me?'

Little things, small details, mostly she hadn't listened. 'It wouldn't have been to his advantage.'

'That sounds too much like him.' Gaira shook her head. 'He demanded I come here. He demanded it. Given my history with him and Robert's protectiveness, he must have been desperate to make such a demand.'

Why would the almighty Laird Colquhoun be desperate to reveal the truth to her? He had to know she'd want nothing to do with him once she knew of Robert.

'He wrote to me about you.' Gaira raised her hand. 'Not a lot, but enough.'

'For what?'

Gaira looked at the opened doors. 'Bram wants me here…for you. You mean something to him. He's never done anything like this. He's trying to change.'

Lioslath could see no evidence of that. 'He didn't tell me you were coming.'

'Can you blame him?'

'Aye,' she said.

Gaira laughed again. 'Good, then for once he did something right.'

It wasn't only Bram she didn't understand. It was the entire Colquhoun clan. 'You think lying and manipulating me was right?'

'Nae, I think marrying you was right.'

Before she could answer, Donaldo and Cook brought in platters of food.

'Oh, thank you for this,' Gaira said, already helping herself to slices of venison. 'I'm so hungry!'

It had to be the oddest conversation she'd ever had. She should be throwing daggers at this woman for fleeing her father, for causing his death. For marrying his murderer.

And all she did was pour ale into cups as if she was the lady of the manor. Then she remembered that it was Bram who requested the food and drink. Had he expected this to happen? How could she trust a man who was so good at understanding people, when she didn't understand them at all and never did?

Perhaps Gaira believed them happily married. As if this were a joyous affair. Apparently, Bram didn't tell his sister all the details either.

'Your brother didn't choose to marry me and he didn't intend to stay married.'

Gaira lifted a cup to her lips. 'My brother never does anything he doesn't want to do. So this is a story I'd like to hear, if you'd care to tell it.'

Lioslath did. From the very beginning, from the siege to the present, and all the while Gaira ate, drank, listened. When she was done, Gaira said, 'You can't tell me he didn't want to marry you. He declared it before all.'

'I ruined his plans. Backed him into a corner.'

'I see how he looks at you, and nae man has ever backed Bram into a corner he couldn't talk himself out of.'

Lioslath almost believed her.

'But as for it being temporary at the beginning?' Gaira took a small bite of bread. 'He is Laird Colquhoun. He has duties which conflict with him being here.'

'He told me of the Jewel of Kings.' And it bothered her. If he had such a duty to his clan over the jewel, why had he come here at all? Why did he stay when Malcolm was certainly in danger? Another reason why he couldn't be dependable.

'If he told you, he must have wanted to marry you. Even though you may not trust him.'

Lioslath shrugged and took a drink. She couldn't trust him.

'This is difficult when it's clear you already love him.'

Lioslath choked.

'You do. You must or else the moment you saw us coming, you would have been gone. You waited to hear what I had to say. You wanted to hear what I had to say. Bram was right, you needed me here so you could trust him.'

She blamed her watering eyes on her difficulty swallowing. Was it true? Was any of it true?

'That being said, I still would like to ask a favour.'

'A favour?'

Gaira nodded, a light to her eyes. 'Please wait to tell my ragabash loun of a brother you trust him. He needs to apologise and I *like* it when he does.'

* * *

Bram walked with Robert outside the gates and they continued to walk. Much had to be discussed and it wasn't for anyone else's ears.

Still, he felt only unease as he left Lioslath behind with Gaira. He could tell from her eyes she felt betrayed. He never wanted to see that look in her eyes again. He'd done it once already in that moment before the wolves. Then it looked as though he shoved a sword in her gut. Now her expression was worse. Now she looked as if she expected it.

And she was right. He purposely hadn't told Lioslath that Robert and Gaira were coming.

He thought he learned his lessons when he almost lost her to the wolves. But still there was more to learn. He should have told her.

He hoped Gaira would find the words he could not. He had to believe that Lioslath would believe his sister. It was his sister's story, not his. But it was a painful story. Robert was Gaira's husband. But he was also Lioslath's father's murderer.

It had been a fair fight. The only thing Robert could have done, but how would Lioslath feel about it? He hoped Lioslath would find some understanding, some peace by knowing.

'So you married,' Robert said.

'Aye.' He had, though he fought to keep it so.

'And I see you lead Lioslath well.'

Bram expected this conversation and knew he deserved it.

'Aye,' Robert continued. 'The way she drew her fist up as if to fight you and threatened banishment? You couldn't find a more biddable woman in all of Scotland. Congratulations, Bram.'

Bram laughed. 'You didn't wait long to remind me of that conversation.'

'It's taken every effort to wait this long. In fact, I intend to repeat it again merely to relish it.'

Bram shook his head. He'd been so arrogant when he met Robert. So sure that women were only for marriage and children. How miserable his life would be if he hadn't met Lioslath. 'Lioslath isn't biddable and I thank every star at night because of that. But I wish at times she wasn't so stubborn.'

'I often told you others don't laugh or forgive as easily as you. The rest of us need time.'

'My actions to her have been unforgivable, yet she says she has forgiven me.'

'Ah, then you are well matched.'

Bram shook his head. 'But she does not trust me.'

Robert stopped. 'That is another matter altogether.'

'I ken.'

'Time, Bram. Time.'

'I ran out of it when you arrived.'

'Yet you requested us here. You risked her knowing everything and never forgiving you against lying to her. You think she will not recognise that?'

'She's been hurt, more than I realised, and I added more. I'd apologise for the rest of my life if she'd let me.'

'Now, what biddable woman would pass on that opportunity?'

'Ah, aye, just push that dagger in my arrogance some more.'

'With pleasure.' Robert exhaled and stopped. 'We have other…important matters to discuss.'

'Important?'

'Grave, and I hope they are mistaken.'

It was too soon. Bram's heart went to his throat. 'Malcolm. You've heard from Malcolm.'

'No, it's not Malcolm. It has to do with Caird and Mairead. Of the Jewel of Kings and the Englishman.'

'I wanted you to know. You are my brother now.'

Robert rubbed the back of his neck. 'Aye, brothers.'

It hadn't yet been a year since Robert found Gaira and the children at Doonhill. Robert still hadn't discussed with Bram why he had gone to Doonhill or what haunted his past. Bram would wait for his story because he didn't doubt Robert's love of Gaira. But he liked to push against Robert's natural reserve, since he wasn't quite used to the boisterous Colquhouns yet.

Robert looked over Bram's shoulder. 'I need to talk of Doonhill.'

Grief sliced through him, quick and insistent, before Bram could breathe freely again. He thought he buried it more deeply than this, but with Gaira and Robert here, Irvette's death was all too present. Yet Robert said matters were grave, and it needed to be discussed. 'Go ahead.'

'As you know, the deaths at Doonhill were caused by Sir Howe and his men. However, it may be possible that the Englishman, the man responsible for threatening Caird and Mairead, for chasing after the Jewel of Kings, is also Sir Howe.'

'It must be coincidence. What… Why would there be a connection?'

Robert looked around them as if realising how far they walked. 'It's troubling, I agree,' Robert said. 'I could understand an Englishman chasing the legendary Jewel of Kings for its power and its value as treasure. But Doonhill was random and violent. There wasn't anything there to gain. It was all…loss.'

'Nae connection,' Bram said, even as he thought of Irvette. How precious she still was to him. How she was a Colquhoun. The Jewel of Kings had been on its way to the Colquhoun clan when it was intercepted by the Englishman, who murdered to recover it. Had Irvette anything to do with the jewel? He couldn't think. She'd been so young, innocent. So dearly loved by her husband and their fair-haired daughter, Maisie.

He knew the horror Caird and Mairead suffered while escaping the Englishman. He couldn't bear that his sister might have suffered like them, but in his heart he knew she had. Two sword thrusts to her stomach. Irvette had been murdered at Doonhill.

'Do you intend to stay here?'

He was taken again by grief over his sister. A need for revenge and to correct wrongs. And his feelings for Lioslath. His Lioslath, who was needing a lifetime of apologies from him.

'Irvette, Doonhill, it all changes nothing. If Lioslath will have me, this is where I belong.'

Chapter Twenty-Two

He found Lioslath in the stables. She was several stalls down, leaning heavily on her staff and stroking a horse's nose.

He'd left Gaira, who was tired from the journey, and Robert, who was worried about her because of her pregnancy.

Bram's insides continued to stutter with the news. His sister was to have a baby and had made the journey here. She risked much to give him the chance with Lioslath. He didn't even know if he had one.

He left the door open so he could see Lioslath now. So lovely and looking far too alone. He didn't want her to be alone any more.

'I came here to escape you.' She kept her eyes on the horse.

'I know, but you have to know I'll keep looking for you.' He searched the darkness. 'Is Dog here?'

'He ran off.' She darted a glance at him before she went into the stall and grabbed clean straw. 'Why did you request your sister here? You haven't proved that you're dependable or that we're family. Because that's why you did it, isn't it? Because if I'm married to you in truth, then Gaira becomes my sister. Did you honestly think you could force this?'

'I asked her here so you'd know the truth. We both need to have the truth between us. And I have more to tell you.'

'I'm through negotiating with you,' she said.

A muscle ticked in his jaw. 'I may not be a traitor because of Dunbar, but I am a traitor because Robert of Dent is Black Robert. King Edward thinks he's dead. I intend to protect that lie.'

She shrugged. Black Robert was the English King's sword. Greatly feared and legendary.

'You know?'

'The timing fits his disappearance and it doesn't matter to me. He's English all the same.'

'And unforgivable because of it?'

'The English weren't kind here.' She gently brushed the straw along the horse's muddy flank until some came off. 'But I will not judge Robert by those same standards.'

Bram exhaled. 'I could do nothing else for a

man as honourable as Robert, nor one who is
loved as much as Gaira loves him.'

Everything she believed of the Colquhouns
was wrong. Gaira hadn't acted with dishonour
and neither had Robert. There was no one to
blame for her father's death…except her father.
No one to blame for the fall of the Fergusson
clan except…circumstances. She couldn't throw
buckets or daggers at Fate.

'I do not begrudge their feelings for each
other,' she said. 'Now that I have met her, I know
you had nae choice. She wouldn't give you a
choice.'

'You must know the king will not take their
love for each other into consideration if he discovers the treasonous lie.'

Treason. Aye, but only if Robert was caught,
or someone told. Now it was all clear to her why
he had told her. 'You tell me, not knowing my
feelings for you, not knowing if you can trust
me not to use this against you.'

'Aye.'

'You think to earn my trust with this? He murdered my father! I doona care if a legend killed
him. He's dead all the same.'

'And your feelings on this?'

'What do you care for my feelings on this?'

'Everything. I want everything from you, but
I could not expect it if I didn't give it as well.

Having you understand, having you choose me even so, that is everything to me.' He looked down the narrow corridor where it remained dark. 'Will you talk to me of your father?'

'So you can use the information for some future manipulation?' She picked some of the mud off with her fingers. 'To get me to give you something else? You've taken it all.'

'So you stop hurting. You're hurting so much. Do you even know you're crying? I can see your tears from here, like streams of grief that you didn't know were trapped inside you. It's killing me watching you.'

First she fainted in front of him and now she cried. 'Good, then stay until the deed's done.'

'Not until we've talked.'

'So says the great negotiator.'

'So says a man who loves you.' A tender smile reached his face as she stumbled her hand across the horse. The horse stamped in agitation, but Bram didn't give up. 'Aye, loves you,' he continued. 'Who merely wants to hold you, to know your heart, but you have it so protected under layers of grief, and hatred, and fear, you may never let me know you.'

'Fear?' She stroked the horse.

'There are many different types of fear, lass. Some are dearer than others. In some ways you are not like your father, and yet you are also his image, too.'

'I'm like my father?' She stopped and looked over the horse at him. 'Who attacked Robert from the back?'

Bram felt the verbal blow.

'Aye, I know,' she said. 'He was my father, remember? I saw what had become of him. Did you think me so simple I couldn't guess what Robert hadn't said? What Gaira was about to say in his defence?'

'I never wanted you to know that.'

'I think you did. You brought them here and now you're saying I'm like him. That I'm a coward.'

'Maybe you are.' He took a step towards her. 'You may face a man when you hold a knife to him, but you still hold a knife. You still keep the fear as your father kept his.'

Had he called her a coward? Anger and then something else broke within her. Her vision blurred as tears welled and fell to join the others on her cheeks. She hated that she could feel their weakness now. At some point Bram came too close and penetrated whatever defences she put against him because his words were sharp, cruel. Fear? Aye, she had it. She feared that he spoke the truth.

'I know about your stepmother, Irman, and

of how you grew up,' he said. 'I see how that pains you still. I doona know everything. I want to know.'

'As if you deserve to know!'

'That may be true, but, Lioslath, I'm not letting go of your hand.'

'You make nae sense. I have my hands over here.'

'Lioslath. I'm staying here. I'm begging for this marriage to be true.'

'It's not what I want. How could I want it?'

'Tell me. Let us find the truth. Then when all is revealed, if you doona want me, I'll go.'

'You're negotiating.'

A curt shake of his head. 'I have nothing left to bargain with. I'm asking.'

Lioslath tried to ignore him as she picked more straw and brushed the other side. But as always Bram's patience was vast. She watched him lean against the wall as if he had all the time in the world. The stables were full now, but not large, she couldn't do this all night. She didn't want to do this all night. She felt the tears on her face making her cold. So cold.

'Why do you want me to talk of him? You already know of him.'

'What you've said in anger. In worry. I want to hear something else.'

She stopped again. 'Why now?'

'Because I've been…listening.'

Listening. Could Bram be changing as Gaira said? Since the wolf attack, he had done things differently. He had patience with her clan and with her siblings. He listened to her suggestions. He *was* different from when he first arrived. Back then he demanded she take his gifts, ordered a feast and a competition. Now she couldn't see him doing anything without consulting.

'For the first time, I've been listening,' he continued, 'and I'm beginning to believe your father died a poignant death.'

How could he know? But it was how she felt. Her father, dying a bittersweet death. If Bram knew, if he guessed, then he listened to many people during her recovery.

Yet instantly she knew he wasn't talking of only her father. 'Irvette,' she whispered.

He gave a quick blink of surprise. 'Aye, Irvette. She was happy, joyous. And she was only happy because she followed Aengus south to Doonhill. She wouldn't have been there if she hadn't married him and followed him there.'

Then his sister had been killed. 'You doona regret her death?'

'Aye, I do, a thousand times, but not that she followed Aengus.'

Bittersweet. 'Isn't all death this way?'

'Nae, but it seems it is for the loved ones we lost.'

She paused, thinking. Did she love her father still, even knowing what he had done?

'Tell me of your father,' he repeated.

If what he said was true, if what Gaira said was true, could she open up and talk? 'Why do you want to know now?'

'I had to be ready to hear it.'

She quickly shook her head.

'When a death is poignant, when it is bittersweet, a person has to be ready and prepared to listen and learn about it. It's something you'll be remembering and carrying the rest of your life.'

She felt his words, felt them trailing a knife of pain along her skin. It hurt to think of her father, but his words somehow released something as well. Like a winter brook that needed the sharpness of a blade to release the flowing spring water underneath.

'I've been laird for so long, but I'm starting to listen and I'm ready to hear your view on this.'

She gave the horse a few quick strokes, then leaned into him. Maybe it was time. 'My mother died when I was six. She had a cough that wouldn't go away. Then one day she couldn't breathe any more.'

'Before that what was she like?'

'She was like…light. Everything about her.

Her hair was so white, it was almost like snow, but her eyes were changeable shades of blue and green.'

'Like seeing winter and spring all at once? Or night and day?'

Bram was using fancy words again, but that was exactly how her mother felt to her. 'I think I know what you mean.'

He smiled. 'That's a start.'

'She was gentle, kind, and something about her was able to withstand my father. Or maybe he wasn't quite as fierce. I do know he was happier then, he smiled...'

'You frown,' he said. 'Was it not a happy memory?'

She didn't realise her feelings were so near the surface, but she wasn't surprised Bram could guess her feelings. She'd seen him interact with too many people. But his words didn't feel like manipulation.

Lumbering to the stool, she shook her head when Bram gestured to help. 'Nae—' she gave a quick glance up, settled on the seat '—it's only I forgot his smile. My father always smiled, but his smile after my mother died was different. Harder. His eyes weren't as clear of worry. It's been a long time since I remembered what he used to be like.'

'Life changes a man.'

Her father had changed irrevocably. 'You're saying this because he became a coward and a murderer.'

'Life changes all men…as it should. It's what we make of that change. If your father was unhappy, I doona believe he wanted to stay that way. He came to my clan for help. There was still some good in him.'

That Bram could say this even after Gaira feared and fled him… Even after he attacked Robert from the back. She'd been hurt by her father, by Irman. But could she look at them differently?

If she did, she'd have to face that there was still goodness in her father, and if that was true, then she would have lost him twice over.

'I can't talk like this,' she said. 'Think like this.'

'You think it's easy for me?'

She saw a glimpse in Bram's eyes of something more behind the flow of this conversation. He flirted and laughed with ease and yet she glimpsed these moments from him, more so now after the accident, when she was beginning to see another Bram.

'I know how you feel. Irvette and your father died poignant deaths. You think there's some way you could have prevented it. But I couldn't do anything for Irvette and you couldn't for your father.'

Her father. The fierce, reckless giant of a man, with his deeply ingrained anger and bitterness.

'I didn't try.'

The words simply fell out of her. They were whispered softly, but they rang through the stables. She wanted to take them back. Hadn't meant to say them. It was too personal...too painful. The second time her father had left with overwhelming anger, she hadn't even wished him goodbye.

Bram adjusted himself against the wall, but his silence was absolute. He now knew she hadn't tried to stop her father. He understood how weak she was. 'So, tell me more of your mother.'

She wasn't prepared for the change of subject. The tightness coiled inside her whipped loose. Bram hadn't accused her of weakness, and there wasn't pity in his eyes. There was only understanding...kindness.

With her confession echoing in the stables, she appreciated talking of something else. 'She liked to cook. I helped her.'

'You spent time in the kitchens?' he teased.

'I did the menial jobs. My favourite was sitting on the back steps and plucking out thrush feathers. In fact, it was that which caused me to…'

'What is it?'

'I always wondered why I sought out Niall and Aindreas when my mother died and Irman came. I now know I must have known them already from my mother. Them giving the birds to us and us sitting on the steps together to pluck them.'

'So it wasn't out of desperation.'

'Nae, I think it was…a happy memory.'

He straightened, moving away from the wall. 'It hasn't been easy for us, Lioslath, but there could be happy memories for us, too.'

Something skittered in her heart at his words and it wasn't so she could deny him. The feeling fluttering in her heart felt something like…a wish. And it made her focus on what was before her. What she could see so clearly in Bram's eyes.

Hope. He was showing her hope. Could she dare take it again?

'I know you want things differently,' he said. 'When you realise it, you'll know you could have done nothing to prevent your father from going. That others couldn't have stopped him either.' He looked over her shoulder and outside the window to the near-empty courtyard. She'd seen him go to many windows over the past weeks. She knew that when he wanted to say something important, he looked outside to gather his thoughts. But he couldn't get to the window now because a horse blocked the way.

Still, he must have succeeded for he looked at her again. 'I know you doona want to be separate any more. I know how you do care for your clan, who are as stubborn as you. I've seen how you look at your siblings and how you've been trying with them. They are also afraid, like you, but everything can be relearned.'

'How am I to teach them something I doona know?'

'See, this is why I won't let go. You care, Lioslath, you care so much for them. You already know what you want to do.'

She found she did, at least in part. 'Fyfa. She just turned eight. I'd like to...celebrate that.'

Bram's full smile was swift now, blinding and all too knowing.

'You're good at this bartering you do,' she said, feeling that familiar caution warning inside her again.

His smile eased, but not the warmth in his eyes. 'Nae, I come to you a beggar now, lass, with nothing to barter except a hope. I won't let go of your hand and I can only hope you won't let go of mine.'

He was determined, relentless...dependable. Bram was telling her he was dependable.

He showed her that. Never giving up when she barred the gates, or when the villagers shunned him. Not even when she purposely foiled his competition. He took her hunting and cared for her when she was injured. And he was here again, asking Gaira to help her understand the truth. At what point had Bram become…dependable?

She looked away. Too soon. Too easy. Everything outside her pushing her to believe, everything inside her telling her she was mistaken. Experience had taught her never to trust. Bram couldn't be dependable. He laughed all the time. He joked. He played tricks.

'This won't work. This…' She waved at the space between them. 'Whatever this is, how could you expect it to work? Just because you want it to, merely because you're *trying*, doesn't mean we can have a marriage in truth.'

He huffed as if she jabbed him in the stomach. 'Why do you think I'm trying?'

'Because you're Laird Colquhoun. Because—'

'Lioslath,' he said.

That was all, but it was enough. The fact he was laird didn't matter and he knew it. There was something more there behind his determination, his relentless bartering and controlling things.

It echoed too painfully of the things her father had done. His relentless pursuits to remedy past mistakes propelling him to make more. She knew Bram had that same drive. He laughed, acted as if he was carefree. But he brought Gaira and Robert here. He talked about Malcolm and Dunbar, about Irvette. He might be able to forgive and laugh more easily than most, but he wasn't carefree. She knew why he was relentless.

'Because you doona want to be proved you're wrong,' she said.

Bram took a step back, then another. It was enough so the shafts of light no longer illuminated him. He was in the shadows, but she already saw the emotion in his eyes he tried to hide.

She still didn't understand people. Didn't know how to talk to them, bargain or play. But she was beginning to understand him. ''Tis the truth, isn't it?'

'Aye,' he said.

'So you'll do anything, control anything… anybody, to avoid it.'

She waited.

'You're right,' Bram said. 'When I came here, I didn't want to be proved wrong. Couldn't be. I made errors I needed to remedy. Coming here made everything right. I could help rebuild the Fergusson clan, hide from an English king and wait here for news of the jewel. It fit to be here. Everything fit, everything was right…except you.'

She wanted to protest, but he gave a quick shake of his head. He was telling her now so she'd understand and she'd let him speak. Even though he was in the shadows, he wasn't hiding from her now.

'Everything I did with you was wrong because I tried to make you fit into what I thought you were and should be. But there was nothing wrong with you.' He paused. 'It's your contrasts, you see. Your passionate need to help your clan and yet you doona know you're being loyal. Your need to be close and yet the way you doona know how. Your hair is the colour of night and your eyes the colour of day. You're a woman and yet you hunt with such deathly skill. You weren't what I expected because you're…perfect.'

She couldn't believe the words Bram gave her now. He wasn't teasing and this wasn't flirting. She was seeing the man underneath the laughter and play. He meant these words.

'I doona like being proved wrong, I may never,' he said. 'I may always need to negotiate and to plan.

'When I was young, my father hoped, some day, I'd be laird,' Bram continued, his voice softer now. 'So for one planting season, he let me make the decisions. I knew I'd be laird and let everyone know it. I wanted to prove myself.' He breathed out harshly, as if the air had been trapped inside him. 'To this day, I doona understand why they let me do it. Were they humouring me? Teaching me a lesson? Seeing what kind of laird I'd be?'

She turned to face him. 'What happened?'

'Everything wrong happened. I didn't listen. I only ordered and demanded. I was old enough, had seen enough plantings. I thought I knew everything.' His eyes riveted on hers. 'There wasn't enough food that spring.'

The Colquhouns always planned, always had enough stores. They'd been wealthy for generations, and yet, from his voice, she knew he spoke the truth.

'There wasn't enough food, but only my family went hungry. My father gave the clan our stores. It was only my brothers and sisters whose stomachs were empty.'

Bram shook his head as if dislodging memories and stepped out of the shadows.

'Everything I did after that point was to ensure my family never went hungry and neither did my clan. I was determined that I would never be wrong again.'

He took steps towards her until suddenly he knelt at her feet. 'I've wronged you, Lioslath of Clan Fergusson. I took advantage of your clan's desperate position. I took advantage of your father's desire to better his people. I took advantage of my sister's love for her family. Then I took advantage of you.

'But worse, I cannot be truly sorry for any of it. If I had not done these things, I would not have known you.'

His dark spiked lashes framed grey eyes that sheened like storm-filled seas. She was falling into his eyes, drowning in everything he was showing her. 'Could you ever trust me?'

So many wrongs had been done to the clan, and to her, but he admitted those wrongs. Gaira told her how Bram was changing. More important, she understood him now. Understood why he did what he did. He didn't negotiate for something so shallow as a laird's dominion and gain. He did it because he was still trying to remedy a mistake from his childhood.

If he said he was listening, the least she could do was hear what he said. Crucially, she was understanding. But there was something more she had to do. To trust him, she had to hope again. Could she?

Bram was kneeling at her feet, waiting patiently. He wasn't demanding her trust. He was listening to her now, though she was quiet.

That something skittered in her heart again. That wish, but it felt stronger this time. It had to be stronger because it withstood all she and Bram had been through.

He wanted her trust again, but she knew better. 'I haven't given you any.'

Bram stood, his hand taking hers and tightening with emotion. 'Lass?'

'Trust. Even when I willingly married you, I didn't trust you.'

'Of course you didn't,' Bram said, a small smile at the corner of his lips. 'I never gave you cause to. I know now I need to tell you everything, to bare myself to you. It's why telling you wasn't enough, why you needed to meet Gaira and Robert. Even though I could do *nothing* to protect you.'

'You didn't need to protect me from Gaira or Robert. I…understood. I understood almost immediately.' He bared himself to her. 'The moment I knew Gaira travelled here regardless of her pregnancy, I knew there was more to you than I wanted to see.'

'What is it you do see?' He helped her return to the stool and crouched before her.

She saw Bram changing…for her. He was showing her he could be there for her and her clan. After everything, could she hope? The feeling fluttering constantly now inside her and his baring all to her told her the answer. She *understood* now.

In the forest, Bram had said life wasn't easy, but how one approached it could be. Bram had lost his mother, but his father hadn't turned to bitterness as her father had done. She and Bram shared similar childhoods; they both experienced loss and yet—

'It hasn't been easy. Your life. Has it?' She swallowed. 'When I accused you of wanting only your comforts, of being demanding and greedy, I never knew of your childhood, of what had happened to Irvette, of what you must have faced, of what you *are* facing.' She looked around, waved her hand. 'Yet you laugh. You laugh though I make fun of your laughing.'

'I vowed to find laughter again after that winter. My family never blamed me. I realised people can be forgiven and so I vowed that each day since would be made anew. I merely had to find a way.'

He said people could be forgiven, but it was clear Bram hadn't ever forgiven himself. Not truly. And with those few words, he told her so much more. About his love for his family, and theirs for him. About his determination and joy he found in life.

'But you are wrong about my greed,' he said. There was light, an ease in his eyes again. 'I've always wanted more. Like now.'

He was talking of wanting her. And she was beginning to believe she wanted him, too. They both suffered for and wanted to help their clans.

But after all he had done to protect his family, how could he stay here?

'What will you do with your clan?' she asked.

'I received a response from Caird accepting his position as laird.' He made it sound easy. As if he hadn't sacrificed most of his life for his family and clan. Yet he wrote those letters. He intended to stay.

'And the king?'

'I can't avoid his missives forever. I will be replying soon.'

'The jewel and Malcolm?'

'It doesn't matter. I'm staying here, with you.'

'How can you say this?'

'There's so much more to say.' He eased back on his heels. 'I didn't tell Malcolm why he couldn't go to Dunbar. If I had, he wouldn't have gone. Instead, he almost *died.* I had…I had almost lost him before when he was young. I tend to be protective of him, of all my family. But I regret. I grieve. And I can never forget that if I had told Malcolm the truth, he wouldn't have a scar across half his body. He wouldn't *hurt.*'

Bram wasn't only talking about Malcolm's wound. Something worse hurt his brother now. Bram was telling her everything so she wouldn't hurt. How could she not trust this man?

'He's in danger now.'

'Aye, but he needs to set things right himself.

More wrongs have been committed against him than simply my not telling him the truth. It's a dangerous plan, avoiding kings and protecting legends, but a worthwhile one.'

Such simple words outlined a dangerous and precarious future for her and her clan. 'There's a lot of work to be done here,' she said.

'With you by my side, I'll hardly notice.'

Diplomatic Colquhoun. 'I won't keep house, or make sure there's nae stones in your bread.'

'We'll find a steward.'

'I'll never be genteel, or know how to talk to traders or kings.'

'I doona want genteel or biddable. I doona want easy. I want contrasts and a woman who looks like night and day. And as far as those traders and kings? You're so beautiful, you could smile and kingdoms would fall.'

He was flirting again, even now. He changed, but not in this. 'There won't be time for all your…play.'

'Ah, I won't barter that. There's always time for play.' A small smile, an inner secret. He was so determined. His strength apparent in his very size, but there was a strength deeply imbedded inside him as well.

'There's time for love,' he said. 'I want your love, despite your knowing of Gaira, of Robert, of the jewel. Even though you know staying married to me is dangerous. People calling me a traitor will follow me, your family and this clan forever.' His face was suddenly grave. 'Lioslath, I won't force you. Our marriage is nae final. There are reasons for you to walk away. You could have someone who doesn't have dangers and treason. Someone who would be more—'

'Dependable?'

A curt nod.

'Haven't you proved that? After all the strife and obstacles upon your arriving here. After all the danger you and your clan faced and will continue to face. After the sacrifices you've made here. I've seen how your clan, how mine, look to you for leadership and hope.'

Raw emotions flitted with light. Grey eyes told her he was listening.

'*I* look to you for hope,' she said. 'I thought it lost and you keep revealing it to me. I doona need someone who is dependable all the time. I want someone who strives to be dependable. I have nae doubt that it's you.'

'Lass. Love. What are you telling me?'

So much. Couldn't this magnificent male see? 'I've been listening to your words, your voice, Bram.' She took his hand and clasped it with hers. 'It's time to use your hands and kisses.'

Chapter Twenty-Three

'Aye?' Bram whispered, as if he couldn't believe it was that simple. As if it was her turn for tricks and jests.

'Aye,' Lioslath said, never releasing his hand as he swept her up and carried her across the empty courtyard. Along the way, she caressed her fingers against his palm, feeling his body tighten with each sweep of her fingertips. She didn't let go when they entered her room and he set her down on a chair.

Then she looked up and saw Bram's uneven breaths, the way his throat worked as he swallowed, and as he carefully knelt before her again.

He brushed his thumb against the back of her hand. 'Lioslath, if you hold my hand much longer—'

'You'll be using it?'

He gave a short nod. When his eyes turned to a storm, she could feel the lightning in them.

That moment when the darkness of the sky clashed with the warm of the earth. How the very air prickled across her skin. Like now.

His eyes darkened further, and she swore she could smell the onset of the storm. That clash of damp earth with the salt of the air. But she wasn't prepared for how his scent, his heat, would affect her. She wasn't prepared at all.

'I want you to. I want you to use your hand.' She grabbed the other one. 'This one, too.'

Lioslath was before him. Trusting him; trusting them. He showed her every black spot in his soul. Told her every wrong he ever committed and she wanted him to touch her. Love her.

'You are my night and day, Lioslath.'

Her brow suddenly furrowed, driving him crazy with want and need and love.

'Night and day?' she said. 'Oh, because of my hair and eyes.'

She remembered his previous words and he took heart at that. 'Nae, because those are the times of day I want you.'

'Are there other times of day?'

Leaning in, he skimmed his lips and tongue around the shell of her ear. He loved the shape of her ear, the way his touch made her shiver. 'Nae.'

She pulled away. He couldn't stop his smiling. Couldn't hold back the joy he felt when he was with her.

'Are you saying you want me all the time?' she said almost crossly.

'Aye.' He wasn't nearly finished with her ear or the spots underneath. This close he could smell and taste her. This close he knew she wanted him, because of the frantic fluttering of her heart.

'Then why wouldn't you simply say that?'

'I did.' If he thought about her moles, he wouldn't make it through this night.

'I'll never ken your jests and flirting.'

'You will, lass. You will because we fit. My games, your work. My irritating smiles and that crease between your brows. Unexpected, aye, but we fit. And I love you.'

'Love me...?'

'From my head to the soles of my feet.' He'd never tire of surprising or teasing her. 'Are you wondering if the soles of feet can feel love?'

She shook her head, the puzzlement easing in her eyes. 'Nae, because I believe they can.'

'Lioslath?'

'I thought it was a wish, or hope, or trust. But it's stronger. All-consuming. I think...'

She looked down, which hid her eyes from him. He let her. He'd let her do anything so he could hear the words. 'I think the soles of my feet love you...as well as the top of my head.'

He was stunned as joy burst through him. Still…

'And?' he prompted.

'There's more?' She looked at him again.

'There's everything else in between,' he said, chuckling low.

'Are you wanting more?'

More? Only their hands touched and his body tightened with want, need, lust, love. More? He wanted…everything. So she knew it, he kept the wicked glint in his eyes. 'Are we, are you, wanting more?'

'I think I am.' Her eyes widened. 'How did this happen?'

He laughed suddenly and tugged her towards him. 'Joy?' He looked at her puzzled, surprised eyes and wanted to drag her off the chair and crush her to him. 'I know it happened for me when I first watched you at the gates.'

She tried to find some purchase on the chair. 'That was…vexation.'

'Nae, I watched you throwing buckets at me with the fiercest of yells. I couldn't see you clearly, didn't know the colour of your eyes or… about this.' His eyes riveted on the mole above her lip and he brushed his thumb across it. 'Your beauty was hidden to me, but not your spirit. I admired your spirit. So when I saw your beauty, I changed directions, I started following you and will continue following you. You're my star in the night sky now.'

He trailed his fingers along the moles on the side of her neck. 'I was a fool not treating you well. I lost my way when I hurt you and your light went out. But I want to find my way towards you again. I want you to find your way to me.'

'Are you apologising?'

He sighed, and his hands stilled. 'Aye, lass. I was saying how sorry I was.'

She pressed her fingertips to his lips. 'Nae more apologising.'

'I have a feeling I'll keep apologising to you,' he said, leaning in against her lips and pressing a kiss there.

'I wouldn't want you to. I want you to use your hands and your voice.'

He swept her up in his arms and sat with her on the bed. 'Words, love. You doona know what you do with your words.' He unlaced their shoes and threw them in a corner, unwrapping his belt and tossing it in the same direction. Then he trailed his hands behind her.

'It's your words, Bram, with your voice. Then you...' As he unlaced her, he brushed his fingers along the open bits of her bodice. 'Then you... do this thing with your fingers.' The huskiness in her voice told him how his touch affected her.

'This thing with my fingers,' he prompted.

She tilted her body to give him more access, her eyes closed and her lips parted as an invitation to kiss her.

'Lioslath?' he questioned. 'Are you finding parts of me pleasing now?'

'You please me, Bram. I find all of you pleasing.' She opened her eyes, the blue dark with desire. 'Only, do that thing with your hands and voice.'

Laughter was contained only by desire. The laces at her back were loose and he tackled the ones at her sides.

'Will you tell me?' he said.

'Tell you?'

'You told me your head and your feet love me. It's not the same thing.'

It was her turn to sigh. 'I love you, Bram.'

'So now that you love me, will you tell me where they are?' he whispered, liking that she was distracted, and he meant to keep distracting her.

'I thought you'd know… You haven't done this before?'

Oh, that was it. That perplexed look. He wanted to take this slower, but his slipping control was lost and he pulled at the lacing, yanked at her gown until she sat before him in her chemise. The fire's light illuminated her, but she was as bright as a star to him.

He reached over his head and yanked off his own tunic, and was heartened at the little sound she made.

'It's time, Lioslath,' he said. 'I've wanted you night and day, and I'll want you night and day for the rest of our lives, and beyond that. Until all the nights and days burn out.'

'It'll be awfully dark then,' she whispered, as her hands tentatively reached out. He grabbed them and placed them on his upper chest.

Did she know she teased him? He saw the light in her eyes, but he couldn't be sure. She never teased him. She never even laughed.

'You'll be my light,' he said.

Lioslath knew Bram was flirting with her. Playing in that way of his. She didn't understand it, but she accepted it, wanted it, because as much as there was darkness inside him she wanted his light as well.

When Bram pulled her closer, he held perfectly still. He was close enough to kiss her, but he didn't. Instead, he seemed to be waiting for something, but she didn't know what it would be. Couldn't think of what it would be. Not when he held her like this and he was bared to her.

She'd seen Bram without his tunic when he

worked, when the sheen of sweat highlighted his strength.

She'd touched him before, but not like this. Not when the texture and heat of his skin beckoned her to trace her own fingertips along his skin the way he did hers. So she did. Along the cords of his arms, the dips at the top of his shoulders. She flattened her palms to feel the plane of his chest, down along the ridges of his stomach.

She only noticed his breathing increasing when it matched hers. That breathlessness was now becoming familiar to her, though it continued to surprise her.

He kept his hands carefully at his sides while she explored him with her hands, but she saw his fingers flexing and fisting as if he restrained himself. When she glanced up, his expression was just as still as the rest of him, but his eyes were burning and swirling hotly at her.

'You do know what you're doing,' she whispered, stopping her hands. He had to know because her nervousness eased by merely feeling the texture of his skin.

He clasped her hands between his own. 'Not in this. Not with you. Is it too soon? What of your leg?'

She felt the texture of his skin and wanted more. 'It pains me very little.' She barely felt her leg, not when Bram held her like this. But her chemise suddenly chafed and pained. 'If you take the chemise off, I think it will feel better.'

He flashed a grin. 'Aye, but then I'm afraid it'll all be over.'

'Oh, I thought…there was more.'

He kissed her until she clung to the warmth of his skin heating her own.

'There is more, but my imagination has been very vividly imagining you with that chemise off and I want to give you the pleasure you need.'

'I doona ken, Bram. You know I doona. Do you know what you're doing or not?'

'It's your moles, lass. I take this chemise off and I'll see them. You said you had more than these three. I mean to kiss and touch each one, to taste them with my tongue and heat them with my breath. I mean to explore them and see where they lead me, and I mean to do it all over again. But I fear it'll be too fast once this chemise is gone. So it's better if I doona see them yet.'

'My moles are making you…wait.'

'Aye.' He traced his fingers along the folds and creases of her chemise. His eyes roamed everywhere till she wanted to pull it off herself. Because he was making her wait.

Bram lowered his head, skimmed his mouth and tongue along the shell of her ear again, as he whispered, 'A bit more, just a bit.'

She wanted to sob with need as his fingers

deftly caressed the chemise again. The soft fabric felt like silk and like the coarsest wool against her stomach, her breasts, her nipples.

When he locked his eyes with hers, she knew he was aware of the torture he was causing.

'I doona want to wait,' she whispered.

'Your words, I've warned you.'

'I'll use them less, if you—'

'Negotiating, Lioslath?' His fingers, his hands a bit rougher, a bit firmer, clenched and released the fabric. She wanted them on her skin, on her body.

'Aye.'

'Oh,' he said, his voice lower yet. 'That's worse. I didn't think. But that's worse.'

He didn't release his eyes, but he released the torture as his hands touched under her chemise, lifting it until it fell to the ground. Then he cradled her in his arms and laid her on the bed.

The linen's coolness provided a sweet contrast as he leaned over her and whispered, 'Ah, aye, there are more.' There was heat in his eyes and heat in his touch as he softly and deliberately circled the moles along her neck and down along the one on her chest, the one on her right breast.

His eyes and his fingertips circled along her left hip bone. 'And one here, too? Open your legs for me, love.'

His hands were skimming, his tone conversational, casual, as if there wasn't a restrained tension thrumming between them.

She widened her legs and felt his fingers startle. She heard his breath hitch and she widened her legs more. She didn't know what gave her this boldness, but it was something in the ease of his request. He merely wanted to see her spots and she opened her legs so he could see.

The heat of his breath was exquisite torture and she heard him then, she heard him whispering. Like tiny prayers.

'Are you…kissing them?' she asked, trying to be offended, but failing. Not when she felt like this.

'I'm revering them, but I have to know if there are more. Turn over.'

The casual tone now gone from his voice, he lifted himself off the bed. There was an urgency about him now. Completely bared, lying on her stomach would make her vulnerable to him. But she realised there was an urgency in her, too.

'I think I needed to barter more for this,' she said.

'Have mercy.' His eyes darted across her body, as his hands went to the ties on his hose. 'I am so far in your debt and you want more?' His eyes settled on hers and he dropped his braies.

He was…magnificent. His shoulders, the tapering to his waist. The locking of his thighs as he held himself still for her to see. His hands, his hands flexing beside him as if he was still caressing her.

She rolled onto her stomach and coveted what he no longer hid from her eyes. What her eyes and body so greedily needed.

When he sat on the bed, his body was out of her view, but she felt every single touch of his hands. Sure strokes now, no longer lingering or skimming, and she couldn't feel vulnerable, not when he leaned down and kissed along her back. His breaths spreading hot, moist heat.

'You'll make a beggar of me, lass. You have three along your back.' He kissed, he touched, along with his words. 'Here and here…and here.' The rough calluses of his hands, the heated softness of his lips.

He pulled up and she almost turned over, but he stopped her with his hand on her thigh. 'You have one here, too.' His voice was unbearably husky, low, full of wickedness.

Then he touched her…there. Just where she ached the most. A slow, soft slide of a finger against her wetness. And again.

'You're so wet for me, lass, and if I press my body against yours like this, I'll feel your moles pressed to me.' He slid up her body, bracing his weight above her.

'Bram, are we to, like this?' Her voice was almost a keen and she didn't care.

'That's it,' he whispered. 'You've done it.'

She felt him shudder above her as he pulled away, cradled her in his arms and turned her around. His hands cupped her face before he kissed her possessively.

'Done what?' she asked, when he moved his lips away.

'Your words have broken me and I cannot wait. Cannot take my time, cannot linger and taste along your skin. I both knew and feared it'd be like this.'

Yet he continued to kiss, his hands wandering, cupping her breasts now. His thumbs flickering against her nipples until there was nothing but heat and want and him. He whispered his encouraging words as he adjusted himself between her legs, as he circled the mole along her inner thigh and she felt his fingertips tremble.

'Are you ready, Lioslath, are you ready for me?' His eyes shone with love and need and want of her.

'Please,' she said, widening her legs, pulling on his shoulders. She revelled in the trembling under his sweat-slicked skin as he complied. As she felt his hand beneath lifting her, as he grasped himself and edged closer yet. She gasped, expecting the pain, but he adjusted his movement until he rubbed against her. Just there.

Her gaze flew to his, amusement curving his lips even now, and heavy-lidded eyes belied his restraint as he moved his hips again. Amusement. As if he knew.

'Oh,' she gasped. Her fingers bit into his shoulders.

He stroked against her again.

'Bram,' she whispered, she pleaded, and he did it again.

'Aye, lass, that's it. I can feel you. I need you to—' He whispered with his breaths, his body, with his voice.

When his fingers caressed her around his strokes, she broke. Waves of clenching need as he entered in one full thrust and her pleasure intensified. Her gasps turned to deeper sounds as Bram clasped her closer to him, as he took her hands in his and locked their fingers together. He was there, he was there, and she never wanted him to let go.

Lioslath woke to the faint light streaming into their bedroom. It was early yet, but she knew the keep was already stirring despite the softly falling rain. Another day for them, but infinitely more to her.

She was happy. Happy. She knew what it was,

though she hadn't expected it. Even though she never could have guessed the tragedies of their pasts would result in her being here. In the dead of night before sleep claimed them, she asked how it happened. How she began with throwing buckets of dung at him to being enfolded in the warmth of his arms. She didn't understand him, or his words, or the way he continued to confuse her, but she understood what he told her of love and how she felt inside.

Like now, as she woke to this morning with happiness warming inside her.

When Bram stirred next to her, when she felt the press of his lips against her bare back, she felt her happiness burst like a spring brook breaking free of ice. She couldn't contain it and a small sound escaped her lips.

'You're awake?' At his words, Bram's kisses changed direction, although still touching the same places along her back. He was repeating a pattern she didn't understand. And then… And then she did.

'Are you,' she asked, finally comprehending, barely containing some bubbling force within her, 'are you playing a game with my moles?'

She felt his lips curve, felt his kisses become more tender, more intent. 'Aye, I mean to keep you, Lioslath, fill you with pleasure, with play. But I need to find the way that pleases you most.'

He was playing games. Even now. Her Bram was finding ways to play in bed. She couldn't help it.

She laughed.

He immediately stopped his kisses and adjusted himself until he faced her. His eyes were the same mesmerising grey she was always lost in, but more so now because they were wide and filled with joy. 'You have to marry me now,' he said.

'We're already married.' She felt her own eyes must reflect the wonderment in his. 'And I already gave myself to you.'

He smiled and the curve of his lips only added to the joy inside her. 'I thought I gave myself to you,' he said in that voice of his.

Wondering if she'd ever get used to his teasing, she blushed.

'You have to be my wife now, Lioslath, because you laughed,' he added, taking pity on her shyness. 'And it was the most beautiful sound I've ever heard, lass. Not even angels could sound better. In truth, I fervently hope it is the last sound I hear on this green earth.'

No, she'd never get used to his teasing. Why would he want to hear laughter while he died? If she was with him, why would she be laughing? 'My laughter's the last thing you want to hear?' she asked, unable to keep the confusion from her voice.

He sighed exaggeratedly. ''Tis romantic sentiment, lass. Teasing, flirting, coaxing. Love. I see I'll need the rest of my life to teach you these.'

Love. That was something she could understand. She brushed her fingers against his cheek. She loved his constant smiles. She loved him. 'You'll teach me love for the rest of my life?'

'Aye, love for the rest of our married lives.' He gave her a true, wide smile as a joyful determination glinted in his very grey eyes. 'You can depend on it.'

Epilogue

~~~~~~~~~~~~~~~~~~~~~~~~

They both jumped at the banging on the door.

'Shh, be quiet, they won't know we're here,' Bram whispered low.

Lioslath giggled against his chest.

'Laird, Lioslath!'

'It's Aindreas.' Lioslath met Bram's gaze and disentangled herself. There'd be nae reason Aindreas would dare disturb them now. Nae reason except an emergency. Bram came to the same conclusion.

'Aye!' Bram called out.

'There's a rider heading towards the keep.'

Aindreas's feet retreated as they quickly dressed. Bram carried Lioslath until they reached the courtyard, where he abruptly stopped.

Robert and Gaira were there in the easing rain. Gaira was pacing, her hand to her stomach.

'The baby!' Lioslath exclaimed, as Bram ran

the remaining distance and set her down so she could lean on him.

'There's a Colquhoun messenger coming up fast,' Robert said. 'Aindreas is notifying Cook and seeing about the horses in case more are needed.'

The gates were open as a lone rider curved around into the empty courtyard. He dismounted before the horse stopped.

Deep breaths as he addressed them. 'It's the clan, Laird.'

Lioslath grabbed Bram's hand, felt him answer her squeeze with one of his own.

'It's Maisie.' The messenger stumbled. 'She's been taken.'

The colour left Gaira's face as she fell and Robert caught her.

Bram's eyes were locked on the messenger. 'What happened?'

Aindreas and Colin ran to greet them. Colin took the horse, while Aindreas supported the messenger, who struggled to stay upright.

'She's…gone,' he panted. 'Caird—'

Bram looked to Aindreas. 'Tend him. He has an hour of rest, nae more.'

Robert cradled Gaira, his eyes fierce and protective on her waxen features, but his words were pointed to Bram. 'I don't give a damn if this has to do with the Jewel of Kings or the Englishman.' His eyes pinned Bram. 'My duty is to her and my family. You understand?'

Bram looked to Lioslath. 'Aye, I do.'

'Then take care of it. We'll leave for Colquhoun keep today,' Robert said, as he swept Gaira into the keep.

Bram's arm went around Lioslath.

'You worry,' she said.

'My sister's fierce. She's never fainted before.'

'It's the baby. She'll be…' Lioslath stopped. 'It's not over, is it? What will Robert do?'

'He'll protect them with his sword. If the Englishman is the kidnapper, he doesn't know the wrath he has brought upon himself.' Bram clenched his jaw. 'Why would he take Maisie? It makes nae sense. Malcolm has the jewel.'

'But the Englishman was there…wasn't he… at Doonhill?' Lioslath said.

'Aye, it's the only connection, but Doonhill's destroyed.' The muscle in Bram's jaw twitched before he took a ragged deep breath. 'By him. The Englishman set fire to Doonhill. The Englishman massacred everyone there.'

'Not everyone,' she whispered. 'There were children.'

'Aye, the children, but they fled to the woods…except for Maisie.' Bram's eyes became fierce. 'This kidnapping. I think it's not a question of why the Englishman isn't after Malcolm and the jewel. We need to discover why Doonhill burned to the ground and Maisie survived.'

Lioslath's heart clenched, but it did not waver. 'I understand.'

'Lioslath, I have to—'

She laid her hand against his heart. 'I understand, Bram. Please, after all the confusion and changes this year, in this I ken. You have to protect your family as well.'

'My duties and my heart are here now.'

'People are depending on you,' she said. 'It makes me happy they can depend on you. Is it wrong to feel this way?'

'I feel I can't hold my heart in my chest any more when I'm with you. If it's wrong, we both are.' He lost his smile and held her hand to his chest. 'It's too soon. After everything, it's too soon, but I must go. It's Irvette's daughter. I cannot stay.'

'Clan Fergusson will be fine. You've ensured we'll survive the winter.'

'Nae throwing buckets or daggers at me when I return?'

'The only thing I'll throw to you is my heart.'

'Lioslath.' He gathered her close and trapped their hands between them. 'Romantic sentiment from you. Now? Ah, how can I leave you?'

'It matters not, since I'm going with you.'

He pulled away but did not let go of her hands. 'Never. Not when I— It's dangerous.'

'Nae negotiation or bartering, Colquhoun, I'm going with you.' She linked her fingers through his. She'd always link her fingers through his, just as she knew he'd clasp hers in return. 'You can depend on it.'

* * * * *

If you enjoyed this story, you won't want to miss these other great reads in Nicole Locke's LOVERS AND LEGENDS *miniseries*

THE KNIGHT'S BROKEN PROMISE
HER ENEMY HIGHLANDER

Lynne Graham has sold 35 million books!

To settle a debt, she'll have to become his mistress...

Nikolai Drakos is determined to have his revenge against the man who destroyed his sister. So stealing his enemy's intended fiancé seems like the perfect solution! Until Nikolai discovers that woman is Ella Davies...

Read on for a tantalising excerpt from Lynne Graham's 100th book,

BOUGHT FOR THE GREEK'S REVENGE

'Mistress,' Nikolai slotted in cool as ice.

Shock had welded Ella's tongue to the roof of her mouth because he was sexually propositioning her and nothing could have prepared her for that. She wasn't drop-dead gorgeous... *he* was! Male heads didn't swivel when Ella walked down the street because she had neither the length of leg nor the curves usually deemed necessary to attract such attention. Why on earth could he be making *her* such an offer?

'But we don't even know each other,' she framed dazedly. 'You're a stranger...'

'If you live with me I won't be a stranger for long,' Nikolai pointed out with monumental calm. And the very sound of that inhuman calm and cool forced her to flip round and settle distraught eyes on his lean darkly handsome face.

'You can't be serious about this!'

'I assure you that I am deadly serious. Move in and I'll forget your family's debts.'

'But it's a *crazy* idea!' she gasped.

'It's not crazy to me,' Nikolai asserted. 'When I want anything, I go after it hard and fast.'

Her lashes dipped. Did he want her like that? Enough to track her down, buy up her father's debts, and try and buy rights to her and her body along with those debts? The very idea of that made her dizzy and plunged her brain into even greater turmoil. 'It's immoral… it's blackmail.'

'It's definitely *not* blackmail. I'm giving you the benefit of a choice you didn't have before I came through that door,' Nikolai Drakos welded with a glittering cool. 'That choice is yours to make.'

'Like hell it is!' Ella fired back. 'It's a complete cheat of a supposed offer!'

Nikolai sent her a gleaming sideways glance. 'No the real cheat was you kissing me the way you did last year and then saying no and acting as if I had grossly insulted you,' he murmured with lethal quietness.

'You *did* insult me!' Ella flung back, her cheeks hot as fire while she wondered if her refusal that night had started off his whole chain reaction. What else could possibly be driving him?

Nikolai straightened lazily as he opened the door. 'If you take offence that easily, maybe it's just as well that the answer is no.'

MILLS & BOON®

The One Summer Collection!

Join these heroines on a relaxing
holiday escape, where a summer fling
could turn in to so much more!

Order yours at **www.millsandboon.co.uk/onesummer**

0616_MB523_OSA

MILLS & BOON®

Mills & Boon have been at the heart of romance since 1908… and while the fashions may have changed, one thing remains the same: from pulse-pounding passion to the gentlest caress, we're always known how to bring romance alive.

Now, we're delighted to present you with these irresistible illustrations, inspired by the vintage glamour of our covers. So indulge your wildest dreams and unleash your imagination as we present the most iconic Mills & Boon moments of the last century.

Visit **www.millsandboon.co.uk/ArtofRomance** to order yours!